THE SIREN SONG

By the same author

THE
Siren Song

BY

David Beaty

New York, 1964
William Morrow & Company

For B,
as always.

In this novel, I would like to make it clear that the characters are fictitious and the Allen Autoland is not intended to be one of the fully automatic systems which will soon be making completely blind landings a commonplace commercial operation. Inevitably the names of some organizations are used, but these in no way refer to their real-life counterparts.

BOOK ONE
Anne Corby

ONE

As I came out of the shower, I heard our front door close and Maurice's footsteps crossing the hall.

I went out onto the landing and called over the balustrade, "You're late!" drumming my fingers on its wrought iron curli-cues. I heard my husband walk into the cloakroom to hang up his uniform cap. I heard the water running in the basin, as he washed the dust of the car drive off his hands. I heard him put down his brief case on the hall table and check the grand-father clock with his own wrist watch. I heard his hissing in-drawn breath of displeasure as he saw me standing above him —naked except for a towel flung round my shoulders and a frilly pink cap over my hair, my feet making dark wet marks on our expensive rose-red carpet.

Seen from above, eyes upturned, lines and puffiness high-lighted, my husband looks even older than he is, which God knows is old enough. He has very fine grey hair, which in the August light that filtered through the hall window looked silver. His face is broad at the brow, coming to a point at the chin, wedge-shaped and clever. His skin is colourless without actually being pale. But his eyes are pale, very narrow and grey. In fact, Maurice's predominant colour is grey. Even his voice is grey: soft and suave, seldom raised, seldon hurried.

"I apologize, my dear," he said, beginning to climb the long staircase towards me. "But you know how it is at the airfield. I'm afraid the delay was unavoidable."

I could see his eyes travelling over my body. His small mouth remained moulded in an inverted crescent of aloof displeasure, but already his eyes had become alert, alive and interested. That look of his made me think of a dog pointing.

For a moment, I stood there like a naked fairy at the top of a crimson Christmas tree, while unhurried step by unhurried step my husband came up towards me. Suddenly it reminded me of years ago, at a little convent I'd been sent to when my mother ran off. It was a French order and they had a mother house in Africa and all the nuns were strong on the missionary angle. For the sum of half a crown, a black baby (or what the nuns called a poor pagan) could be baptized in any name you chose. And as half a crown might appear steep to a seven-year-old child, you could get your poor pagan on the H.P. The hire-purchase was a sort of Jacob's ladder for which you paid threepence a rung. And after ten rungs, the poor pagan got into heaven, where an angel waited to welcome him with outstretched hand.

By the time Maurice reached heaven, it was his hand that was outstretched. It siphoned off a little of my irritation to abruptly turn away, and snatch myself out of his reach.

"Why was there a delay?" I stalked ahead of him into our bedroom. I flung the wet towel on the bed cover, and shouldered my way into a wrapper. "Couldn't you arrange it better than that? With a party tonight? After all, they're *your* guests!"

Not that I cared a hoot about the party or his guests. Every four months or so Maurice in his capacity of Flight Captain, British Empire Airways, gave a very formal cocktail party at what the magazine articles would call our elegant home in Hanfield, the smartest suburb of London. The guests were always the same personnel and their wives, of captain's rank and over, for in this horrid little inlet of society, we practice our own apartheid—and no one more devotedly than Maurice. The only difference between our parties and say Carruthers', the Training Captain's, was that with Maurice having money of his own, the drink flowed faster, the food was richer, and we could have hired help (normally Company stewards) to do the serving and the clearing up.

Actually, it was the party and not Maurice being late that had put me in what Maurice always labelled one of my perverse little moods. Maybe it wasn't even the party. Maybe it was first the mood, and then the party. The party being the legs and arms to take the mood somewhere.

Sometimes during our little sessions in front of the television—for my husband, when he is not genning up on new aircraft what-nots or entertaining suitable people, enjoys as he puts it the more informative programmes—I watch the weather forecaster with models of bulging cloud banks pregnant with rain, putting them down over Manchester and the Midlands, Torquay or the southeast. They remind me of my moods. Suddenly they're there, thick with rage and tears, waiting for somewhere to be unloaded, having filled up God knows where or when.

Maurice picked up my discarded towel, and took it through into the bathroom before replying. "We've just had a demonstration of our first Allen Autoland. I would not have felt it permissible to hurry that."

"Not *another* new gadget!"

"But this is a very special one, my dear. American. A robot pilot that lands the aircraft in nil visibility."

I shrugged and said nothing to let him know I wasn't interested. I began to pull my underwear out of the drawers, searching for the particular pieces I wanted. Maurice brought his dinner jacket out of the dressing room and said, "I'll change in here while I tell you about it."

Which made me laugh, because I knew perfectly well the real reason why.

". . . we've put it in the simulator . . . you've heard me talk of the simulator, that wonderful device we do our training in . . . that's exactly like a 909 but never leaves the ground . . ."

"When is an aeroplane not an aeroplane?" I asked as I pulled on my stockings.

But Maurice has never been keen on riddles. Now he was taking off his jacket, still going on talking. ". . . works beautifully . . . right down the runway centre line . . . never a waver . . . !"

In the blue uniform of Empire Airways, he doesn't look unhandsome. I suppose in the days of his youth, he wasn't either. He hasn't a bad figure—medium height, compactly built, neat and nondescript. The jacket is padded over the shoulders, and the double-breasted style cuts away the folds, soft as baker's pastry, over his diaphragm. The gold bars and brass buttons give him that *je-ne-sais-quoi* that Balmain would do for me. But taking off his uniform is like depetalling a flower.

". . . the throttles and controls moving back without human hand . . . quite uncanny to watch . . ."

Usually I don't look. Purely for aesthetic reasons, I don't watch him hop from the tortoise shell of his uniform to the less splendid but quite adequate one of his D.J.'s, which is Maurice's horrid abbreviation. But tonight because the clouds were building up inside me, while I dressed I kept my eyes on him all the time.

". . . the pilots will have to be trained on it . . . but then we'll be the first airline to run a clockwork all-weather schedule."

"Talking of clockwork schedules," I said, "everything here was dead on time, but you. I got Mrs. Thorpe to make some of those lobster canapés Carruthers wolfed last time. The stewards came half an hour ago."

"Good show!" Maurice padded over towards me in his stockinged feet. Even his suspenders are grey. He has small calves and the skin of them is pale and hairless like mutton fat. I knew this storm was going to be a big one, because I began to make the sort of remarks to myself about Maurice that Essie Somerville and I used to giggle over about people at school. In his underwear he looked grub-like and ridiculous . . . like . . . like . . . like . . . I shook inside with rising bubbles of laughter . . . like something that comes out of the cheese.

"You smell delightful, darling." Maurice brushed my newly set hair with his lips.

"Do I? Thank you . . . well, you smell . . . now let me think . . . officey. Aren't you going to shower?"

"Presently." He didn't hurry. He never does hurry. Now he remembered something about his new gadget. "Oh by the way, about the Autoland, I'll have to go to their New York factory soon. I wonder whether you'd like to come along . . . I shall be busy but it might be a little holiday for you. . . ."

Maurice doesn't like me staying here on my own. He thinks of all the things I might get up to. I hadn't been to New York, and I would rather like to have gone. But at the moment a holiday from Maurice was what I wanted, and I just murmured something noncommittal. He didn't pursue the subject. He began to move with his cat-like tread into the bathroom—stealthily, as if it were a bird that might get away. Any schoolgirl's giggles had burst and died, leaving behind a cold flat sourness like stale champagne.

I opened the door of my closet and fingered through my dresses. Finally I chose one of dark blue brocade. I bought it in Paris on our trip there last spring. It's topless and back-less. It's cut as low as any dress I dare buy with Maurice, and it's the same colour as my eyes—which are almost navy.

Oddly enough, it makes my hair look blue-black, and it does things for my skin and figure which aren't really necessary. With it I wear long chandelier earrings of Indian diamonds— a piece of family jewelry which Maurice's mother gave me two years ago for a wedding present.

Maurice emerged from the bathroom and began deodorizing his armpits, while I slipped the dress over my head. He uses a little puffer of some discreet manly scent and I could hear its faint rhythmic wheezes abruptly pause.

I zipped up the side-fastener without looking at him. I hummed under my breath as I slipped my feet into a pair of shoes.

"Do you really think *that* dress, darling?"

"I wouldn't have put it on if I didn't!"

I bent down and adjusted the silver buckles on my left shoe. I felt a sudden wriggle of excitement low in my stomach, a curious dragging spasm that you first get as a child on a too-fast merry-go-round. I imagined what would happen if I'd spoken to a young man as crossly as that . . . a young man like that First Officer who'd flown us over to Paris or that hot-tempered Italian customs man or that tall bronzed Norwegian who'd sat next to us at dinner. I imagined him coming to me over the floor, as Maurice was doing now. I still kept my head down. Maurice's patent-leather shoes moved into my few feet of vision. The spasm in my stomach fanned out over my body, pebbling my skin with gooseflesh.

"You see, you're cold in it," Maurice said. "Even in August."

He still stood beside me. I straightened up. He was holding the ends of his tie out invitingly. It was one of my wifely duties and his husbandly pleasures that I tie the bow.

I tied it for him—quickly, crossly and therefore perversely successfully. As always, he kissed the tip of my nose.

"You taste delicious too, darling." He squinted down the

bosom of my dress. "All the same, it *is* a little low. More the dress for a gala occasion."

"No one will notice." I stared at myself in the mirror. There are times when one's own beauty is an added insult to the situation you find yourself in, like being born with a silver spoon in your mouth and ending up a pauper.

Maurice shouldered his way into his dinner jacket. "I shall notice, darling."

"No one," I said over and over again to myself, spraying perfume behind my ears for no one to smell.

I heard Maurice changing over his keys and wallet and small change, filing a nail, brushing a speck off his trouser leg.

Then the front-door bell rang. Distantly below us, Mrs. Thorpe emerged from the kitchen. Maurice with a brief smile and a "Don't be too long! Don't go to sleep at your dressing table, darling!" hurried down to the lounge to greet, as of new, the first of our perennial guests.

I sat there for a long time. My mood seemed now to fill my whole body, and my legs seemed too tired to take it to the party. I heard the doorbell ring five or six times. I heard fragments of voices I could identify as Jack and Dorothea Snaith, Carruthers with his wife and daughter, a manager of something-or-other whom the wives called Must-Touch-Flesh.

I made remarks to myself about them all, but I couldn't raise a giggle inside myself. Finally, I hooked in mother-in-law's earrings, and with them tugging gently and persistently like twin consciences as I walked, I descended to the lounge and my own party.

It was in this sort of mood that I met Philip Matherson— and it was then that it all began.

Maurice introduced us, and apologized at the same time. "My wife is always late . . . but then, she is well worth waiting for."

My husband was standing at the head of the first and larg-

est group by the door. Back in the element of the airline com-
munity, he becomes assured, authoritative, deferred to.
Empire Airways is a private company, running smaller jet aircraft than the nationalized lines across the Atlantic and parts
of the Pacific. He is its gen man, its elder statesman. In the
wave of sycophantic smiles and applause which followed his
remark, I had time to look this new man over.

He was a good three or four inches taller than my husband
—Maurice had to angle his eyes upwards each time he ad-
dressed a remark to him, and because Matherson's body and
limbs were built in proportion, I could imagine him being
able to lift my husband up bodily like a child. He had brown
hair which stood up from his forehead in a thick coxcomb. I
couldn't see the colour of his eyes in this mixture of evening
and artificial light, but they were bright and blessedly young
and unwrinkled. He had what my aunt would have called a
nice open countenance. His teeth were strong and even, and
the gums wouldn't be receding and have to be rubbed every
night with an equal part solution of water and H_2O_2.

My stare appeared to make Matherson self-conscious, so I
turned brightly to Dorothea Snaith. I said, "Sorry I wasn't
here, Dotty darling, when you arrived." I squeezed her arm.
"Still, you're an old enough friend to find your way around.
I laddered my stocking just as I was coming down. So I had
to go back and change it." I held one foot out and pointed to
my ankle. "I caught it just there . . . I think it was the damned
buckle of my other shoe."

And when I saw Matherson staring appreciatively at my
ankles, I gave him a special kind of look which highlighted
what a more conventional girl would have pretended she
didn't notice.

"Maddening!" Dorothea said. "They always ladder at the
wrong moment. I find the American ones are stronger. I always get Jack to buy me this kind in New York. Guess how
long I've had these?"

But no one was interested enough to look at *her* legs. I told her what a pretty dress she was wearing, and I assured her that particular shade of salmon pink looked very becoming with her complexion. I asked Jack Snaith how the golf was going these days, and I told Wilson, who breeds poodles for a hobby, that one of these days I was going to ask his advice about buying a dog. Dutifully, after a few minutes, I left our little group to say hello to other people who had arrived. I collected half a dozen whisky-flavoured kisses. "Now quickly, Anne, while Jill isn't looking." Or Margot, or Daphne or Phyl.

"Oh, but I *am* looking. You old rogue! If everyone didn't know what a devoted couple Anne and Maurice are, I'd drag you off home right now!"

"Anne, what a charming dress, how nice to see you!"

Each whisky kiss was mated with a soft powdery one of Coty Airspun or Max Factor or Arden Invisible Veil.

"What a beautiful room . . . I love the new drapes . . . did Maurice get them at Saks? No, I agree, Maples take a lot of beating. . . ."

"The flowers . . . you cheated and had them done professionally, now didn't you?"

"The children? Oh, they're fine, thank you, Anne dear . . . no, no trouble getting baby-sitters . . . quite the reverse, eh, Jack? . . . his mother, she lives with us now . . . it's a problem, you can say that again . . . Anne, you don't know how fortunate you are . . . where does yours live? Norwich or something, isn't it? And quite independent . . . lucky you!"

"Yes, we must have a get-together when the boys are off. . . ."

When I got back to the original group by the door, Matherson had gone. So had Maurice. He was greeting some new arrivals in the hall. I took around dishes filled with olives and savouries, because now the room was getting crowded and I am not tall enough to be able to see far. Though I had never heard him laugh before, somehow I located him by just that. It was unmistakably like his face, spontaneous and unmannered.

He was talking to Carruthers, the Training Captain. There were just the two of them, heads close together, both glass in hand, both drinking whisky.

"Oh, there you are, Bill," I said to Carruthers. "Where have you been hiding yourself? Joanna's been looking all over for you. She says my lobster canapés are better than last time. You're to pronounce on them, before I tell her my secret ingredient."

And when obediently he shambled off, I picked up a glass from the waiter's tray and I raised it to my lips, "Tell me, Captain Matherson," I said, looking up at him over the rim, "why haven't you been to our house before?"

"Because I didn't know till tonight that Captain Corby had such a beautiful wife."

"Liar," I said. "Liar! You've only just been made up to Captain. You didn't qualify. You weren't gazetted."

And my laughter joined his so that people near us turned to look. I suppose I knew then that I was going to have an affair with Philip. I think Maurice knew too, for not many minutes afterwards, I saw he had established himself by the fireplace, and that already he had begun to watch both of us in the mirror.

Maurice and I bought that mirror on our first shopping trip after we were married, at a midweek sale at Sotheby's. From the beginning, it had been his choice rather than mine, though I don't suppose he had any idea then of the use he would put it to. It is late Georgian, and the glass itself has a particular blue-lead cast which pleases Maurice. But to me, its elongated oval, belashed within a ribbed gilt frame, looks exactly like an eye, which is what my husband now uses it for . . . his third eye, the eye of inner knowledge and prescience, the eye that watches me. Mirror, mirror on the wall, who is the unfaithfulest one of all? Sometimes, I toy with the idea that it can actually not only reflect but record, that it can save up for Maurice's return all the small things that happen while he is away, that like some computing machine it can assess the cool embraces we indulge in when he is home. And hanging as it does over the hearth, the centre of our home, sometimes it is more to me than that—it is a false glass heart, full of surface moving pictures. The symbol of a cold and barren marriage.

Or at least that's what I think in some of my moods. But only in some of them. Tonight, I rather liked the mirror. Tonight I was going to be amused. I watched my husband manoeuvre the little group which surrounded him until he stood with his back to the empty fireplace, his arm resting nonchalantly on the white chimney piece. He made some remark, and the group gusted with laughter, their heads moving almost in unison like heads of grey blighted corn. He put up one foot on the brass fender, and he put his glass down by the clock, so that each time he reached for it, he saw Matherson and me.

"And how long," I said to Matherson, "have you had the three-ring carte blanche to airline society?"

"Just two weeks I'm afraid, Mrs. Corby. I'm a brash new boy."

He gave a rueful little laugh and I promised it didn't show, and I could see him relaxing and making mental remarks to himself about Mrs. Corby being a rather good sort, not at all the type you'd have expected Corby to marry.

I took a cigarette from one of the boxes. I held it out for Matherson's lighter. And Maurice reached over for his glass.

He was a long time taking it to his lips—longer than Matherson in lighting my cigarette, longer even than I was to slowly inhale.

When first I'd discovered this horrid little spying habit, I'd loathed him for it. There was something stealthy and key-holeish about it, grey and creepy as fog. It was the opposite of the technicolour stories Essie Somerville and I told each other at school. We used to read historical romances because we liked the way they used to deal with their women. And the only piece of academic knowledge that seemed to stick was the rape of the Sabine women. We both decided we would marry passionate jealous possessive men. . . .

And then Essie hadn't married at all. And I had married Maurice.

So it wasn't that I minded him being jealous. What I objected to was the way his jealousy took him. All the same, I'd got used to it, just as I'd got used to a number of other things. In fact, like a lot of bad habits, I'd acquired a taste for it. So that now I could only do my best flirting with my husband indirectly watching. It was queer that his greyness could give it such colour, his reflected shadowy profile such depth and dimensions. It was as if when he took up his position by the mirror, the curtain came up, the conductor raised his baton.

"This being August," I said, "I suppose I should ask you about holidays. Where did you get that elegant tan, Captain Matherson?"

"All in the line of duty, ma'am. Bermuda. Nassau. New York." He touched his shoulders. "But you should see the Honolulu colour!"

"I'd like to," I said. "Next time, I'll tell Maurice to make it a swimming party."

He laughed again—but less certainly. And I went on, dropping into a bright hostessy manner. "Talking of holidays, I'm hoping to go with my husband to New York very soon."

"You'll enjoy that. Though this isn't the best time to go."

"I suppose it isn't. But then Maurice *has* to go over about some new gadget."

"The Autoland?"

"That's it. He told me about it tonight. So I thought I'd twist his arm to make him take me along."

"I shouldn't think he'll need much persuading."

"Oh, but he will, I promise you."

"I find that very hard to believe."

I think he found it easy to say the right things to me. I think he really did like me. I know he found me attractive. A woman always does know. It isn't what a man says or how he says it, or even how he looks. It's a kind of aura he exudes as elusive and as positive as perfume.

When I didn't make any acknowledgment of that last remark except a faint lifting of my brows, he said, "You airline wives don't know how lucky you are . . . being able to go on these expensive holidays at the drop of a hat!"

"Nonsense, it's you men! Being able to slough us off, and get up to God knows what. A carte blanche for a couple of weeks at a time in some glamorous place! You ask your wife. She'll be on my side."

"I'm sure she would . . . if I had one."

"Don't tell me a man of your mature years . . ."

"Here, steady on!"

"Hasn't married already! Aren't you even engaged?"

"Sorry!"

"But I bet you have a pretty little girl tucked away somewhere who's trying to get round to Captain's marriage allowances."

"Not guilty. No one in sight."

I mimicked his voice. "I find that very hard to believe." We both laughed immoderately, swimming somehow in laughter, coming up for air, with our eyes moist, our glances suddenly and briefly tender.

"Then," I said, standing on tiptoe, "I shall find you a girl. I am now going to find the prettiest girl in the room and when I have found her I shall take you over and introduce you to her."

He bent down and whispered in my ear, "Look in the mirror, Mrs. C. Don't you *know?*"

But I tossed my head as if discarding his compliment. I searched the whole dreary bunch of our guests, as if to discover a hitherto unrecognized nubile girl. I pointed out Snaith's elder daughter eating a sausage on a stick. And a plain-looking girl whom the Carrutherses had asked if they could bring along.

"No sale?" I asked when he shook his head.

"Positively none."

"Then all the rest are married." I clasped my hands and looked down at them. "Alas!"

"Yes, alas!"

A silence, cupped by the party murmur all around, held us uneasily. "Tell me about New York," I said, looking up. "How many times have you been there?"

"Oh, dozens. More than dozens, I suppose."

"Then you'll know all the places to go. All the shops. All the sights."

"Not *all.*"

"Some of them then?"

"Yes, some."

"Tell me a few."

He reeled off names of Fifth Avenue shops which I'd heard of anyway, and a few restaurants.

"Those all sound so upstage. What about the cheap dives? The places you go to—save dollars to buy nylons for non-existent girl friends?"

He told me about automats and drugstores and a Hungarian restaurant off Forty-third Street, much frequented by the boys.

"Then of course there's Coney Island. You'd love that. I'd like to—"

He stopped abruptly.

"Go on. What would you like to?"

"I'd like to see you and Captain Corby there," he impro-
vized. Briefly the idea amused him. Laughter seemed to radi-
ate under his skin.

"Maurice won't have the time, I'm afraid. Nor the inclina-
tion."

"Then I'd like to see *you* there."

"But you're not likely to see me, are you?"

"I might. You never know the roster."

"No."

"Nor your luck."

"No," I said, "you never know that."

"You sound very solemn all of a sudden, Mrs. C."

"Do I? I didn't mean to. All right then, luck and the roster
permitting, is it a date?"

"Coney Island? If you like. Yes, sure it is!"

I held out my hand half in fun, and after a moment's hesitation, he took it. This was the first time we had touched—
and without really meaning to, and without him meaning to
either, that touch was both prolonged and somehow momentous.

Involuntarily I looked past Matherson to the mirror. He
half turned to follow my eyes.

Momentarily our three reflected glances—Matherson's, my
husband's and mine—met and held. It was as if their apex
splintered the mirror. Maurice turned away. Carruthers came
back to reclaim Matherson. The group in front of the mirror
opened up to include me. Movement shivered the surface like
cracks. Our three faces disappeared.

But they had been there. The mirror had already recorded
that the next step had been taken.

"Good night, Anne dear, and thank you for such a lovely
party!"

"Anne, I positively intend to find out your secret! Why are
your do's such a success."

"Now have a marvellous time in New York. Take care of yourself. And don't forget! Ring me about bridge the moment you get back."

I stood in the hall, finding scarves and hats, brushed with a snowstorm of farewell kisses. I promised cakes for a bring-and-buy, a subscription for Freedom from Hunger. I admired furs bought tax-free from Montreal to Afghanistan. I helped the men on with their coats, and patted their arms good-bye. And if they said, "Come, come! Why so formal all of a sudden, Anne?" I raised my brows at Maurice, seeking his permission, and then I stood on tiptoe and kissed them prettily on their cheeks. The night air blowing in the open door smelled curiously of the country. A flower smell, night-scented stock perhaps from our formal front garden, the leafy smell of the beeches that filter the lights of the street lamps beside them, all fixed and made permanent by the pungency of car exhausts and the smoke pall of London.

"Nice night," someone said, poised like a dark bird in the doorway.

If I closed my eyes, I could imagine it was two and a half years ago, all over again. I was standing in the Prentices' hall. I had just met Maurice. He was somewhere behind me, shouldering his way into his coat. I listened to him thank Mrs. Prentice, knowing that he would be drawn to me down some invisible lane of my making. Just as I knew tonight about Matherson. One can feel the certainty of it inside you, warm and fertile—a thin thread spun, a red banderilla pricked just behind the shoulder.

I opened my eyes and helped Dorothea Snaith to find a glove. I stood in the doorway and waved to the Carrutherses' departing car.

"Corby, what the hell did you put in that liquor . . . because I'm telling you . . . it's not often old Raynor . . . all right, dear, stop pulling me . . . just coming."

"Good night, Mrs. Corby, and thank you."

"Good night, Captain Matherson. You must come again soon."

Then the front door closed behind him and the party was over.

The house seemed to buckle and collapse like an empty can with the air sucked out of it. I stood for a moment, leaning against the front door. Faintly I could hear from the kitchen the stewards finishing their cleaning up, Maurice padding about in the lounge, the last guest's car—Philip's probably—fading like a contrail into nothing.

I turned off the lights in the cloakroom, and walked across the hall and into the lounge. Maurice had his back to me. I stood in front of the electric fire as if to warm myself by its artificially glowing coal.

Now it was my turn to watch Maurice in the mirror. Momentarily he was absorbed in his little tasks, apparently oblivious of me. I saw him straightening the ornaments—a cloisonné vase, the twin Delft cows on the alcove shelves. He studied their position carefully from a distance before smoothing the brocade curtains, bending to examine a cigarette burn drilled like a bullet hole through our pale green carpet. I held out my hands to the fire, while Maurice moved in the mirror bubble above my head—a small dark figure, a tadpole in a furnished pool.

Dislike absorbed me in him, as jealousy absorbed him in me.

I watched him pounce on two dirty ashtrays and carry them through into the kitchen. Though he never raises his voice, I heard him talking to the stewards. I heard their deferential good nights, the rattle of the bolts on the back door. Now there was no one but Maurice and me. I should have felt trapped, awaiting the inevitable questioning. But it was Maurice I felt was trapped, maybe Matherson too—but not me.

When he reappeared Maurice said, "Three glasses broken

and that nice sweetmeat dish cracked. There's a stain on the table and a burn in the carpet. But not bad damages for such a good party!"

But all the time, I knew *that* wasn't the real damage he was looking for. Very soon, in his own good time, he would get around to the damage the party had done to me.

"No, not bad at all," I said. "I thought it went very well. Everyone enjoyed themselves."

"Yes, indeed. A highly successful effort. You are to be congratulated, my dear." He came and stood beside me, both of us backs to the fire, and put his hand on my shoulder. "For being a good girl and a beautiful hostess."

He kissed my cheek. His lips are always cool and soft. I tried to imagine Matherson kissing me. It would be nothing like that.

"What are you thinking about?" Maurice said. "Just now?"

"Oh, I don't know. Why do you ask?"

"You closed your eyes."

"Did I? Then I must be tired, mustn't I?" I put my hand to my mouth and yawned. And when he still waited for an answer, "Actually, I was thinking about the party."

"And the people who came?"

"Yes."

"Who did you notice specially?"

"Raynor, I suppose. But then I usually do notice Raynor because he always gets drunk."

"Yes. I'm afraid one of these days I shall have to have him in."

I glanced sideways at Maurice. "What shall you say to him?"

I like to imagine Maurice wielding the whip. Sometimes imagining that is as attractive as pretending I'm being made love to by somebody else. I toyed with the idea of teasing Maurice a little . . . just a little . . . with Matherson. I wondered if I might see Maurice in a fine red-coloured rage. But

Maurice was in no mood to discuss Raynor and discipline. "I don't know," he said, "I haven't thought about it."

Prissily, like a schoolmaster, he was not going to be diverted from his subject. He pursed his lips before speaking again.

"What I did feel, though," Maurice said, "was that the new fellow was rather a dead loss."

"The new fellow?"

"Captain Matherson. You talked to him a good deal . . . remember?"

"I remember. Yes, he was a dead loss."

"He didn't circulate. I do like people to circulate. I'd have thought he would have liked to meet the other wives."

"I pointed out several interesting people."

"But he wouldn't go over?"

"I think he was shy."

"Possibly."

"Anyway, he was just a brash young boy." I got a mild kick out of using Matherson's own words. I smiled pertly and secretly, as if he were there and I were caricaturing him.

My husband put his fingers under my chin to turn my face round preparatory to kissing me. "Why are you smiling like that?" His expression froze with a fresh chill of suspicion.

"Am I? I didn't know."

"Yes, you were. You were smiling in a very peculiar way."

"But then I am very peculiar." I stared up at him still smiling, shuttering my thoughts from the fingering of those cold eyes. "Besides . . . d'you really want to know why I was smiling?"

"I do."

"I was smiling because I knew you were going to kiss me. And because that was what I wanted you to do."

I brought my face close to his, my lips parted, my eyes half closed. His small mouth fastened eagerly and greedily over mine. For a few seconds I kissed my husband as I myself always want to be kissed. But Maurice's kiss is just putting two damp orifices together, and making them stick for a while. All the same, I could feel his body tauten in response. I could feel a pleased surprise jerking his nerves. His hands dropped from my bare shoulder to my bare arms, moved purposefully across to the curve of my breast.

Abruptly I opened my eyes. Maurice's were always open. One huge grey eye, ugly as a Cyclops, seemed to fill my vision.

I hate eyes. I drown in eyes. I'm sucked through them. I disappear, like Alice in the looking glass. Partly it was that. Partly it was because he wasn't Matherson. But mostly it was because I was suddenly filled with the sheer beastliness of being married to Maurice, and I wanted to leap, leap, *leap* back again to my really young, really free days, when Essie and I used to laugh over the men we went out with.

I pulled myself away from Maurice. His whole face had a curiously elated sensual look. His hands were trembling. When I moved away from him, he blinked as if it was dark and I'd suddenly switched on the lights.

"Well," I said brightly, "I don't know about you, but I'm frightfully tired. I'm going straight to bed. I shall take an aspirin. Don't wake me when you come up, will you, darling?"

TWO

Augusт 5th dawned clear and fine—a good omen for the start of my New York holiday.

I had after the party made my preparation for accompanying Maurice as though that murmur of mine in our bedroom had just been meek acquiescence. Maurice was pleased. He suggested I buy some light clothes because it would be hot, told me I would have a wonderful experience in the New York shops, said he only wished he wasn't going to be tied up so much with the Allen Autoland people, but that afterwards we would go off together to some holiday resort—just the two of us.

"Who will you be dealing with at the factory, Maurice?" I asked.

"Oh, the manager . . . Groger. He's the Big Wheel."

I rather enjoy my husband in this authoritative light. When the stately prow of the Company's management limousine came looming up to our door to collect us, I was feeling almost at peace with the world. At times like these, I could get a kick out of being married to Maurice. I like all the *yes, sir, no, sir, three bags full, sir* routine, not from any snobbish angle, but because it reassures me that to some people at

least Maurice is quite a man. We were both travelling free,
because he was travelling on such important business that a
wife was considered a necessity.

All the same, he fussed and clucked over my eight bleached
pigskin suitcases the driver began loading into the boot.

"We'll have to pay excess just the same as everyone else.
There's no special law for Flight Captains."

"Then there should be, Maurice darling."

It's not that Maurice is mean. But he manages our fi-
nances, as he manages everything else, with a razor-edged
efficiency. If money could be saved by careful planning, then
Maurice would save it. On the other hand, he gives me a
rather staggering dress allowance and he is a lavish giver of
presents. Of course, I knew and he knew and no doubt everyone in the Company knew, too, that it was really to offset the
unbalanced years between us. Fifty and twenty-five is quite
a difference. A childhood, a schooldays, a coming of age and
a maturing. Someone, my aunt most likely, had said a coming
of age of trouble.

Sitting at the back of the car, I let him hold my hand and
said, "Besides, this will be absolutely nothing to what I bring
back. I'm going on a shopping spree, don't forget."

The car started moving—and we were away. Setting off
anywhere is exciting. Besides, I love beginnings. Beginnings
of holidays, beginnings of affairs. I like it best when they
both might come together.

I'm sure that at this stage, Maurice didn't know who the
pilot of our aircraft would be. He'd spent the last days going down to Riverly Airport which is near Bournemouth,
preparing for the flying training down there of his new toy,
this robot pilot. I certainly didn't know. I've never regarded
myself as being a particularly lucky person. Though I usually get what I want, the bill follows almost immediately and
the price is frequently one I hadn't expected to pay. In many
ways, I think whoever dreamed up the maxim *take what you*

want, said the Lord, take it and pay for it must have had me specially in mind.

This time, however, the fact that Philip Matherson was flying us over was a pure bonus. I don't think I'm unduly superstitious, but luck comes into everything too damned much not to give it the odd bit of credit. And the fact that this was my bit of luck seemed as well as the weather to be a good omen for the trip.

We reached London Airport, and the car dropped us at the passenger reception lounge, where Maurice installed me with a martini while he went along to Operations. It was the first time I had noticed that like our mirror at home, the walls there have the theme of eyes. Heavenly, all-seeing eyes, looking down at you from just below God and judging your little ways accordingly. Maybe it's because secretly most pilots get a bit of a God-complex and come back from their trips as if with the Tablets.

I had just got myself another martini when Maurice slid onto the stool next to mine.

"Well," he said, ordering a grapefruit squash, and then rubbing the dry white palms of his hands together so that they made a curious papery sound. "Good weather forecast, my dear. Tail wind. Looks like being a fast trip over."

He smiled, apparently unaffectedly, but his eyes had what I have christened their feathery look—the irises muffled and depthless like a pigeon's breast, the pupils pin-point size. I knew before he spoke that there was going to be a little test.

Besides watching me in the mirror, my husband has other endearing ways of checking up on me. These tests are his favourite. In the midst of an apparently surface conversation, he lets fall a weighted remark, a piece of information likely to disturb, at the same time watching my reaction, his eyes charting every tiny expression like a seismograph pen.

"By the bye," he said. "Captain Matherson is flying us over."

It was information that pleased me so much I almost caught my breath. There are times, of course, when even though I know it's a test, I don't bother to pass it. I get what Essie Somerville used to call bloody-minded. I flounder and look guilty as Maurice gets jealous, and I have exquisite fun.

But today I knew it was highly politic to pass. "Matherson? Do I know him? He's a good pilot, is he?"

"All our pilots are good. But you've met Matherson."

"*Have* I?"

"It was only the other day."

"Was it?"

"You *must* remember!"

"Is he so remarkable then? What does he look like?"

A tannoy came on then, announcing a departure by some unpronounceable airline to Bombay and Jakarta. I watched the dribble of passengers pick up their bits and pieces and disappear before saying, "Wait a minute! Isn't he the one with the potbelly and the son at Repton?"

"That's Brayshaw to a T." Maurice shook the silent laughter from his face like sea water. "What a naughty girl you are! And what a dreadful memory for a Flight Captain's wife! No, I don't think Matherson has any family. I don't think he's married at all, come to that." He went on to remind me that I had met Matherson at our own party. He even described him—tall, reasonably good-looking, rather American in appearance, he thought, an extrovert, not greatly gifted up *there*, he wouldn't say.

"I was never any good at names," I said. "Especially at a party. But yes . . . the penny's beginning to drop! Wasn't he the one who was rather a dead loss?"

"At last . . . that's right!" And then: "What a vague child you are!"

I opened my bag and brought out my compact. I examined my smooth oval face, my dark blue clever eyes. This holiday was *really* going to be a success. "Which all goes to show,"

I dabbed my nose and smiled sweetly, "that I never really notice any man when my husband is around."

I snapped my compact shut, put my fingers to my lips and dropped the postal kiss onto his hand.

I think Maurice, too, had decided for his own reasons that at all costs this holiday must go well, for he didn't contradict me. In fact, by his sudden almost youthful smile, I think momentarily he actually made himself believe me.

He went up to the flight deck about fifteen minutes after we were airborne. A great streak of propriety runs through Maurice. If he was going to do a murder, he would boil the instruments first, and make all the proper inquiries about last wishes and next of kin.

The stewardess came around while he was up there, with the usual magazines and cigarettes and boiled sweets. We looked each other over. I wonder if all women see every other woman as a potential body-snatcher, or whether it's just me. She was a nice-looking girl, tall and blonde with big capable hands and an antiseptic smile. Pretty, I would have said, but not sexy. Which was probably quite wrong, because Dorothea Snaith told me all the stewardesses are as sexy as hell. It was the effect, so Dotty said, of high altitudes—which was an interesting theory. I reminded myself to ask Matherson what it did to men. It was the sort of question I might fling at him when he took me to . . . where was it? . . . Coney Island. While Maurice worked himself up all day and every day on the Autoland.

I smiled at the stewardess as she came back down the aisle, stopping here and there to take an order for drinks or cigarettes. I was pleased that she was the girl on the crew. I would take a bet with myself there was very little competition there.

She smiled back and asked me if she could get me anything? Coffee? Tea? An iced drink?

"No, thank you," I said, "I'm fine. I'm rather enjoying just looking out."

I pointed to the cloud carpet below us, the hollows through which dark blue sea shone back at the sky like ragged holes in a frozen pond.

She was pleased that I, the wife of a man as unapproach-able as Captain Corby, should be so friendly. I could imagine her talking me over in her bed-sitter with the other girls, saying Mrs. Corby was such a sweetie, she couldn't under-stand how on earth those two . . .

"How many trips have you done?"

"Eight, Mrs. Corby, on this particular line."

"Do you always fly with the same captain and crew?"

She shook her head. "Not usually. But I have flown before with Captain Matherson. He's a very good pilot," she added, mistaking my interest.

I wanted to ask her more about him, to pick up some scraps of information to paste into my picture book of him. But in-stead, I murmured that I was sure he was. I let her go on her way then, back to the galley, both of us deviously pleased with our little conversation.

I leaned back against the headrest and half closed my eyes. We were flying like Icarus straight to the sun. I watched just below our wing tip the pink-topped clouds insubstantial as candy floss . . .

Candy floss . . . Brighton pier ten years ago . . . the candy-floss stall . . . a whole holiday from St. Bride's . . . the boy had spun me an extra large one . . . he'd twirled the sugary stuff round and round the stick while he watched my face . . . making the candy floss as big as one of those clouds, as light as air. He was Italian, I thought, with big brown sexy eyes. He tickled the palm of my hand deliberately when he took my sixpence. There's always a wind blowing round that side of the pier. The candy floss was so big and light, it was whipped from my hand and over the railings. It lobbed down

lightly into the sea. I remember Essie laughing, and me leaning over and watching it float round the rusty uprights of
the pier. Brighton pier . . . Brighton Rock, hadn't someone
written a murder story called that?

We went to a night club once, Essie and I. She said it was
madly sordid . . . Brighton-rockish. The proprietor had been
inside and the pianist had strangled some woman or other.
But nothing happened. Nothing much did with Essie.

Yet it was through Essie I met Maurice. Essie and I were
staying with her uncle and aunt, the Prentices. I was always
looking out for a weekend invitation after we left school and
the Prentices were high on my list. They live about ten miles
from Maurice's mother. He was home at the time and they
were having a party, so he was invited. I remember we'd
had a natter in Essie's bedroom about who was coming, and
when Essie had torn every man in shreds, because Essie isn't
very successful with men, she told me about Maurice. I suppose there's something about a confirmed bachelor that is
half attractive and half repellent. The destructive part of me,
which is healthily developed, immediately wants to *uncon-
firm* him, just as some men want to rape nuns or scribble on
a Leonardo. Essie, of course, egged me on. She was a soft
boneless-looking girl, and she had a bad complexion which
her mother used to say was from eating too many sweets, but
which I think was heredity. She had mousy hair and a floury
skin, and she got her chief colour in her adolescent life from
me.

She bet I couldn't. She was always betting with me. And
she was always losing. That way I'd got myself a very nice
little collection of presentable jewellery from almost scratch.
Anyway, she bet me her sapphire earrings to my culture-
pearl necklace.

Of course with stakes like that, she wasn't going to take
my word for it. It wasn't going to be enough that he paid
me a lot of attention. It had to be done properly. Maurice

Corby had to ask me for a date, and I had to accept. Otherwise she didn't trust me not to just pretend that he had, but that I'd turned him down flat.

One thing about Essie was that she always paid up promptly. We each had a bed-sitter in the same house at the less fashionable end of Chelsea. The morning I was lunching with Maurice, she came up, and without a word she dropped the earrings one at a time on my dressing table. I put them on straight away and admired myself in them. Actually, they were wasted on Essie, because her eyes were pale and those sapphires were darkest, richest blue, almost the exact colour for mine. I wore them to that lunch. They were a bit opulent with my new blue dress, but they gave an added tang to the occasion.

After that first date, I didn't really need any other tang. Just to have Maurice watching me was enough. Not because I was in love with him. But because he seemed mature and authoritative and because he was utterly obsessed with me. And having someone obsessed with you isn't like being loved. It's like living inside a giant magnifier or moving within huge halls of mirrors. Your tiniest action is of supreme importance —dream-like or nightmarish according to your mood. Sometimes, especially after we were married, I hated and despised Maurice for his obsession. Sometimes I felt that I could hardly exist without it.

Before we were married, I had gaudy images of what he would do to me when he was jealous. Sometimes after an evening out, Essie would come up to my room and we'd make coffee and talk about Maurice and shiver over the real physical violence Essie said she was sure he was capable of. I suppose I was as near then as I ever was to physically desiring him. On our first night, I didn't try to pretend I was a virgin. But if Maurice realized I wasn't, he said nothing. At the time, that is. Afterwards on our honeymoon, he kept making me go over all the men I'd known before him. But his jealousy never comes to anything. No real explosion. It is quiet and insistent, like perpetual snow. That's why it never goes away, and never gets any less. It has the same quality as sound waves, going on and on without ever reaching the relief of a crescendo. I remember feeling oddly cheated that first night, as if he'd been an incompetent lover—which for me I suppose he was.

From Maurice my mind drifted to Philip and I wondered pleasurably what sort of lover he would be. When Maurice put his hand lightly on my shoulder, I started up guiltily. I was glad that my eyes were half closed, for under their lids I had so much sealed away.

I knew, just before I looked up, that he had brought Matherson back with him. I pretended to be flustered and embarrassed because I'd been asleep.

"Far too many late nights," my husband said.

"Good evening, Mrs. Corby. It's nice to see you again. That was a very successful party you gave the other day."

He gave a stiff half-nod, half-bow, as a shy person does who knows the right things to say.

"Hello, Captain Matherson. And this appears to be a very successful flight you're giving us now."

He looked different in uniform. I should have known from Maurice that uniform improves most people. He looked older, fined down, more remote and therefore, to me, more attractive.

Matherson stood aside and smiled at the passengers across the aisle, while Maurice eased himself into the seat beside me. It's in movements like these that he betrays his age. He stiffens, tucking in his chin, holding his hand over his stomach as if he had a middle-aged paunch, which he hasn't. Then Matherson leaned over to talk to us both.

"How long will you be staying in New York?"

His eyes were brown, not the dark velvety kind, but lightish brown, the colour of amontillado. They went from one to

the other of us with a fine impartiality, which in itself was
revealing. No one given his free and natural choice would
as soon look at Maurice as at me.

"Five days in all. Hard labour for me . . . hard shopping
for Anne. After which we shall have a short holiday in the
country somewhere."

"Then if you've time you must let me take you out to dinner one night?" Matherson said politely. "I'll be in New
York for three clear days. Of course, it won't be such good
fun as your party, Mrs. Corby. But I know one or two good
places where we might get a decent meal."

"Thank you, we'd like that," I said.

Philip kept his eyes on Maurice. "Perhaps you'd give me a
ring when you're free, sir?"

"Will do, old chap . . . if I can."

Maurice nodded his head in dismissal. Philip moved a
pace towards the couple sitting behind. Maurice made as if
to open the *Times*. Then as an afterthought, he touched
Matherson's sleeve.

"Oh, by the bye, if you have three days kicking your heels,
old chap . . . you might do me a favour."

He spoke even more softly than usual, so that Matherson
had to bend down to hear him. Their profiles seemed almost
to touch. I had a momentary glimpse of the pair of them,
cameoed by the clear high Atlantic light, like two sides of
some bizarre counterfeit coin—one sharp as silver, the other
blunt and uncomprehending in bronze.

"You might look after Anne here . . . show her one or two
of the sights . . . keep her out of mischief for me, perhaps?"

It might just have been that he was perfectly satisfied I
thought Matherson the Company bore, and that he was better than my finding my own amusements from morn till night
nearly every day for a week in a wicked city. But I'm pretty
sure it wasn't. It was another of my husband's little tests. On
Matherson this time.

They say the onlooker sees most of the game. So does a test-watcher. And one thing was immediately apparent to me. Philip Matherson isn't nearly as clever as I am. He failed. Quite definitely failed. His whole body stiffened. His eyes narrowed, not so much guiltily or suspiciously, but as if he were genuinely puzzled.

Briefly, before saying the conventional, "Of course. I'd be delighted," he looked at Maurice almost sympathetically, as if my devious clever husband was slightly mad.

THREE

Philip Matherson phoned the following morning, just after ten. In fact, it was less than an hour after the transport had swept my husband off from our hotel to the Autoland factory fifteen miles west on the other side of the river. This gave to the call a certain conspiratorial urgency which probably didn't exist outside my imagination. I was lying in bed with the remains of breakfast still on the bedside table. Even before I lifted the receiver, I knew it would be him.

I had wakened early. Maurice would say it was because of the time difference, or because I'd insisted on having the windows too wide, or left the Venetian blinds with their slats fully open. But it wasn't any of those things. Awareness of the day was as palpable as something squatting on my chest. As dawn broke I was awake and alert—pounded out of sleep by my own quickened blood.

I had not wakened my husband. I wanted to preserve the aura of the day which Maurice's consciousness would invade and break. I had listened to the sounds far below of a city not so much waking up (for it had never seemed to sleep) but of accelerating its tempo, the traffic getting more continuous—thicker and slower, louder and crosser. I had lain quite still for hours, it seemed, and watched the bars of light on the ceiling deepen from pale grey to lemon gold, and slide down until they almost caged my head.

I had got out of bed then, zipped up the blind and dissolved the cage in a flood of sunlight. I had leaned out of the open window. White clouds, frothy as egg whites, suspended themselves just out of reach of the tallest skyscrapers. Sunshine blinded their columns of windows to gilded reflectors. The walled-in sky above my head was a bland picture-postcard blue.

It was going to be a *beautiful* day.

My second bit of luck. Luck and the roster after all *were* permitting.

Behind me, almost in his dreams, Maurice tut-tutted at the sudden current of air. I could hear his tongue go *sklap-sklap* against the roof of his mouth as he swallowed away sleep. I listened to all the horrid sounds of a deep sleeper waking up, as if their distastefulness automatically gave me carte blanche.

"Just seeing what sort of day it is," I said, figuratively and physically dragging myself back in. "Making up my mind what I should do."

Though I knew precisely. Just as I knew when Matherson phoned. Though being me, I didn't come straight out with it. Maurice says all women are by nature crooked and crab-like, but then Maurice only really knows me. I know I find it difficult to approach anything in a completely straight line. I do sometimes, of course. But mostly I'm like one of those toys which are set to run in life-like deviations, who double back on themselves and whose complicated pattern is as pre-set for them as the righteous engine that charges loud and clear down shining straight and narrow tracks.

Matherson was speaking from his hotel bedroom a couple of floors above us. I heard the operator say, "You're through to 4095 now."

Then I said, "Hello?"

"Good morning . . . is that Mrs. Corby?"

His telephone voice, like his party manner, has a slight attractive hesitation. But being me, I pretended that I spoke to a stranger. "Good morning. Yes, this is Mrs. Corby speaking. I'm afraid if it's my husband you . . ."

"No, thank you, Mrs. Corby. I don't want to speak to him. I wanted you."

"Who is that?"

"Don't you know?"

"I'm no good at telephone voices. Ah, I know! Bill . . . Bill Carruthers! I didn't know you were over here!"

"I'm not. I'm back in the Training Section. Try again, Mrs. C."

"Let me think . . ."

There was a pause.

"You know, of course . . . don't you, Mrs. C.?"

"I haven't really a clue, Captain M."

"Well, we'll just have to sort it out sometime later."

"Sometime later *when*?"

"Later this morning. You've seen what sort of day it is?"

"To tell you the truth, I've hardly noticed."

"Fine and clear, with a bit of wind. Just right for a day out."

"Well actually, that's exactly what I was going to do. I'd told Maurice I would spend a day out at the shops. I was just on my way when the telephone rang. In fact, I was just closing the door. I had to come back in to answer it."

"In that case," Matherson said, "I'll expect you down right away. I'll wait for you in the foyer. By the lifts. Mind you're on the next one!"

I made no promises. I simply laughed into the receiver and put it back into its cradle. I didn't hurry either. I wanted to make sure I should wear something fairly devastating, and as I have a fairly comprehensive wardrobe that made the decision somewhat lengthy and difficult. I finally plumped for a new pink linen suit which we had bought on a three-day visit with my husband to Rome. It has with it a wild silk blouse of just the right green, and the whole thing is by La Goncha. I'd bought its accessories in Rome too, and though the shoes have heels that are too spiky for sightseeing, I put them on nevertheless.

I suppose I arrived down on the foyer about fifty minutes after he phoned, which considering the results was quick. If I'd known him a little better, if I could have been certain he'd have waited, I'd have made it still longer.

He was standing with his hands in his trouser pockets, head a little down, his eyes fixed on the crowd of us that spilled out of the lift. Though he's by no means bull-like in build, his stance was oddly so. I went towards him smiling, unabashed, offering him my small gloved hand as one offers something of exquisite value.

"Captain Matherson! How nice of you to invite me out like this"—and in the same breath—"you look like the wrath of God."

"I am the wrath of God."

I giggled. "My humblest apologies. But it wasn't really my fault. There was a lightning strike of lift operators. You know how these things happen. I was marooned at the thirtieth floor."

He looked me over, raising one eyebrow in schoolboy derision.

"God help the lift operator!"

"I'm afraid He didn't."

I noticed again his clear golden brown eyes—rather effective under thick scrubby eyelashes—the way he held his head, and his good thick discus-player neck, so different from my husband's, which secretly under his white collar is beginning to fold like a tortoise on the move.

"All the same, I'll forgive you. You didn't actually waste your time."

"Heavens, that *is* a compliment!"

"Mind you, you wasted mine."

Across the foyer, I fell into step beside him. He walked in a slow unhurried relaxed way that was designed to be the true opposite of Maurice's cat-like prowl.

This was the first time I'd seen the foyer by daylight, if that was what you could call its metallic illumination. Daylight, like the air, was sucked in, blinded, denatured, splintered by chromium, stainless steel, glittering tiles, and conflicting rainbow signs. People milled, shoved and shouted. Lifts whooped up and down. Telephones buzzed. Bells rang.

To guide me through its buffeting, Philip held my arm lightly just above the elbows. I could feel the pressure of his fingers through the thin sleeve of my jacket. Even that small physical contact swelled the pleasure of my mood. I took three steps to every one of his, making my heels click across the tiles like castanets. From time to time I looked up into his face to see what his reaction was to me.

But I think he is, as Maurice said, an extrovert, unimaginative, uncomplicated and outward-looking. Now he was absorbed in steering us both through the crowd and out into the street.

"Actually," I said, "the real reason I'm late . . . I wasn't going to the shops when you rang, I was in the bath. I dashed out and came dripping to answer it . . . without a stitch on."

"That's the way most people bathe, isn't it?" His eyes just crinkled up at the corners.

Then he had to take his hand away from my arm to push open the swing door ahead of me, and once we were out on the pavement he thrust both of them in his pockets. We stood for a moment under the hotel's blue and gilt awning which cut out a sharp rectangle of shadow from the now bright sunlight.

"Well, Mrs. C.?"

"Well, Captain M.?"

"Is it to be Coney Island?"

"That's what I came over for!"

"Fibber!" he laughed. "All right, if that's what you want."

"Isn't it what you want?"

"Yes."

"Is that why you phoned?"

"Of course. What else?"

"You might have phoned to please Maurice." I had to say that somehow, though I knew I shouldn't have. I saw him frown at me, as though a hitherto unrecognized situation had abruptly dawned on him.

Then he looked at my face. I know that he was suddenly conscious of me, of all of me, in a way my husband has never been. Maurice would never have enough warmth to quicken his knowledge, and Matherson would never be able to analyze his. I saw the recognition of his desire for me cross his face with a sudden surprise, like a quick blink of sunshine. To be followed by a wariness, an instinct to escape, at once titillating and amusing.

"Well, come on," I said impatiently. "If we're going, let's go!"

He held up his arm to try to get a taxi . . . and it was as if, after that, the day itself took over, and we were just aware of the fun of being with each other, and I for one didn't care about anything else.

After a few minutes of standing outside the hotel with the doorman doing absolutely nothing, because as Matherson said even with me he didn't look prosperous enough for the man to bother, we decided we'd get a cab better along Fifth Avenue itself. So off we hared, waving and whistling, cursing when they didn't stop, holding hands because that was the only way he could stop me in my high heels being run down by the traffic.

We got one at last. We slumped against its upholstery, laughing and breathless, looking at each other with an odd sort of camaraderie as if we'd just climbed Everest together.

"You're a fine runner, Mrs. C."

"You're not so bad yourself, Captain M."

"Of course with you," he said, "it's on account of being so young."

"I'm twenty-five."

"My, my! Who'd have thought it?"

"How old are you?"

"Thirty."

"Maurice," I said, looking down at my hands, "is fifty."

"So what?"

"So nothing. Just telling you."

As the taxi sped through high bare caverns of streets full of tenements, I asked him about himself. Where did he live? Were his parents still alive? Had he any brothers or sisters? "I know you're not married," I said. "Because you haven't a single grey hair."

"Not because I told you before?"

"No. *Did* you tell me?"

That was the first time I noticed his way of biting off a smile when I said something which was irritatingly untrue. I rather liked that expression. It made something inside me shiver and melt. To amuse him and to amuse myself too, I gave him a few half-edited, half-fictitious accounts of things that had happened—some to Essie and some to me.

"You must have been quite a gal before you married."

"I'm quite a gal *still*."

When we arrived at Coney Island, he took my arm quite automatically. And without my having to tell him, he began calling me Anne. By this time the day itself had got going. There was real heat in the sun. But the little egg-white clouds had swollen up into huge bull-bosomed ones, higher than any skyscraper, and a brisk wind trundled them at intervals between us and the sun.

Coney Island itself was a mammoth bastard village of commercial fun . . . a dirty dollar-grubbing place that made Brighton look like Cheltenham Spa, and I loved every inch of it.

We wandered around the alleys and the roadways hand in hand, putting money in slot machines, having our fortunes told on printed cards and reading them out aloud.

" 'You have a gentle retiring artistic nature,' " mine said. " 'You will marry a handsome farmer from the Middle West. A widower with independent means.' "

Philip's said his neurotic wife didn't understand him, that he must try to be patient, for happiness was on the way.

All of which Philip said was absolute gospel and he didn't know how those machines did it. I invented stories about my Middle West farmer, and he dreamed up dreams about his neurotic wife.

We ate lunch-time hamburgers with double rations of onions out of paper bags, while we still wandered aimlessly, blissfully around. We smelled each other's breaths afterwards and said they were so awful that both the Middle West farmer and the neurotic wife would certainly turn us out. Then we kissed each other lightly on the lips to show that anyway we didn't mind.

We went on the cakewalk, and I held on to him tightly . . . purely for Empire Airways' sake, lest he fall and break a leg and be unfit for duty. We nibbled clams from a fish-food stall.

"God!" I said. "They've got eyes!" And I spat mine out on the sidewalk, though Philip chewed his. We went in a foul place which blew your skirts over your head—which as I pointed out was all right for *him*. We went on the Ghost Train and I avoided all those vile wet sponges that trail over your face by holding mine against Philip's chest.

"I can feel your heart beating." I could, even through his jacket. And he said, "Christ, do you wonder?"

We went down on the roller coaster. I got my hair set ruined by the Big Dipper, and then had it stood on end by some surprisingly old-fashioned swings.

It was exactly like rolling away twenty years. It was like eating good food after years of elderly cooking. It was like getting the strength back in your legs after being an invalid. I remember Philip's face watching me indulgently as we whirled along the Scenic Railway, with me holding his hand so hard that the diamonds of my engagement ring made my fingers bleed. We went on the Dodgem cars, and I steered and each time we banged into someone, he said, "You got me, pal!" Which seemed very funny at the time, as I whirled like some sand devil up some dizzy emotional spiral.

I remember him saying as I hurled wooden balls at an ugly pursed-faced Aunt Sally which immediately reminded me of Maurice, "This is a fine place to get rid of all those childish inhibitions!"

But it wasn't. I didn't get rid of anything childish. I was wallowing in it. My mood revolved in a delicious sound-and-colour-blinded ecstasy, like those flying cars orbiting round and round.

And the central supporting column was him.

When he looked at his watch and said, "Don't you think it's time we weren't here, Mrs. C.? What time is your husband expecting you back from shopping, all of a piece?" I felt as if that column had broken, as if he had aroused me and then withdrawn from me. Even the very mention of my husband seemed inept and wrong. For today, the years between Maurice and me had become a tunnel, a giant telescope, and he had diminished to a tiny figure at the wrong end of it.

"You mean the farmer from the Middle West?" I said, trying to climb back into the dream. "Oh, any time really. He's not fussy. And I'd like just one more look around . . ."

But it's always a mistake. There is, I suppose, a perfect end to everything perfect. I should have let it end there— but I couldn't. I asked him to buy some popcorn and a carton of juice to make do for tea and we picnicked on a grey wooden parapet that bordered the beach.

Behind us, loudspeakers rattled out pop music, klaxons wailed, joy bells rang, the whole place creaked with its wooden laughter. While in front of us, the Atlantic rolled in long blue-grey serpents over a dirty foreshore, frothed with paper bags and milk cartons. Mixed with the rank smell of fat and onions and fried meats and boiling sugar and dust and the fumes of panting diesels came the tang of the sea, so much the same here as in my childhood that I seemed to slip through some crack of emotional time, and be where it all began. And with the prescience of childhood, I knew that this place was the nearest I would ever get to Heaven and that already even this was passing away.

As if he recognized my change of mood, Matherson leaned forward. He tossed the empty paper bags away and put both his hands on my shoulders. I think he merely meant to give me a quick kiss to break the spell and bring me back into myself again.

But I couldn't leave it at that. I slipped my hands round his neck, so that his lips were pressed hard on mine. Then I let my finger tips trail soft as shivers up and down the nape of his neck, just as Maurice likes me to. I felt the outline of his teeth, his hard cheekbone, the whole stiffening of his body which made mine melt softly against him. Perhaps most yearning of all, I smelled the air on his skin, which gave it that sandy sweetness of youth, which an old skin never has. And I kept thinking of that, and letting my senses draw it in, as if Maurice were near and watching—and if my senses let go, he would come forward and snatch me to himself again.

I tried then very hard to tell Philip with my mouth and with my body that whatever he wanted I would do. Then

abruptly his hands tightened. He pushed me away. When I
looked at the expression of his face, I knew that like most
devious people, mine was a devious fate.

I had in my own way won Philip Matherson—and just as
certainly I had in my own way lost him, too.

FOUR

FOR ONCE, I had no desire to make my husband jealous. I suppose that might be taken as a compliment to Matherson. Whatever he had for me didn't require Maurice's jealousy to make it three-dimensional.

Or so I thought.

Usually when I've been attracted to another man, sooner or later I can't help letting the odd clue drop to Maurice, and watching him pounce. It's all part of the fun. But this time, no. I hugged that day out to me as if its very secrecy made it personal, real, *mine*. I even went out of my way to please Maurice. When he came back from the factory—late, because they'd laid on a special full-scale demonstration of all the blind landing qualities of their robot—I had already showered and changed into his favourite dress of long-sleeved black velvet. The neck is scooped out wide over the shoulders, and I have a dramatically white skin. With it I wear a double choker of pearls, so that the whole effect is as Maurice once said (hopefully, I think) quite virginal and nun-like. I always have a sympathy with the wolf in sheep's clothing or the one in Grandmama's best bonnet. It's a necessity sometimes to appear as one's true opposite, a curious refreshment,

as if you were two people, light and dark. And it pleased me
that night to wear it, when I could hardly have felt less nun-
like.

More important still, it pleased Maurice.

"Ah, my dress, darling," he said as he closed our bedroom
door behind him. "How charming you look!"

He brushed his lips against my cheek and patted my shoulder. I smiled back at him and said I'd ordered bottles for the
drinks cupboard, and should I mix him a martini while he
changed? He smelled fusty and indoorish, and I could smell
somebody else's tobacco smoke on his clothes.

"Delightful thought!" Maurice said. "You can bring it into
the bathroom while I shower."

He also insisted with the forced gaiety which is his pro-
prietory brand on changing into his dinner jacket. He
hummed to himself as he chose his shirt and found his socks,
and while I tied his tie, he told me about the Autoland, and
what a splendid show the Company had put on that day. He
was taking his evening shoes off their trees, when he said,
"Well, that's quite enough about me. What has my little girl
done with herself all day?"

I never considered telling him the truth, though I paused
a moment before answering. But the reason I lied was neither
because I didn't want to make him jealous nor because I was
afraid. I lied because I preferred to. Because a secret binds
its sharers together and cements what relationship they already have. And because in some curious way, I knew Matherson would feel impelled to keep it a secret, too.

"Well, nothing very much really. I looked around mostly.
Getting the feel of the place, I suppose."

"I hope you remembered to eat properly."

"Oh, but I did. I had a lovely lunch."

"And where did you get this lovely lunch?"

"I forget the name of the place. A little restaurant on
Fourth Avenue. Morelli's I think it was called."

"I'm glad they did you well. How did you find the shops?"

"Blissful! But heavens, aren't they vast?"

"Well, Saks is, of course. I suppose you went there?"

"Oh, yes. But lots of others, too."

Maurice laughed and said he hoped I hadn't tried to buy them all up. He was cleaning out his fingernails with an orange stick when he said, "And when are we to have the fashion show?"

"The fashion show?"

"Of what you bought, darling. Don't tell me you didn't buy anything!"

"Oh, I bought *lots*. But I'm having it sent. You'll have to wait a little longer." I tickled him under the chin, and he seized the tips of my fingers and kissed them and said I was beautiful, no matter what I wore. Then as he was dressed, he made us stand side by side in front of the cheval mirror.

"There, darling," he said while his eyes devoured me like a cat, tiny bit by well-chewed tiny bit. "Don't we make a handsome couple? We shall have the Grand Seigneur treatment, I promise you!"

But privately I reckoned I had ceased even to look nun-like. We looked like a couple of magpies out after some carrion, the one young and shiny, the other old and dull. But both all black and white.

And I longed for rich colours, throbbing colours, gold and red and green—colours of fire and blood and jealousy, the colours of life.

The next day was both their faults—Matherson's and Maurice's. To begin with, Matherson should have phoned me. If he had, things might have worked out very differently. He didn't have to invite me out. All he had to say was that Coney Island had been fun, and that we must see each other again.

Soon.

After all, the only thing I wanted was something to look

forward to. I wanted it so much that I didn't go out all the following morning. And in the afternoon, only to Saks to choose three dresses and two suits and ask for them to be sent round as soon as possible so Maurice wouldn't get suspicious. Even then, I left a message with the telephone operator. And as soon as I got back I lifted the receiver and checked up.

No, there had been no calls.

I think I knew even then what had happened. Men are much more conventional than women—I'd always recognized that. And pilots are more so than other men. That doesn't mean they're more moral—far from it. They just detest being found out. So Matherson had decided to play safe. That wary look that had crossed his face when he stood outside the hotel yesterday had won. He had decided to back out while the back door was still open.

But though I knew it, I didn't let myself be convinced. I went on hoping. I lay on the bed and listened to the lifts hissing up to our floor, stopping to let out invisible passengers, and then I tried to imagine that Philip might be one of them. And I waited for footsteps . . . and when I heard them I waited for them to stop outside our door.

But they didn't. Not until I myself rang, mostly to make sure the damned phone was working . . . sometimes phones do go out of order just when you're waiting for an important call . . . to order a tray of tea to be sent up. And then it was only the bellhop, and he wanted nothing more from me than a dollar bill.

They stopped again, of course, when Maurice arrived back . . . early and breezily pleased. But he recognized I was in a bad mood the moment he came in.

He said, "Hello, my sweet," and padded over and stood by the bed. "Not feeling under the weather, are you?"

"Yes, I am."

He tut-tutted and patted my hand. "It's the change, I expect. Or the richer food." He put his fingers on my forehead, but I turned my face away, and said, "I haven't got a temperature. I know that."

"You don't think you're starting with a summer cold?"

"No, I don't."

Maurice took his jacket off and hung it inside the closet. "What!" he said with sudden surprise. "Haven't they arrived yet?"

"Haven't what arrived?"

"Your new clothes."

"No, I phoned up. They're delivering tomorrow."

"Maybe that's why you're feeling downhearted, darling." He went to the drinks cupboard and mixed me a martini. "My little girl's disappointed that her dresses didn't arrive."

"Maybe," I said, sitting up and taking it from him. "Maybe it's just that I'm bored. It's not much of a holiday, kicking your heels all day while your husband works."

I know I made work sound an immoral occupation, and Maurice laughed chidingly, though he was not displeased that I seemed to have missed him.

"Well, never you mind, my dear! I shan't be working much longer. And besides, we're going out tonight. It's all arranged."

"I'm not sure I want to."

"But if you're bored, that's exactly what you must do."

"I might be bored going out."

"I don't think somehow you will be. Besides I've accepted."

"Accepted what?"

"A dinner invitation."

"Who with?"

"No one very exciting, I'm afraid. But he knows his way around New York. Philip Matherson. I met him in the foyer. He apologized for the short notice. But he's out on service again back to England tomorrow."

I turned on my side and said nothing. I watched Maurice

take off his tie and haul his shirt over his head. He has a pale
flabby back and sloping shoulders. There is a brown mole
under his left shoulder. A long grey hair grows out of it. I
focused my eyes on it. I didn't know then who I resented
more, Maurice or Matherson. I didn't really care. Somehow
between them, they had made it all legal and formal and
conventional. They had drained what looked like a promising
affair of all its colour and life. And they had presented it
back to me—grey as suet pudding, lifeless as stone.

Matherson took us to a place that under any other circumstances I would have liked. It was quite a taxi ride out of
New York, and if Matherson noticed anything nostalgic in
our being in a taxi again together so soon, he gave not the
slightest sign of it. There was a small Hungarian orchestra,
and a floor show of vigorously dancing girls which Matherson
made a point of paying attention to. The food was good, the
beef Stroganoff tender and clotted, exactly as I like it. I wore
an off-the-shoulder frock, brilliant with red sequins.

But from the beginning, the evening was designed to put
me in my place. I was Mrs. Corby and I was a stranger. I
wondered quite honestly just for whose benefit Matherson
was putting all this on. I rather hoped it was for Maurice's.
But really I knew it was for mine.

It reminded me of those horrid advertisements you see in
the newspapers . . . *Mr. Righteous X announces that from
the date as above he will not be responsible for any debts in-
curred in his name by Mrs. Unrighteous X.*

He didn't know me. He wasn't interested in me. He had
witnesses to prove it. The best witness of all, my husband.
Mind you, he didn't do it as clumsily as that. In fact, he was
fairly subtle. He included me in the conversation as if I were
someone like Dorothea Snaith, middle-aged, placid, domes-
ticated. How did I find New York? It was my first visit,
wasn't it? Yes, of course Maurice had told him that. Had I

been to the shops? Did I enjoy the food or did I think American cooking overfried?

I tried to rally us both by asking him exactly the same things I'd asked him as long ago as yesterday, when we existed, it seemed, on the other side of the moon. But he answered stolidly, politely, without an answering gleam in his eyes. In fact, his eyes seemed glassed up against me, as if he wore contact lenses. The whole of him did, for that matter—like some moral Space Age man, completely glassed-in and proofed-up against any sort of moral corruption.

Most damnable of all, he brought other girls' names into the conversation . . . that was the time he was coming back from a twenty-first party at Windsor with a girl friend of his sister's he'd taken out . . . the social hostess at the Elbow Beach Hotel . . . did Maurice remember that attractive stewardess who'd left last month to go to B.O.A.C.? Well, he'd run into her last week, taken her to the flicks, as a matter of fact . . . and she was saying à propos B.O.A.C.'s pay loads . . .

From there, the conversation went on to Operational costs, maintenance, stopovers, and inevitably as Maurice took over the conversation—the Autoland.

There it stayed, with Maurice's outstretched hand demonstrating blind landings onto the tablecloth, till the waiters began pointedly to tidy up, and Matherson got our coats. As he put mine over my shoulders he said, "I hope we haven't bored you too much, Mrs. Corby?"

"Far from it," I said. "It's been a most interesting and instructive evening."

I had only one small grain of comfort to hold to myself— Matherson was a fellow conspirator. I had been right. He had said nothing about yesterday. Nor would he ever. And no one conceals something that is of no value.

"Don't you think you were a little ungracious to Captain Matherson?" my husband said, as back in the hotel we walked down our corridor.

He was pleased with himself. Whatever doubts he might have felt had been apparently put to rest. He hummed under his breath as he put the key in the door.

"I don't think so."

I could hardly bear to speak to him. Even his good humour underlined my failure. My spirits worked in an inverse ratio to his. I couldn't wait for him to open the door. I felt like someone who feels sick and who thinks they won't ever get to the bathroom, like someone with unbearably tight shoes who simply must get them off. Something was pressing inside me that could only be released within our room—with Maurice.

I flung into the bedroom and threw my gloves and bag onto the bed. I kicked off my shoes. I pulled so hard on my dress that one of the straps broke and the red sequins slid silently down onto the carpet like drops of blood. I stepped out of my underwear and left it where it was. Then I walked into the bathroom without any clothes.

I didn't know what I wanted then. But Maurice should have done. He was crouched over the washbowl cleaning his teeth, dutifully round and round . . . gargle and spit, gargle and spit.

Hearing me behind him, he glanced in the mirror. I saw him raise his eyebrows and tighten his lips in moral surprise. But he said nothing.

I didn't bother to brush my hair or remove my make-up. I didn't care if my lipstick left crimson smudges on the pillows. I just lay with my eyes closed, hating Matherson and hating Maurice, yet willing my husband to come now and come in vengeance and drive Matherson out of me.

He came to me, of course. He was always only too glad to. But first, heavy-breathed with disapproval, he picked up my shoes, tidied my underwear, and scrabbled up the sequins. Then he came to me—pajamaed, cleaned, deodorized, devitalized. And when he started quietly, methodically, unappeasingly . . . slow, slow, quick, quick, slow . . . an elderly passionless dancing master's beat, something inside me, something savage, something alive, something untouched screamed out.

And I told him I had been so apparently ungracious to Captain Matherson because that evening I had found myself rather attracted to him.

Abruptly my husband's hand stopped its mechanical rousing.

I waited.

I waited for his anger and jealousy to exorcise Matherson. I waited for what I suppose I've always been waiting for. For Maurice's violence. At that time, that was what would have saved us. I wasn't in love with Matherson. And I hadn't, as Essie and my aunt and everyone had supposed, just married Maurice for his money. Maurice did have something for me. Some promise of something. I waited with my heart beating so fast, it was like something thick and heavy, swelling in my throat. I heard Maurice's hard indrawn breath. I waited then, passive and compliant—waiting for whatever was going to come.

Then Maurice switched on the bedside lamp. Light as cold as frozen water drenched my face. Whatever bright colours were imprinted on my mind now paled. Whatever was warm and melting now congealed. Wrinkling my eyes up against the dazzle, I looked up at Maurice, half crouching above me.

At first, I couldn't get his face into focus. It was like coming to after an anaesthetic. And then I saw that his expression had hardly changed, except that it had got sharper and more cunning.

I don't know how long he went on staring at me, but in those few seconds we had moved from bright jungle to the Arctic tundra. For all the heat of the evening, I shivered. My anger had cooled. Whatever climax I sought would, I knew, never come. But my body remained half aroused, heavy and burdensome, how I imagine it would feel to be drowned. And now all I wanted was to be left in peace—and settle for the half-relief of Maurice's body.

"Where did you go yesterday?"

"I told you. To the shops."

"Which shops?"

"Saks mostly."

"Why hasn't the stuff you bought come?"

"I've told you . . . it'll be here tomorrow."

"What did you buy?"

"Two suits and three dresses."

"Where did you lunch?"

"I told you. Mantovani's."

"You told me Morelli's."

"What's the difference Mantovani's . . . Morelli's? Everyone forgets names."

"Are you attracted to Captain Matherson?"

"No."

"It was a lie?"

"Yes. A lie."

"Why did you lie?"

Now it was my turn to look into his face searchingly. Suddenly, I didn't know why—and because I didn't, I closed tight my eyes.

Mistaking my reason, Maurice pulled the bedside lamp nearer. With one cold clinical hand he forced my screwed-up eyelids open.

"I lied," I said, "I lied . . . I lied because—"

And then I smacked my head up and down on the pillow in sheer frustration, and cried so that Maurice had to put his hand over my mouth, lest, as he said, everyone in the hotel should hear.

"I lied . . ." I sobbed. "Because I wanted *you*."

I don't know whether he believed me. I don't even know myself if it was true or only half true or maybe not true at all.

He didn't say anything for a very long time. Then he switched off the light and said almost gently, "You shouldn't lie, darling. Husbands have to teach their wives not to lie."

Then he stretched himself down beside me. And with a quick little movement like the pursing of lips or the closing of a dirty book, he flicked down my nightdress. "Good night," he said, turning away from me. "Good night. Sleep well."

FIVE

"Maurice said I was to apologize humbly, and ring you to-day *without fail.*"

I lay back on our drawing-room sofa, cradling the telephone, whilst I smiled into it as innocently as if Philip had been there in person.

"Apologize, Mrs. Corby? For what?"

He was speaking from Operations at London Airport, where I'd finally run him to ground. His voice was as neutral and polite as if we'd just recently been introduced. He was still trying to maintain the attitude that he had done at our dinner in New York.

"Oh, for *not* returning your awfully kind hospitality. For *not* thanking you properly for that lovely day out. For, to quote Maurice, dragging you around some childish fairground when you had more intelligent interests to pursue."

Naturally Maurice had said nothing of the kind. But I am a fair mimic. I caught Maurice's small-mouthed tone. Anyway, it made Matherson laugh suddenly and spontaneously. Maybe it even convinced him that my husband was grateful. He seemed even relieved that apparently Maurice knew—it made everything above-board.

"You can tell Maurice from me I enjoyed it enormously."

"I will, I promise."

We both waited for the other to continue, like two polite dithery people in a narrow doorway. "Anyway," Philip said after a moment. "You had a nice holiday, did you?"

"Marvellous, thank you. One of the best we've ever had. We went up to the Adirondacks for a couple of days. Maurice did some fishing. I did some walking. Then we came back to New York and did a *few* shows, and a *lot* of shopping."

We both laughed again. There was another pause.

"Did you have a good trip back?"

"Yes, *quite*. Not so good as the trip over, of course. Snaith" —Jack Snaith was one of the most senior pilots—"couldn't handle her quite so well as our westbound Captain did. But he's coming along nicely."

Even in fun, these pilots lap up flattery. You can't make it too sweet, or lay it on too thick. I think they have an Achilles' heel large enough to drive a tank through, never mind an arrow. Anyway, we laughed together again, and I could feel Philip Matherson softening up under me, as if I massaged away little tensed-up knots of muscle.

I asked him if they were working him hard these days and he said so-so.

I told him it was much the same with Maurice, except that these days he was always at the office, working on his beloved Autoland. He would not be going off on Service for quite a while.

"Actually, that was why he wanted me to phone you. We wondered if you'd care to come round for a bite of supper?"

And when he mumbled he'd love to, I said smoothly, "Tomorrow would suit *us* best. About seven-thirty, if you can make it."

It was all very conventional and harmless and proper. The wife of the Flight Captain to the up-and-coming junior Captain. Come, dear boy, be honoured at our table.

"That's very kind of you. May I just think for a moment if I've got anything fixed for tomorrow?"

"Do," I said.

I held the earpiece away from me. I wasn't really in suspense, though from the other end of it I could almost hear the cogs and wheels and chains of his guilts and suspicions working. But I'd heard something else, too. Once again the faint surprise that underlined his courtesy. As if he knew that he was attracted to me, and was puzzled as to why Maurice should appear to encourage him, and why I should seem so blissfully unaware of it. "Anyway," I went on briskly. "We *both* hope you can come. You were very kind to me in New York. It made all the difference while Maurice was busy."

There's absolutely nothing in this invitation, dear boy. Not a spark of affection or warmth. Think nothing of it. Just tit for tat. True-blue suburban hospitality. You eat my food, I eat yours. Supper for supper. Coffee for coffee. Drink for drink. Eye for eye.

"Yes, that's fine. I *am* free tomorrow. I shall look forward to it."

"So shall we. We're not inviting anyone else. So Maurice won't be changing."

And only when I'd said good-bye and replaced the receiver did I laugh out loud. I walked over to the mirror on the wall, still smiling.

"Why should Maurice change?" I asked the clever girl in the mirror. "For Maurice won't be here."

And the clever girl and I laughed so long and so loud that our breath steamed the mirror and almost blurred us from sight.

But not for long. The clever girl and I were on top of our form. She had been much in evidence that day. And together we shared a secret.

Maurice's visits to his mother.

Coolly and methodically, not with the beat of love but with the turning of the calendar, my husband paid her a three-monthly duty visit. Almost like a conscientious bailiff, come Candlemas, come Michaelmas . . . Maurice would drive up to Norfolk.

Very rarely did I go with him. Mother-in-law and I did not exactly get on. I think the sight of my "hideously young face" (as she once described it to Maurice) got in between her and whatever pleasure my husband's visits gave her.

At seven-thirty in the morning precisely, Maurice would leave our house to arrive at Market Railford in time for Mrs. Corby senior's eleven o'clock glass of madeira. And the following day after an early dinner, he would start the return journey. As with everything Maurice did, the schedule worked like clock work. Unlike other people who got held up in traffic jams or diversions, Maurice arrived home exactly the same time, no matter the weather conditions or the volume of traffic.

I knew when precisely to make his hot Horlick's, and when to switch on the spotlight above the garage door. I knew exactly what presents he would bring in return for the box of Fortnum and Mason's goodies which I had sent—cut flowers from his mother's walled garden (for she had bewitched green fingers) off-set probably by an old photograph of Maurice, or some ancient lace from some ancient drawer which smelled, like Maurice did, of mothballs.

I knew exactly what he would say when he closed the door behind him and brushed my cheek. "Mother sends you her dear love. There! She asked me to kiss you."

Well, this morning, I had sent her an extra kiss. Two large soft mulberry ones, full on his lips. "One for you, dear," I said. "And one for Mother-in-law. Now don't speed, will you, darling? You've got lots of time."

I didn't try to hurry him away because I knew that it

would be at least a couple of hours before I could decently
phone Matherson. What I really wanted to beg my husband
was, "Please, darling, don't hurry back tomorrow."

And somehow along the ether or whatever medium lies
between his mind and mine, the message must have got over.
For a few hours after I'd invited Philip, about six o'clock to
be precise, when the cheap calls come in, Maurice phoned
from Mother-in-law's home to say he had arrived safely after
a splendid journey. Then he said "Darling" very quietly, and
paused.

I recognized the tone and I was wary. "God," I thought.
"Don't tell me he's going to say he's coming back *early!*"

And as the drowning are purported to do, my poor mind
reviewed not so much my past life as the beautiful preparations I had made for the man who was coming to dinner . . .
the Nuits St. Georges burgundy . . . the food I'd ordered . . .
the silver I'd made Mrs. Thorpe bring out from the cupboard
and clean . . . the lavish pay I'd promised her for serving and
waitressing . . . my hair-do booked with Charles, and my
manicure with Peggy . . . everything.

Momentarily I swore in silence. But I was splendidly
wrong.

"Darling," Maurice repeated in that confidential bad-news-
coming voice. "I'm a little concerned about Mother. She's a
little under the weather. Nothing serious. Nothing physical.
I don't want to worry you, but it may mean I'll be a little
late back tomorrow."

He paused. Before I spoke, I had to sieve the grin out of
my voice which thickened it like peach pulp.

"Oh," I said, at last. "I *am* sorry." I think I sounded something like it. At least I sounded husky, and Maurice did not
appear displeased. And because he would want me to, and
because I wanted to know, I asked practically, "How late,
darling, do you suppose you'll be?"

"It's rather difficult to say, my love. I hope not *too* late."

"Won't you be awfully tired? Shouldn't you stay the whole night?"

"Well, if I'm tired I shall. I promise. In which case, I'll phone you. Thanks, darling. I knew you'd understand."

He made a horrid sucking noise at the end which he sometimes does to indicate a wired kiss.

"Give Mother-in-law my love," I said with real warmth. "Tell her to look after herself."

"Will do, darling. Good night. God bless."

I blessed him back. I blessed Mother-in-law too. I felt warm with things going well.

And yet for all that, a slight nerve of uneasiness stirred. Why, I didn't know. Except . . . except that somehow I *knew* Maurice.

The niggle of uneasiness was still with me the next morning when I woke. It produced the kind of formless unnameable greyness that I associate more with waking with Maurice than with waking alone. I put it down quite correctly, I think, to pre-something-or-other nerves. Apart from an intimate meal, I hadn't *planned* for this evening. I hadn't made up my mind how far I intended to go. All I was quite sure of was that there was something in Philip Matherson's make-up that called to something in me, and that for the first time I had glimpsed what I'd missed, and I was damned if I was going totally to lose sight of it again.

For once, I was punctual for my hair appointment. I made Charles set me rather differently this time, in a style that Maurice would have called cheap. I think Charles thought so, too. He bent rather warmly and breathily over my hand as I tipped him, as if he scented adultery, like some people can smell spring in the air.

When I returned home, Mrs. Thorpe was looking rather pink-faced over the oven. I gave her a glass of sherry to sip while she made the béchamel sauce, and when I'd had my bath I told her to come upstairs to admire another new dress I'd got—a dark Chinese green this time. I said to her, as I stood in front of the dressing table in my slip, "I have to entertain a colleague for my husband this evening. He's rather a bore but a clever man at his job. The Company have their eyes on him."

The irony of it amused me. It also reassured me that sometime I intended to tell Maurice—or at least it was possible I might. It all rather depended.

I was ready a good ten minutes before he arrived, walking up and down the bedroom, not smoking lest it spoiled my perfume, catching glimpses of myself in various mirrors— bright kaleidoscopic patterns of black piled-up hair, green low-cut dress and white shoulders, mixed in with a fragment of curtain, the corner of our big double bed. As I walked, the tight silk of the dress whispered against my stockings like gossiping women. Absurdly, I wondered what Maurice and his mother were talking about . . . Snap, just then.

I was almost biting my freshly varnished nails when he came. I heard Mrs. Thorpe go to the door as properly as a housemaid, and I heard the drawing-room door close behind him. It sounded as sweet as the shutting of a very comfortable no-cruelty-guaranteed trap. Then and only then, my mood lifted like a dream. I felt electric, quick, shimmering, dangerous. I hurried down the stairs, admiring briefly the little blood-red droplets of my fingernails against the white balustrade. Now the whispering of my skirt was gasped applause, now muffled laughter. I paused outside the door to switch my face to the one marked *hostess*.

I felt breathless with changing moods. I saw my half-bare breasts rising and falling too quickly and betrayingly, and I drew in slow deep breaths to drag my lungs back into rhythm.

Then I opened the door.

He was standing with his back towards me, thumbing through some magazine. His whole attitude was relaxed, and he turned slowly, smiling, expecting to see Maurice. His face therefore was unprepared against me. And that first expression was worth a whole month's living to me.

Then he made the excuse of putting down the magazine in the rack by the sofa, to take his eyes away. When they looked back they were shielded and again armed against me. He put out his hand.

"Good evening, Mrs. Corby."

"Anne, please. Good evening, Philip. I'm so glad you could come. Do sit down." I perched myself on the arm of the sofa. He waited for me to say, "Maurice will be down in a minute."

Instead I asked him what he would have to drink, and at this assumption of Maurice's duty, he frowned slightly, and said he'd have gin and something, he didn't mind what.

"Well, *what?*" I smiled. "Vermouth? Tonic? Bitters? Lemon? Maurice has just about everything."

The mention of Maurice reassured him for a moment. He chose tonic and when I struggled with the bottle opener, he came over and took it from me. I stood very close to him, and I kept my eyes on his face as he poured his drink. I saw a small pulse beat under his eye, and he was avoiding looking too closely at me.

He wasn't reassured for long. He suddenly saw that there was no third glass on the cocktail tray, and he stared ahead of him—thoughtfully, almost grimly.

"How is Maurice?" he said after a moment, rather levelly and shiveringly.

"Fine. Simply fine." I lifted my glass. "Cheers!"

There was a silence—angry, I think, within him, rich in humour within me.

"Why?" I said at last. "Did you think he wasn't well or something?"

As always when a man is more or less on the end of my string, I felt as light and clever and devious as a spider. Or maybe a spider doesn't feel anything at all. Except hungry. And I'm sure spiders can't laugh inside, or they'd break their webs. And I was laughing inside myself so much that my brain seemed dew-bubbled with it.

I heard Mrs. Thorpe cross the hall to the dining room to light the candles. Philip heard, too. He glanced towards the door waiting for it to open and Maurice to come in.

I sighed theatrically. "Mrs. Thorpe has the feet of a herd of wild elephants, hasn't she?"

He said nothing.

"Here," I jumped up. "Let me get you another drink. The other wing."

But he held the glass out of my reach. "No, thanks," he said. "We'll wait for Captain Corby."

Inside my dizzily spinning head, I murmured, "So long?" But it was only for myself to laugh at. Aloud I murmured, "Oh, Philip, Maurice asked me to apologize . . ."

"Again?" He actually caught hold of my wrist, and the feel of his fingers made me shiver with pleasure.

"Again? What d'you mean? Again . . . oh, yes. I see what you mean. But this time it's to apologize for *him*, not *me*. He had to drive up to Norfolk. It's his mother, poor darling. She's frantically old, as you can imagine. And not very well, and . . ."

My voice trailed, for I had seen the changing expression of his face, and I thought . . .

Mrs. Thorpe opened the door then and said, "Dinner is served."

Seeing us standing close together with that sort of intensity between us, perhaps she thought she had caught us in the act. Certainly she eyed us closely as we walked across the hall into the dining room. As for myself, my own mood had suddenly deepened. My laughter had died away into a dark, almost suffocating excitement. I felt I walked in an aura of awareness that Mrs. Thorpe could actually *see*. I saw her big bold eyes go from me to Philip. I saw her look at his mouth, searching out telltale smudges of lipstick. I wondered wryly what she made of its cold set line. But I knew she saw the way he deliberately avoided looking at me as he held out my chair, sat himself down opposite me and unfolded his napkin. And that her conclusions were one hundred and eighty degrees out.

"I hope you like shrimp cocktail," I said, recovering some semblance of aplomb first. I made myself feel amused that the dinner table should act like some surgeon's paraphernalia, cutting off, shrouding physical desire. "And I hope," I went on gently, as he nodded, "that you won't be too bored just with me."

I saw him glance at me once or twice, as if telling himself he'd only imagined what he'd guessed, reassuring himself that after all it was only exactly as I'd said. Dear old Maurice called to his dear old mother, while his nice little wife did duty for him. I saw with a sudden piercing longing, the genuine handicap which Philip Matherson suffered from. This curious niceness of mind. Illogically, I wanted to stretch my hands across the table and tell him . . . for God's sake, I really *am* as devious as he at first suspected. And then at the thought of stretching my hands across the table to him, I didn't want to do anything of the sort. And somehow out of all the mixture, I knew that was as near as I would ever get.

I pored over this knowledge like an illness. I felt all the contradictions of illness, too. One moment I was dizzily, feverishly elevated. Ten feet tall, walking a quiet drowsing world on silent stilts. The next I was earthbound, muffled in a desire that was sick and desperate and furtive.

But I recovered a little. Over the mushroom savoury, I felt sufficiently normal to smile perkily. "After all, Mrs. Thorpe is here, if you feel you must have a chaperone."

But I said it merely to puncture the silence which hung over us. Already I had banished Mrs. Thorpe. Already I could only think with a sort of breathless obsession, "Let's wait till she's gone, and after that . . ."

For it wasn't only I who felt this crackling up of excitement like a sky full of storm, this counting of plodding minutes, this straining after sounds. Now I knew we both listened for Mrs. Thorpe.

I waited, not troubling to talk, for her to come and clear away, to bring in the coffee. I thought her heavy feet would never come flap-flapping across the carpet. I thought when they did, she would never knock, when she knocked that she would never turn the knob, and when she turned the knob, that she would stand forever asking, "Will you have coffee here or in the lounge?" And then: "Black or white?"

And turning in heavy glutinous slow motion back to the kitchen, while I waited another ten thousand barren years for her interrupting return.

For I knew that it was going to happen. That it had to happen. Even in some curious way, that it was *intended* to happen. I felt that it had all worked out for itself, and that in the end I hadn't had much to do with it. One by one, all the little safety devices that might have stopped me had slipped away.

My hand was trembling as we walked back into the lounge. Matherson brought over the cocktail table and put it in front of the sofa. I lay back with my head resting on a cushion, watching him without appearing to—thinking, imagining, wondering where and when . . .

I had taken a bottle of brandy from the cellar. It rattled on the tray that Mrs. Thorpe carried in. She waited, cloth in hand, while Philip uncorked it. Then finally she said, "Shall I go now, Mrs. Corby? I've done the dinner dishes . . . but d'you want me to stay and wash this lot up for you?"

"No," I said sharply. "Go. Leave these."

I had an idea that my tone offended her. She raised her

eyebrows and tightened her mouth, and wobbled her wide
flat middle-aged bottom as she crossed the room. But I didn't
care, I just wanted her to go. Even when she'd closed the
door behind her, I had a horrid suspicion she wouldn't go
home. That she'd hang around on some pretext . . . getting
in the coal or locking up the cellar.

Nervously I picked up a cigarette and Philip lit it straight
away the way Maurice does when he's watching me. I drew
in a long breath of it, not troubling to thank him. I was listening so hard that the silence sounded like a continuous
waterfall. Then I heard the back door slam distantly. I walked
to the south window of the sitting room which gives a corner
view of the gate. I stood behind the curtain, and I was re-
warded with a last glimpse of Mrs. Thorpe's bashed felt hat,
and her moral bottom in the light of a street lamp.

The last hold had slipped easily away, after all. I walked
back towards Philip. He took the cigarette out of my hand,
and ground it out slowly in the ashtray. Then he pulled me
down beside him on the sofa. He made me face him, putting
his hands on my shoulder.

I felt the hardness of his fingers on my skin. I gave a little
gasp, and turned up my face to his, my lips apart. He took a
long time to kiss me, so that every nerve of me seemed to
stretch out quivering.

When it came, it was exactly as I had known it would be
—hard, resentful, fierce, angry, *alive.*

"There," he said, drawing away from me, "that was what
you wanted all along, wasn't it?"

The black pupils of his eyes had swallowed up the irises.
He was breathing quickly and angrily.

"Yes," I said, and then immediately, "*no.*"

I put my mouth quickly up to his, so that he didn't have
time to hate me, making my tongue dart like an adder
through his lips, pressing my body against him. I wanted to
tell him that I had never been alive before. That after him,

making love to Maurice was as obscene as kissing a corpse.

I felt his hands on my back, tracing the notches of my spine, drawing out like wizards' hands little fields of electric shock. I closed my eyes, kissing him back again and again— my mind drugged, unaware of my surroundings, of anything but my own body.

When his hands touched my breasts, I lay back on the sofa, clasping his neck, drawing him down after me, as if I reached for him from some warm dark swelling sea.

"I'm not always like this," I whispered, my mouth on his, now against his cheek, now nibbling his ear, "I promise you I'm not . . . I haven't ever . . . not with anyone else . . . truly, cross my heart . . . I'm not as bad as you think I am."

And muffled, strained but not angry any more, Philip said, "I don't care."

After that, it wasn't me leading him on any more. He led— and I fought and followed. I was a virgin. It was my first night. My hands fought him as he unfastened my dress. Immediately they were captured and held behind me. I wriggled and screamed and bit as he undressed me. But I lay still and moaning as he kissed my breasts and ran his hands over my naked body. Even though I longed for him, I resisted— squeezing my legs tightly together, and then crying out with a pain I had never felt with Maurice. And then we were moving in some galloping magic rhythm through ever-increasing crescendoes of bliss. I remember gabbling that I loved him, and he more softly and meaningly saying the same sort of things back to me. And then we were lying side by side, drowsy and peaceful, my body filled with sunlight, saying nothing, but staring at the darkened ceiling above us.

I thought of nothing and no one but me. My placid sweetness filled the universe.

From the ceiling, my eyes travelled the room, identifying the darkness-shrouded furniture detachedly as one might identify the configurations of the moon. Everything about the place had become removed from reality, made harmless, drained of menace. I admired the straight hang of the un-drawn curtains, the sheen of the marble fireplace, as if this room belonged to a stranger and I saw it for the first time.

Nothing had any history, nothing was real now except me. And every sound, every movement somehow threatened my new reality.

When Philip sat up, and began dressing, I stayed still. I was afraid to speak in case one of us said the wrong thing, and split my mood, and let the things I didn't want in, like germs through the crack.

He had lost his key ring from his jacket pocket, and I heard him fumbling around for it on the carpet. But I made no move to switch on the light, because I didn't want to see the expression on his face. When he said in a neutral offhand voice that he supposed he'd better be going, reluctantly I swung myself onto my feet, and put on my dress, and made weak and feeble attempts to smooth my hair with my hands. Then I followed him across the room at a distance, meekly and slavishly like an Indian wife—head down and still silent.

In the hall, the usually soft lights seemed as penetrating as the all-seeing globes over an operating table. Their glare was so strong it was as harsh as sound. I wrinkled up my eyes and made that the excuse for not looking at him.

"Good night, Anne," he said as I held the door open, and I was afraid he was going to apologize or say something im-possible like thank you for a pleasant evening.

Instead he leaned over and kissed the top of my head, "I'll ring."

"Yes," I said. I wanted him to go because even now he still might not measure up to my image of him. "Yes, do."

I did not quite close the door when he had gone. I listened to his footsteps echoing back to me from the street till they faded away into silence. Then I went back into the lounge, and as if activity was now essential to me, I tidied myself up and went round the room removing every indication that he had ever been here.

The mirror over the mantelpiece watched me. It watched me open the windows, empty the ashtrays, plump out the cushions. I was just taking away the liqueur glasses, when suddenly into its all-seeing oval appeared two enormous bright cats' eyes out of nowhere—and I heard Maurice's car turn into our garage drive.

BOOK TWO
Philip Matherson

ONE

It was a quarter past eleven when I left Anne Corby's house. There's a church clock about half a mile away, and sounds travelled that night. Anyway, I heard its sawn-off quarter sound as I closed the gate behind me, and I cursed because the pubs would be closed. A persistent drizzle had begun to fall, and the sky was overcast. The weather had emptied the streets of casual strollers, and the area looked deserted and grim, like a wet churchyard. I had parked the car down Ainley Close, which is a cul-de-sac, to save leaving on my lights, and I ran the hundred yards, though I didn't give a damn about the rain. I don't know what I did give a damn about at that particular moment, except perhaps getting to hell out of it. I'm not given to undue probing of my feelings, but I had a cold puddle of discomfort inside me right then—not unlike having drunk flat beer on an empty stomach.

I had a moment's panic too, as I turned into Ainley Close from the lighted street. The wet Wolseley melted in with the shadows, and I thought . . . Christ, if it had been stolen that would really have been It. When I opened the door, a hand-ful of rain scattered off the top, and went down my neck, and I stood there swearing aloud just for someone to talk to,

as if I were a kid. The only noises round here were the gut-
ters beginning to tinkle and the drip of trees. I felt I wanted
to make a big noise—bang my fists on the horn, or shout at
those long rectangles and stone-mullioned windows.

Instead, I got into the car and folded my arms over the
wheel, and said, "Oh, for Christ sake, what a bloody stupid
thing to do . . . Corby's wife . . . *Corby's* wife . . . for crying
out loud!"

And crying out loud wasn't so far off what I could have
done. I sat for a moment with the side lights on, and the engine running, and the wipers sweeping backwards and forwards, trying to get things a bit straight in my mind. But my
brain had shrunk to the size of a pea, and I didn't resolve
anything, except that the raindrops were increasing and that
it looked like the cold front was beginning to move in.

Then I put the car into gear and eased her out of Ainley
Close. I had to pass Anne's house to get back onto the North
Circular Road, but I didn't glance out to identify it from all
its solid neighbours, standing a little back from the glow of
the wet street lamps.

All the same, my mind wasn't a hundred per cent on driving, though I was well on my side of the road. So was the
character coming in the other direction. But he must have
had the odd noggin too many. For to begin with he didn't
need what lights he had on, but as he drew almost level with
me, instead of dipping, he switched them full power up.

I had to jam on the brakes, because I couldn't see where
the hell I was going. My eyes ached with the dazzle. For a
few seconds I was caught in the glare like an enemy raider
in a searchlight battery. Though I trod my dipper switch on
and off in protest at him, it didn't dim those lights one watt.
Maybe he thought I was going into a skid, for he slowed
down and crawled past me, and I could distinguish the vague
dark form of the driver turning round to stare at me.

I felt a quick spurt of anger—and with it a sort of trembling. It seemed suddenly that the incident with Anne Corby (and I was going to make damned sure it remained only an incident) had rattled my nerve. Right then I worried more about that than any morals or conventions that might be involved. As a jet captain, you don't get rattled. You should be used to emergencies—weather closing in, firebells going, the lot. I remember feeling a kind of hatred towards the anonymous driver as though he'd tried to do me some harm, and it made me feel a hell of a lot better to drive along cursing him—while the rain came down, and the wipers rattled on and London drowned in dirty grey rivers.

I suppose I must have driven around for the odd half hour, slowing down hopefully at strange pubs that looked as though they had special hours and were still open. But none of them were any good. The light that seemed to come from a functioning bar turned out to be only the wet reflection of a street lamp, or from the recesses of a kitchen where washers-up swilled out the beer glasses.

And then without consciously giving up the search, I found myself driving towards London Airport like a homing pigeon. Though I have never had any aspirations towards psychological egg-headery, I knew I had an almost uncontrollable urge to escape.

If someone had suddenly tapped me on the shoulder and said . . . Matherson, you're out on Service tonight, I'd have thanked him, if not with tears in my eyes at least with considerable enthusiasm. But skating along that flat wet road with my foot hard down, I felt almost as though I was flying. Deserted except for the odd long-distance lorries, the wet tarmac shining back in yellow blobs under the stalked lights, leading like a pitched dart into blackness, it might have been Runway 28 Left itself. And for a while I went nearly fast enough to get airborne. Anyway, the squirts from my tires were coming up on either side of me like water wings, and the wipers could give me only a three-inch fan to see through.

After a couple of miles, I slowed down. That burst of speed had catapulted off my previous mood of uneasy guilt, and acted on my mind like a dunk of cold water. In fact, by Harrington Corner I began to feel a bit like a rabbit who's just crossed the railway line without getting his tail cut off. I even began to have that slightly stimulating shiver you get after a narrow squeak.

And back my nerves bounced to their normal competent level.

As the green lights let me through at Crampton Crossroads, I was already rationalizing it out. It wasn't so much the moral side of it that bothered me. Not because I'm an amoral character, but rather the reverse. It's usually the bods who are on the boil all the time who shout the loudest about moral tone. By and large, I reckon my sex life is a good deal healthier than most pilots'—than most men's for that matter. I don't have to prove anything to myself and I don't have to go around frenziedly looking for it the moment we wear tropical uniform or the thermometer tops seventy. At the same time, I take it as it comes along. And when it comes along, which it does at a very nice average (as most things do if you're not dedicated to finding them) I reckon I cope rather well.

Certainly I don't have any problems. And problems are endemic in this racket. Walk into any bar that serves cool beer and scotch without ice anywhere the airlines touch down, and you'll hear how high flying or pressurization or the phosphorescent instruments or radiation or the time-difference problem or even the vibration through the cheeks of his bottom can fix a pilot. Fix his wife, too, at the same time. It's a wonder the pill merchants haven't cottoned onto the problem.

And that was the heart of the matter. I'd reached the age of thirty. I liked this life—in fact, I suppose I was happy and I didn't have any problems. So I was damned if I was going to walk right up and say *yes, please* to one now. For even then, I knew Anne could be my problem, though I didn't know exactly how or why. The fact that she was Corby's wife would have been enough. And though that was by no means all, it was what bothered me mainly then.

There can't be many men who'd take kindly to their wives whiling away an evening like that. I know I wouldn't, though I have come across a few tit-for-tat, goose-for-gander arrangements. But the Corby ménage wasn't one of them. Even if I hadn't heard it through the airline grapevine—one joker produced a fairy story about Corby being seen buying a gold chastity belt in the market at Jakarta—it stood out a mile when you saw them together. She might not be in love with Corby—and I can't say I blame her—but the sun shone from where it ought to for him. In fact, for all her hints on what he was like, I felt bloody sorry for him. I couldn't even fool myself that I was doing a good turn bringing a bit of sunlight to the bird in the old man's cage. So even if Corby had only been a U/T Traffic Clerk, I'd have been reaching for my hat. But he wasn't just that, he was the Flight Captain, and all my warning systems were screaming *go, man, go.*

But the most important part of all was that he was Corby.

All the same, even Corby hadn't eyes that could see from Norwich. And my newly freshened brain came up with the positive certainty that Anne wasn't going to tell him. Allowing some discount for my male vanity, I think a fair-minded arbiter would have said she'd done the lion's share of the running.

She was a clever girl. She had more to lose than I had. She'd not breathe a word. Everything would be all right, so long as it didn't happen again.

In fact by the time I reached my flat, truisms were running brightly round my head like a neon halo . . . *no harm done . . . least said soonest mended . . . what the eye doesn't see . . .*

My flat is at the top of a block of three, almost but not

quite a penthouse, half a mile from London Airport. It stands
on a very slight plateau, and gives a panoramic view of the
whole field. Seen at midnight from the big lounge window,
especially on a wet night, the aerodrome gives the same
brand of mental satisfaction as working out a mathematical
problem. There is a clean antisepsis about the patterned
lights in unalterable order, the curved taxi-tracks, the runways straight as knives, those flat-chested buildings, stark
and ugly. A rigid masculine place in an uncluttered, undevi-
ous, unfeminine landscape.

Most pilots like to live away from the place. I don't. It's
very convenient. You can be out of bed and onto the aeroplane in no time flat. Or if, as I was tomorrow, you're in for
a session on the simulator, you can get it over and done with,
and not waste a whole day. I like my job so I don't mind
being on top of it. I don't even mind the noise. I enjoy hearing the 404 to Boston and New York thundering off at eleven
fifty-five, as I could hear it now, turning the roster over in
my mind and thinking it would be Jim Brailsford up front,
crouched over the controls. I had a glass of whisky in my
hand, a generous one, though I didn't need it now. I watched
the jet slowly gathering speed down the runway. Then, after
she was airborne, I finished my drink and went through into
the bedroom.

Normally even on trips, I sleep like a log and I don't dream.
But that night I seemed to go on nonstop like a New York
television.

It wouldn't have been so bad if I'd dreamed about Anne.
But I didn't. It was aeroplanes all the time. One damned
aeroplane after another. And always, they were in some attitude that I couldn't get them out of. Either they were climbing up and up and I couldn't level off. Or they had stalled
and were falling out of my hands. I woke in a sweat wondering momentarily where I was, slowly identifying my own
cupboard and chest, the perennial alarm clock ticking away

by my bed, a pair of twin bright lights moving across the ceiling as yet another aircraft flew off.

I remember watching them brush over my head. They reminded me of something. But my memory was foggy with tiredness. I half turned over, closed my eyes—and slipped back into sleep.

TWO

NEXT DAY, when I walked into the Simulator Room, Preston, the Instructor, was already in his chair beside the green metal control table. He's a thin balding man of fifty-odd, who looks as if he'd lived too long on canned air and neon lights. He's precise and economical in his movements. He doesn't raise the hair of an eyebrow unless it's strictly necessary. He's slow to speak and slow to smile, but either is usually worth waiting for.

"Good morning, Captain Matherson." He gave me a brief smile. "Come in. You're early."

"Hello, George." I hung my cap on the stand just inside the door, and then walked over behind him. "What've you got lined up for today?"

"Two blind landings into Riverly. One by you. One by the Allen Autoland."

"Which twin has the Toni, eh?"

"Something like that, Captain. But I don't imagine we'll have great difficulty in telling."

He permitted himself an ironic raising of his bushy grey brows as I flexed my muscles and said, "Well, we'll just have to see about that."

I suppose that behind those bottle-bottom spectacles and his frugal smile, George Preston holds more troublesome secrets about pilots than the average divorce lawyer, which is saying something. Right up there, inside what George Preston calls his pagan idol, the simulator has been the beginning of the end of the road for quite a few of us.

There it stands in the middle of the room, mounted on a mechanical pedestal that allows it to move up or down or sideways, a huge silver truncated nose that does everything a 909 does but never leaves the ground. Its running costs are a fraction of the expense of taking a jet up in the air, so that most of the training these days is done here. Inside you could swear you were in the cockpit, for all the instruments are there. Firebells clang, engines cut, electrics fail, radios blank out, fuel dumping has to be initiated—George Preston or the Training Captain can feed in each and every emergency or the whole lot together so that the pilot can get into a real panic and flap. He can even crash. Simulators vary, of course, in what they can do, but this simulator can stall and spin most dramatically, and when it "hits the ground" a noise like thunder reverberates out like shock waves all over this corner of London Airport. And even though it hasn't been as bad as that for most of us, we've all of us done some bad approaches with a varied selection of balls-ups that it wouldn't have done for anyone but G.P. to witness.

He never said much. He never gossipped about anyone else's performance. I think he was that odd and almost extinct bird, a thoroughly decent type. Or maybe he was saving everything up for his memoirs and when he retired he was going to do a General on all of us.

Whatever it was, G.P. was all right. I never minded these sessions, even when Carruthers, the Training Captain, was checking me, perhaps because usually I put up a reasonably good showing. This morning I intended to do rather better than usual. Like the rest of my fellow pilots, it wasn't ex-

actly love at first sight between me and Corby's pet—the
Allen Automatic Landing System. That's not to say that I
was foaming at the mouth, or beating my breast, or even
talking about the Allen doing away with pilots' jobs and preparing to join the bread queue.

It was simply that I know that flying is a craft which requires the adaptability of the human operator. And this
morning I intended personally to demonstrate that anything
it could do I could do better.

"What d'you reckon to the Allen, George? What's your
honest to God?"

I stood with my hands in my pockets, screwing up my
eyes against the glare of neon lights bouncing off those bald
blue walls.

G.P. took his time about answering. "Just another aviation
instrument. Another *aid*."

"Sure, sure . . . I know all that! It's going to be my best
friend. It's just after my job. But then, not to worry!"

G.P. gave me a reproving shake of his head. "I'd have
thought you'd have been one of the enlightened. I'm surprised at you, Captain Matherson!"

"Oh, you don't have to be. I'm just like the rest of us back-
ward boys. Don't like change. Don't know what's good for
us. Won't move with the times. Have strange ideas that we
like to fly the aeroplane ourselves. And you'd better watch
out, too, George. One of these fine days, *you'll* disappear.
And we'll find a green tin man behind that green tin desk
with wires sticking out of his back."

"So long as he did the job more efficiently."

"Ah, yes. And so long as he didn't get his wires crossed,
and go chasing green tin Traffic girls in office hours!"

"Well, now," G.P. said, cutting me short to peer over his
spectacles at the clock on the wall. "Your crew won't be here
till eleven. So there's time to run through the Allen first with
you before they arrive."

I leaned forward and pinched one of his cigarettes. "Go ahead. See if you can convert me."

"There's nothing to convert you to. You've had the automatic pilot for twenty-five years. And the Instrument Landing System for twenty. All they've done is to connect the one with the other."

Of course, G.P.'s explanation made it all seem as easy as falling off an aeroplane. The Instrument Landing System is a radio beam along which a pilot flies down to the airport runway. In front of him is a round instrument like a mouldy orange, half blue, half yellow. If he goes to the left, a vertical needle on that dial moves to the yellow sector, if he goes to the right, the needle swings into the blue. If he's too high, another needle—this one horizontal—falls to the bottom: if he's too low, it rises to the top. The aim of the manoeuvre (not nearly as easy as it sounds in a fast heavy aircraft flying blind) is to keep both needles forming a cross in the centre of the orange.

"And the Allen does just that!" Perhaps he'd had a pep talk from Corby, but Preston managed to sound even enthusiastic. "From two thousand feet, the autopilot is electronically locked onto the radio beams of the I.L.S.—both localizer for azimuth, and glide path for descent. At *two hundred* feet, because low down the glide-path signals become attenuated, the Autoland disengages them and the aircraft is controlled in descent by an electronic averager, not unlike a clock, that has worked out the rate of descent for the previous eighteen hundred feet, and applies a tenth of it to maintain a constant attitude for the next hundred and eighty feet."

"Sounds simple," I said. "And then it initiates the flare?"

"That's right. The electronic averager controls the pulling back of the stick and the throttles. The actual landing itself is monitored by the radio altimeter."

"And what happens when the autopilot goes on the blink?"

"An identical second autopilot immediately takes over."

"And if that goes too?"

"A third takes over. Three entirely separate systems. Assurance not doubly, but trebly sure. The thing's foolproof. D'you know the complete failure rate in the last crucial two hundred feet?"

I shook my head.

"A hundred million to one! You'd have to fly backwards through time to the Stone Age to get a failure."

"Ah," I said. "Would that I could!"

"And how many times does the human pilot make an error causing an accident in those last two hundred feet?"

"Spare our blushes," I said. "Not back to the Stone Age, I take it?"

"In bad weather, a *thousand* times more often!"

First Officer Holmes and Milligan, the Engineer, came in then, so we all climbed into the simulator, and went over the knobs and tits of the thing.

"I am perhaps rather oversimplifying," G.P. said as he finished. "I'm not the real gen man on the Allen. Captain Corby is the expert. She's his baby."

Holmes, who is a brash young boy, murmured that the likeness was there, and I pretended not to hear. I had no desire to discuss the man right then.

As it was, I'd already begun to feel less confident. Maybe that bloody black box—Captain Frankenstein, some of the pilots called it—was beginning to give me an inferiority complex too. There's something very depressing about perfection, though I knew that no instrument could be perfect all the time. Just the same, as we walked over the polished floor to the simulator the damned thing itself began to look different.

I've never been given to fanciful ideas about it. But today, hostile as the three of us were to the Allen, our walk took on an unwelcome significance, and the simulator standing in the centre of the room in splendid isolation emerged in my mind as curiously like the electric chair.

"I'm sorry, George," I said. "But you've still not convinced me."

G.P. smiled. "Well, we'll see how you make out against it. I hope you're on form."

I took the left-hand seat in the familiar cockpit surroundings. I put up my thumbs. "This," I said, "is where the little black box dies of shame!"

Then G.P. got out of the cockpit and shut the door on the three of us, and I called over my shoulder, "We'll have the Before Starting Engines Check, Mr. Milligan!"

And play commenced.

"Gear up!"

The blind take-off had been good, that I knew. The course had stayed glued on the Runway QDM of 250 degrees. Now as I moved the trim for the climb, I felt more confident.

It's a curious thing, this complete satisfaction that perfect control of an aeroplane—or even for that matter a simulator— can give. It must be one of the most desirable sensations known to man. G.P., who when he isn't turning knobs or explaining instruments in words of one syllable, is a great burrower in obscure books, told me one of his theories. He'd found it in some medico-social tome, and had passed it on to me in one of his brief moments of confidence. The theory was that pilots, like the police say car drivers do, relate their performance on the machine to their sexual prowess, and are consequently highly inflammable about criticism. Of course, I'd laughed like a drain. I'd told him for goodness' sake to get out in the fresh air and stop reading filthy books like that about clean-living boys like us. The theory still made me smile.

"Echo X-ray at two thousand feet, turning downwind," Holmes said.

I was still smiling. I was relaxed. I'm lucky in being a natural pilot, and like a natural car driver, the machine becomes an extension of me. My nerves are its nerves. My mind is its mind. We fuse together and we move in unison.

I can remember feeling particularly pleased. I had everything organized. I had reached that point where I was in perfect control. I had time to look up briefly from the instruments. All around, the windscreens were as opaque as steamed-up bathroom windows. To all intents and purposes, I was coming in for an instrument landing in thick English fog. I moved the stick slightly to the left. Obediently the instruments made their slight alterations, began reading what I intended them to read. I knew exactly each move I was going to make. The whole blind landing manoeuvre was clear as crystal in my mind.

"Echo X-ray on base leg."

If there was anything to G.P.'s bit of nonsense, I had no problems. I reminded myself that some time I must tell Anne about G.P. and his theory. It was the sort of thing she would giggle over. I could see her now with her hands clasped round her knees, and her head thrown back, her small mouth wide with laughter, the muscles of her neck quivering. Then I remembered that as from last night any relationship between Anne and me was strictly past tense.

"Echo X-ray coming into the localizer beam."

I blinked my eyes rapidly. Seconds had run away like water. One moment I was king of the castle—the next, I had slipped sideways. In those seconds, the earth had turned, the aircraft had sped forward without me.

I dragged my mind back to the cockpit—or I tried to. But that's the queer thing about flying, or about any job that demands meticulous concentration. You've got to keep it at one hundred per cent all the time, otherwise the mind refuses. It's hypnotized by something else . . . a mark on the windscreen, a stain on the floor, your mind whirls round it like a Catherine wheel on a pin. I believe some trick cyclists on aviation medicine have got together and come up with the technical term for the affliction—*fascination*.

And not a bad moniker either, for from then on with me it was *Anne*. Not that I deliberately thought of her. But somehow she was there in the centre of my mind, snatching at my concentration, dispersing it to the winds.

"Echo X-ray on final."

I called for the Landing Checks. Holmes, the Engineer, and I chanted them backwards and forwards. That was dead easy. I could have said them in my sleep. Then I gradually eased round onto the localizer beam and stayed on the runway heading of 250 degrees, with the I.L.S. needle in the centre of the instrument. I was sweating a bit with the effort of keeping my concentration. It was as thin as paper. Almost anything could take it back, bust it open. The glide-path needle began moving down from the top, and I started to descend.

I moved the throttles back, as Holmes put the Check List into the container at the side of his seat. It made a tinkling noise as it slipped inside, like a key falling on the floor or the striking of a clock. I remembered the clock in the Corbys' drawing room. I remembered looking at it just before I left last night. Now its gilt ormolu face replaced that of the I.L.S. . . . I screwed up my eyes, dragging my mind back by its shirttails. I saw the localizer needle had gone hard over in the blue sector.

I wrenched over the control column to the left. I put on rudder. Gradually, the needle came back into the centre.

Beside me, I could hear Holmes breathing hard. Maybe it was nervousness. Or maybe it was the way he always breathed. Or maybe he had a cold. Concentration skidded off again, while I flapped around after it like a collector after a jet-propelled butterfly.

"You're well below the glide path, Captain Matherson."

Holmes spoke very quietly. He was only trying to help. But I snapped back at him, "I know! I was just correcting!"

I pulled back, but the altimeter seemed to stick at five hundred feet. Then, incredibly, we began to climb.

Now we were too high. Too high and too slow. The simulator and I had lost touch. We didn't fuse together any more. And I was out of rhythm with my flying. Suddenly too many dials were reading wrong on me. The altimeter, the glide path, the localizer, the airspeed indicator—I began chasing each one of them in turn. No sooner had I corrected one than another was off. I began overcorrecting, zigzagging now left, now right, now up, now down—making the simulator buck like a stallion.

Two hundred feet. Again too low. Again too far starboard. "Full flap!"

I was sweating like a roasting pig. I thought I was going to miss the runway altogether. With a last-ditch effort, I tipped the port wing up, and by violent corkscrewing, picked up the localizer. Then I slammed the throttles shut. With a bang and a squeak of tires—the simulator squawks with pain when you do a bad landing—we were down.

When you've put up a poor show, you watch other people's reactions. Now as I got out my handkerchief and mopped my face, I watched Holmes. If he'd turned and grinned at me, I'd have known it wasn't all that bad. But he didn't look my way. He began fiddling self-consciously with the Check List. Then because the silence had become oppressive, he said awkwardly, "Hot work!"

I nodded.

Then silence again, till over the earphones G.P.'s voice saying neutrally, "Well, now . . . off you go again! Pick up the localizer at two thousand feet. And give yourself a rest while the Autoland does the work!"

I took off again. I did a quick nonchalant circuit. Twelve miles from touchdown on the runway heading, with gear and flap down, I lined up the localizer needle dead centre. Then I leaned forward to engage the Autoland.

Mindful of the existing clutter of aircraft instruments on the flight deck, the Allen people have kept theirs to a minimum. The control box is built into the throttle pedestal. On that are three buttons to give confidence-checks that the Autoland is working and five plug sockets for ground-test checks. The metal cover can be taken off, of course, to get at the works and the wiring. To the left of the main panel is the radio altimeter that monitors the actual landing, and below that is a dial to select the approach speed—which I did now at 140 knots. Then one by one, like you pull a pint at a pub, I moved the three autopilot levels towards me.

And Autoland locked on.

The ordinary I.L.S. indicator monitors the approach. I had less difficulty this time concentrating on its blue and yellow face. We had wandered a little to the left. With a jerk, the autopilot moved the starboard wing down, then steadied again on heading.

I saw Holmes had moved his seat right back, and was whistling silently as much as to say *look, no hands*. I kept my feet and hands off the controls, sure. But just then I was hoping the thing *would* act up.

"Go on," I said, though not aloud. "Make a balls-up of it! Well then, just one mistake! Just to show you're human!"

Meanwhile, just as I'd have done with another pilot, I watched its performance. One thing I spotted straight away. It wasn't a born pilot. There were little hesitations, clicks, wobbles on the control column—though I will say it kept dead in the centre of the beam. As we came up to the glide path it gave a slight shimmy, and then—there was a certain fascination in watching it—back came the throttles, moved by the invisible hand of the invisible man, forward went the stick. And down we began descending at exactly four hundred feet a minute.

Seven-hundred—five-hundred—three-hundred feet. Speed always 140 knots. It was obvious that Captain Frankenstein was untroubled by Anne.

Two hundred feet. There was a cluck like a hen as the glide path (the signals of which were too erratic low down) was disengaged. Now there was a whirring noise as the electronic averager worked out the rate of descent from two thousand feet, and applied a tenth of it to control the remaining descent and the roundout.

Then right back came the throttles, right back went the stick. And we were down.

There was no squeak this time. Just a little purr of pleasure. Holmes held up his thumb. "Nice work, eh?"

Even when we'd done all the After Landing Checks, I didn't answer.

Then everything began to be switched off. Slowly, like a collapsed bellows, the simulator wheezed into silence.

I sat there for a moment, feeling all the air had gone out of me. I'd like to have taken a running jump at that smug black box. I didn't say anything to Holmes or Milligan. I just gave them a nod as I climbed out. I remember being thankful . . . first that mine hadn't been a real landing, and secondly for old G.P.

I wouldn't like to think of any other eyes but his examining the ink results of those two landings—for in every simulated approach each movement is followed by a metal "crab" which inks a thin line on a glass map of the airport on the instructor's table. There's no hedging about those results. They are there, printed for all to see, in bright red.

I walked down the steps slowly, turning over in my mind some joke with which G.P. and I could decently bury it. And then I became aware of another figure standing beside the table.

That figure was Corby.

I suppose that under any circumstances, there'd have been something acutely embarrassing in running into the girl's husband the next day. But bearing in mind my bloody awful approach, and the reason for it, I felt as if I'd just had Anne there in the simulator, and he'd been watching a running commentary on how we made out.

I wouldn't have been in the least surprised if the trace of my approach on the map had suddenly looped into the name *Anne* or spelled out the sort of message you see behind a lavatory door. Certainly it was wavy enough. And certainly Corby stared at it with sufficient distasteful interest. In comparison, the Autoland was a straight red line, never wavering, going plum down the middle of the runway.

"Well," G.P. said, trying to pass it off as a joke, "I don't think there's any doubt which twin has the Toni."

I shook my head. "Come to that, I don't think they were twins to begin with."

G.P. laughed with tactful heartiness. Corby did not. He said very softly, "I think that should convince you of the usefulness of the Autoland."

I shrugged my shoulders. I avoided looking at him. I felt rather than saw that his eyes were still on me, travelling slowly over my face. I had the odd sensation that I could actually feel their contact like a blind man's fingers. Immediately I was reminded of something Anne had told me about those eyes. Something about their ever-watchfulness. And her bobbing up again in my mind increased my discomfort.

I heard Corby draw in his breath. I knew he was going to say something. But he took a long time to get it out, and during that time I really sweated. I decided for the hundredth time that this sort of situation was definitely not up my street.

And while he paused, my guess seesawed between a sarcastic comment on my landing or a hats-in-the-ring accusation about Anne and me.

When he did speak, it was so ordinary a remark that I could have laughed out loud.

"By the bye, Captain Matherson . . . we owe you a dinner, you know. Would Wednesday the twenty-sixth suit you? I know you're in. I've looked at the roster. Shall we say eight-fifteen?"

I was so relieved that I almost salaamed my thanks. Even G.P. looked at me with a mild curiosity. I wasn't owed a dinner, and perhaps I was so obsequious partly because I was being paid back twice. It was only after Corby had gone that I remembered my good intention. But what was a dinner party? There was safety in numbers.

And Wednesday the twenty-sixth seemed a long way off.

THREE

WEDNESDAY the twenty-sixth came round almost without my noticing it. Maybe because I'd been giving my mind even more than usual to the job. I'd done a lot of flying, and a lot of praying (in vain as it happened) for thick soupy terminal weather just to show the Company in general and me in particular exactly how good I am. Maybe it's just that time creeps up.

Anyway, one day it was a fine afternoon with me sunning myself in the fag-end of a Bermuda summer, while dispassionately I admired the chubby shape of the stewardess' bottom. The next, I was greasing her down on a cold English morning that already smelled of autumn, with a planeload of passengers reaching for their overcoats. When I signed the manifest at London Airport, I remember looking at the date, the twenty-fourth . . . and thinking Christ, I'd better see if I had a clean dress shirt, for the Corbys were formal in their entertaining. "Just D.J.'s, old boy," Corby always said, as if at the drop of a hat a fellow pilot would have appeared in white tie and tails. And as quickly as I'd thought about my shirt, I tried to think of a decent excuse for not going.

Not that I didn't want to see Anne. I both wanted to and

didn't. Which was another thing that griped me. Usually I
know my own mind. I know what I want. I also know when
I want it. I don't normally sheer off a thing for days on end,
and then have a yen for it like an outsize bellyache. But I
did with her, which was one good reason for not going to the
Corbys'. And there were a whole lot more where that came
from. Besides, there weren't going to be any kicks for me in
seeing her at that distance, unreachably surrounded by a
legal husband and unadulterous friends.

There was some story I learned at school about some
thirsty sod—Tantalus I think his name was—standing up to
his neck in water, with a bunch of luscious grapes just out of
reach. And every time he tried for them, they were whisked
away, while a rock above his head moved lower. And down
through the years, I remember thinking . . . what a Herbert!
If he was that parched, there was always the water. But now
I could see it wasn't so easy because didn't the water recede?

I couldn't think up a reason fit to tell Corby on the twenty-
fourth. I was too busy making up my sleep on the twenty-
fifth. And by the twenty-sixth it was too late anyway. I'd
upset the balance of their dinner party if I fell out now.

Not that I need have worried. When I decelerated past the
Corby house, there were no cars drawn up by the curb.
Neither were there any in the side turning where I'd parked
before. Of course, I was still a little early. And I'd have preferred not to be the first guest to arrive.

I got out and locked up. It was already almost dark, but
fine, with the odd star just visible high above the pink glow
of the city. It was cold, too, with that faint smell of smoking
leaf fires that you get about the suburbs around autumn. I
stood for a moment looking at the big solid houses with their
formidable high stone walls and their sooty trees. Naturally,
I thought about the last time I'd been here when those walls
were cataracting water and the trees had dripped and I'd
been in a state of some considerable alarm and despondency.

Now with the courtesy of the fine cold evening and our old friend Time, I could think about that night with an ironic smile.

Everything had turned out all right in the end.

Those comfortable words had come true. And here I was, invited by Corby himself, all right and proper and above-board, which regularized the whole situation, like having the marriage lines just before the bastard was born. I wondered why on earth I hadn't wanted to come. Sheer laziness probably. I walked away from the car with a bit of a swagger, and if I felt at the back of my mind that I was something of a shit, I kept that thought firmly in the place where it belonged.

I moved down the road slowly, hands in my pockets. There was, I remembered, a clock that chimed in the neighbour-hood, and I was going to wait till I heard the quarter before I rang their bell. Some of the trees that overhung the pavement had already spilled small conkers. They were so black and swollen with rain that they split as I kicked them into the gut-ter. A Bentley, appearing from behind me, looked as if it meant to slow down, but continued its leisurely progress un-til its red lights winked out at the crossroads. I paused for a second and looked at my watch in the light of the last street lamp before the Corbys'. A minute to go. I walked a few paces further on. Then, as the church clock chimed, I turned in their gate.

Standing in their long lighted porch, I did just wonder ex-actly why Corby had asked me. But only briefly. Not being a formal type, I always have so many jobs to do before any mine host opens the door. A sort of social pre-landing check list. My tie, is it straight? My socks, do they hold up? My handkerchief, have I got it? Most important of all . . . my nose, is it clean?

I'd just completed my check list when Corby opened the door.

I knew then that it wasn't going to be a big impressive

sort of do, otherwise Corby in his social wisdom always hires a Jeeves-type butler to open the door. He also hires the stewards in their off duty to serve the drinks, and call the guests *sir* and *madam* as if they were paying a couple of hundred for the trip.

"Hello, Philip. Come in! What sort of a night have you brought with you? Mmm, cold front coming up by the feel of it!" He stepped back into the lighted hall. "Here, let me take your coat." He stood slightly on tiptoe to help me off with it. Then he glanced at the grandfather clock. "I see you agree with me. Punctuality is the courtesy of kings."

"I haven't heard that one. I suppose we get used to doing things to the clock."

"Yes, indeed."

I am not normally tongue-tied with people, but now my brain seemed muffled. I murmured something about the nights drawing in. And almost in a parody, Corby said that Christmas would be on us in no time.

He waved me towards the cloakroom. "Would you care to wash your hands?"

I didn't care to, but I wanted to see if there was anyone else around to dilute Corby. But there was only a Company cap and a grey burberry to hang my coat beside on the pegs. On the floor, just beside the hot pipes, were some ladies' boots with fur tops and high heels. There were still some leaves stuck to their soles, as if Anne had been out walking in the woods that afternoon. That was the first time I noticed how touching people's belongings are.

As I washed my hands, I could hear Corby padding up and down in the hall outside. There was that same sort of heavily scented soap in the washbowl. It clung to my hands persistently, like it had done that night, jerking me back the way smells do to things I didn't want to remember.

Back in the hall, I glanced around. I remembered that long

polished table, and what looked like a white onyx bowl. It was filled with the same sort of orangey coloured flowers. They couldn't have lasted that long surely? I touched one as I passed to see if it was plastic. But they were real enough. It shed a few petals softly on the table.

"You have a lovely place here," I said.

"I'm glad you like it. But you've seen it before, of course?"

Corby inclined his head. The polite host, proud of his home, pretending attentiveness, not really caring what the answer might be.

"Yes." Corby still waited. "But that was at your party. Difficult to notice much, with a crowd milling around."

"Of course. I was forgetting. That's the only time you've been here then?"

I didn't want to tell a lie for no good reason. But he seemed to expect an answer so I said, "Yes. That's the only time."

"You could still remember your way here?"

"Oh, yes. My navigation's bang on."

"Good show!"

We were halfway across the hall. Corby stopped to point out a water colour they had bought in Holland, at Valkenburg to be precise. What did I think of it?

"Very attractive. Though I'm not much of an expert."

"Nor am I. But I know exactly what I like. And I enjoy having beautiful things around me."

Like Anne, I thought. He looked at me sideways as if I'd spoken aloud.

"You're very lucky," I said.

"I think so, too. By the bye, I should have told you where to park. There's a small turning up on the left. Not many people know about it."

"I found it, as a matter of fact. I'm rather an expert on finding parking lots."

"Yes, I'm sure." He paused. "What's your car?"

"A Wolseley . . . the medium-sized one."

"Ah, yes . . . that's the one with the badge on the bonnet that illuminates with the side lights?"

"That's the one."

"It must be the only type with that distinction?"

"Yes, I believe it is."

"How d'you find it?"

"I'm very satisfied."

The usual sort of conversation between men. Cars first, sport next, shop last and longest. We had reached the white-painted door into the lounge. He opened it, and inclined his head for me to precede him. "Anne won't be a moment." He stepped back and rested his hand on the upright of the wrought-iron balustrade. Without actually raising his voice he called up. "Anne! Anne darling! Our guest has arrived!"

The lounge was empty. Though there was a clean bright fire burning in the grate, and the room was if anything over-warm, its quietness had a chill about it. Or at least, that's what it seemed to me.

"My wife," Corby smiled indulgently, "does *not* have the same respect for punctuality as you and I."

He lifted a silver cigarette box from the drinks tray, opened it and held it out. I noticed there were only three glasses on the tray. Just as the other night, I'd noticed there were only two.

"What woman does have respect for time?" My humour sounded heavy on the runway.

"Oh, that I wouldn't be permitted to know, Philip. You probably have a good deal more information on the subject than I have."

He spun his lighter and held the flame under my nose. Though I'm by no means adverse to discussing women, I couldn't have nattered about them to Corby for a million quid.

"What are you drinking?"

"Scotch, please. Whoa, that's fine! With water. Thanks."

Hospitably he pulled the sofa nearer the fire, and settled me back with the stiff drink. "There," he said, "that should thaw you out."

The heat made me feel uncomfortable. That, and sitting on the sofa. Not that I'm inclined to think here this happened, or there that did. I've read that some foreign police, French, I think, take their murderers to the scene of the crime. They reckon they can spot their guilt by their reaction. Personally I don't think guilt shows all that easily. At least, I hope it doesn't. All the same, I'd have preferred the chair Corby was perched on. Besides, I could see myself in that damned great mirror they have over the mantelpiece, and in contrast to Corby I looked about as smooth as a farmer's boy.

I fished around for something to say. "Have you been out on Service lately?" I didn't know whether to call him Maurice or sir, so I called him nothing. It wasn't many months ago that I was his First Officer.

"Unfortunately not, Philip. I'm tied up with this Autoland business, and I haven't been airborne nearly enough."

It seemed to give Corby the opening he wanted. It began to dawn on me that he had invited me tonight purely to sound me out about the Autoland and pilot reaction to it.

After that, I felt a whole lot better. In fact, we had quite an interesting talk. I told him my point of view, which was that a man should trust himself, not a machine, and he understood it remarkably well. He explained his, which was a clockwork schedule with no postponements or cancellations. He stood with his back to the fire, glass in hand, like an advert for huckstering whisky.

"There's a good deal in what you say, Philip. And you put it very cogently. You're not as hidebound as my lot. And not as brash as the real youngsters."

By the time Anne came down, we'd had three-man sized whiskies, and if I wasn't exactly feeling any pain, I wasn't minding too much what I *did* feel.

She came in very quietly, so quietly that at first I hardly knew she'd arrived. I just saw the door open, and there was Anne, looking about ten times more nubile than my picture of her. Corby didn't see her either. He'd turned round to wind the clock on the mantelpiece, facing the oval mirror, and he had his back to the door. It was a good thing. For I'm certain that until then, Anne didn't know who the guest of the evening was going to be.

She was a few paces in the room before I struggled to my feet. Their sofa is one of those deep affairs that hug you to them like a drowning man.

Seeing it was me, she paused. Her face didn't exactly alter. The formal smile of welcome still remained on her face. She didn't go pale or change colour. It was simply that for the fraction of a second she froze, as if she'd been a figure in a stopped cinematograph film. Then someone released the switch and she moved forward again.

Corby must have heard the slight punch of her heels on the carpet. He turned round, smiling proudly. "*There* you are, Anne!"

"Good evening." She held out her hand to me, but her eyes were on Corby. She gave him a sudden appealing smile—a God-I've-forgotten-his-name-help-me smile. She could act the pants off any actress you care to name. Corby fell for it hook, line and sinker. He put his hand on her bare shoulders. "Well, at last, Anne, we've managed to persuade *Captain Matherson* to dine with us." He moved his fingers over her skin in a way that made mine crawl.

"How nice of you to come, Captain Matherson. Has the Company been working you hard?"

"Oh, so-so. Not too bad really."

Corby somehow blocked her way, so that she had to sit down beside me on the sofa.

"What are you drinking, Anne?"

"Oh, the same as you two. What is it? Whisky?" She leaned forward. "Yes. Not too strong, darling."

While Corby dropped ice cubes into her glass, I passed her the cigarettes. If I'd moved my fingers in her direction one fraction of an inch, I could have done a Corby and touched the bare skin of her arm. She was wearing a very simple-looking dress of dark red velvet, without any ornament. It wasn't particularly low cut, but when she leaned forward for me to light her cigarette, the material just naturally seemed to fall back, and I could see the full white curve of her breasts. I don't know whose hand had the tremble, but it took me a long time to get the bloody thing alight.

Sitting side by side, deliberately not touching, three inches of damask no-man's-land between us, I was aware of an excitement coming out of her as heavy as perfume, as palpable as heat. I caught a glimpse in the mirror of the pair of us framed in guilt, like the principals in a Victorian melodrama.

I felt hazy with whisky. My mind began harping back to the last time. Everything was so different, and yet so alike. It reminded me of one of Priestley's time plays. I half expected Corby to be whisked away, and Anne and I to close that gap. I began to sweat.

Corby stood with his arm on the mantelpiece. He might have been focusing us for guilt. He had his head on one side. Then he licked his lips, preparatory to speaking.

"Anne darling, please excuse us talking shop just once more. I've been thinking over what you've just said about the Autoland, Philip. I like the way you put your point. I like it very much. In fact, I suggest you come in on our next meeting." He smiled paternally, as if he were a headmaster handing a bright boy the term prize. "That's next Monday."

The Autoland . . . that's all the bastard was thinking about! God, the man was bone from the neck up and the navel down!

I glanced at Anne. She was staring at me, her eyebrows

raised, her lips slightly apart. I can't explain the look. It asked a question—though I wasn't at all sure what the question was. Anyway, I nodded.

And then Mrs. Whatever-her-name-is knocked on the door, and the three of us went in to dinner.

FOUR

I LAY on my back in the sand. This part of Nassau beach was a good half mile down the road from our hotel, which is eight hundred yards too far for aircrew to walk. I don't know what it is about being wafted about at five hundred miles an hour, but it makes you like that. One of these days, we'll lose the use of our legs, and we'll have to get an Autoland Mark II to take us to the bar. I'd got myself a shallow hollow with a hump of sand behind me. I'm nobody's pin-up, and I'm never going to be torn in shreds by howling fans, but there are times when I want to be alone.

I was quite safe here from my crew. Safe, for that matter, from anyone.

It wasn't that I didn't like the bastards. The six males were all decent types . . . good in their jobs, affable and ordinary like me. And all the female had done wrong was to feel off-colour so she couldn't do any work on the trip down here. The shrimp cocktail we had for lunch had disagreed with her most likely. Not her fault at all, really.

But I'd had them on the flight over from the U.K., two days in a New York hotel, the flight down here, dinner last night and breakfast this morning. I still had the flight back tonight, another two days in New York before the eastbound back to London.

In any case, it's one of the Captain's perks to get away from it all. And this was the place to get to. Palm trees, speedboats, cheap liquor, well-shaped girls. The Caribbean Sea doesn't roar or hiss or boom—it lisps. The sun beats down on your skin so that you know you've got a body. And the air is full of jasmine and jacaranda and flowers that smell like girls.

Here I wasn't Captain Philip Matherson—who had an unresolved affair with a married woman squashed as far down as it would go inside him, and a balled-up simulated instrument approach still niggling at his manly pride. For since that shocking performance, everywhere I flew had been clear and sunny, hardly a cloud in the sky, nothing to fight against, and almost in disgust I'd given the First Officer most of the landings.

But here I could forget. Here I was just a crustacean clinging to a bit of coral, a bit of seaweed washed in by the frilly tide. Better still, just a body.

A live body, mind. Not a dead one.

It was now nearly a fortnight since that dinner at the Corbys'. Not one word from Anne or about Anne had I heard. Nor had she heard a word from me.

Which was as it should be, of course. Crazy to rush in again, now everything was all over and everybody was still in one piece. No point in putting your head back in the noose —because believe you me, Corby would have no mercy. Remembering myself in that compromising and dangerous situation of August madness—as I can quite detachedly now—it's as though I'm a child at a pantomime again, watching the hero all unwary of the ogre just behind him, so I want to shout look out, *look out!*

Break it off clean, that was the way to do it. And that was what I had done. And yet, sometimes my mind would start out of the strait jacket and begin wandering. That look, for instance, Anne had given me, as we sat side by side on the sofa, just before we went into dinner . . . what did it mean?

I took a small marble-coloured pebble, and threw it at the blue Caribbean sky. At about twenty feet it lost flying speed, stalled and spun in onto a coral outcrop with a rasping noise that brought me right back to Corby's office and the Autoland meeting there just before I came out on Service.

It's close to the engine shops and the maintenance hangars and whatever Corby said was given a dentist's-drill undertone. Now that we'd all had a taste on the simulator, he told us, the Autoland was being fitted to the Astra, a small twin-engined Company aircraft with similar flying characteristics to the 909, mainly used for communications. Corby himself would do the instructing of each Captain in turn down at Riverly Airport, before sending him off solo "preferably in bad weather so as to bolster his confidence." It was only at the end of the meeting that he appeared to remember our conversation. "Now Captain Matherson," he said, "has a point to make, I know." And out I came, unaccustomed as I am to public speaking, with what he'd asked me to say: "I'd rather trust myself than any machine." It was what ninety-nine per cent of the other Line pilots round the table thought, but would any of them, now they were in The Presence, come forward to support me? Not on your life, and there was such a horrible hush that I began to think maybe it was the liquor that had made me say it in the first place.

I took up the same pebble and threw it at the sky once more. This time it came down with a soft *plop* in the sand, as much as to say, "Keep your mouth shut in the future, Matherson. Your mouth shut and your nose clean. And then you'll be able to laze like I do in this sunny paradise for ever and ever, amen."

And that good advice I intended to take. Lying beside my pebble, I erased Captain Matherson again and resumed being a crustacean. I felt soothed by the sun and the slight salt breeze on my skin. Some way behind me was a row of beach-type private houses, screened by oleander bushes. Half a dozen owner-occupiers were splashing in the water, but too far away to be anything but a mild bee-buzz in my ears. All I could see were a few grey-green strands of marram grass on the hump of sand behind me, looking like the last hairs on an old man's head.

And then over the hump, trampling the grass, came two feet. Girl's feet, *nice* girl's feet . . . straight toes, decent arches, pale pink lacquer on the nails. They continued up to nice neat ankles, the size I could have got my fingers round, and nice neat legs. A footful of sand splashed on my bare belly. A nice girl's voice said, "I'm sorry."

I looked up higher. I saw a face that went with it all. Round except for a pointed chin, pinched in afterwards neatly with a potter's fingers, a flat face with low cheekbones and wide eyes. I couldn't see the colour of them, but they were light.

"Don't apologize," I said. "I don't belong here really. I was just washed up by the tide."

But it was no use trying to talk to her as if she were Anne. I didn't want her to be Anne. I wanted her to be what she looked. The real true opposite of Anne—a nice girl. My married sister always says there's no such animal. But she's a cynic, and I'm not so sure.

"Look," I said, standing up and dusting sand from my swim-suit bottom. "I don't know if you go in for this sort of thing. But this little hollow here is quite big enough for two."

She skidded down the slope and eyed me and my habitat doubtfully. Close to, her eyes were light blue, harebell blue, nursery blue, harmless blue. Not like Anne Corby's, mid-night blue, blue as a Jamaica night. She was wearing a neat and decorous one-piece, the same colour as her eyes—if she had been Anne, it would have been a scarlet bikini.

"But aren't you going to bathe?" She seemed a healthy

extrovert, too. Sand, sea and swim suit equalled bathe, Q.E.D. No maundering around thinking of things this girl wouldn't know existed.

"I wasn't," I said. "But now I'm seriously considering it." "The water's absolutely heavenly."

"You've been in?"

"Oh, yes. Before breakfast. But I'm just going in again."

I remember thinking as I got up and walked beside her that she was the sort of girl in the end most aircrew married. Sure, they had their flings with the fringe types, but in the end this was the sort of girl who ironed shirts and pressed uniforms, and trained the au-pairs, and kept herself happy with the W.I. and Good Works while the boys flew off.

We splashed around rather inanely in the water. She pointed out the fronds of Woolworth's coloured weed growing up from the sea bed, and I watched the movements of her legs garbled by mild currents and wavelets. She had a pale skin—not white like Anne's, but pink and white like a schoolgirl's, or at least like a schoolgirl's is supposed to be. Her shoulders were rather wide for a girl, which gave her waist a snappy neatness, and her breasts were small and high. She was a smooth competent swimmer.

We did a decorous breaststroke up to the raft, and then we hauled ourselves on board. I asked her then what she was doing in Nassau, although already my own private computer had deduced her answer. She was a stewardess.

"Well, if it's for Empire Airways, why haven't I seen you before?"

It *was* for Empire Airways, she said. And the nearest she got to sauciness: "Perhaps you weren't looking!"

"Oh, but I was, I promise you." Then I shut myself up because that sort of flippant talk with that sort of girl could bring you in faster than any Autoland. "What's your name?"

"Alison Humphrey."

"It's a nice name, Alison. I like it." I did, too. It was a kind of expurgated edition of Anne. A *Lady Chatterley's Lover* without the best-selling word.

The conversation paused. "I have a name, too," I said at last. And as she still remained uninterested in my identity, "Not such a nice name. In fact, I don't like it at all."

"Actually, I think I know it." She coloured slightly, and with what seemed a characteristic of hers when she was nervous, she gave a shy wriggle on her bottom. "You're Captain Matherson, aren't you?"

Now that the name was out, the last molecule of crustacean gave up the ghost on me, though I amended it to: "Philip Matherson."

"I thought so."

"But how did you know?" I rubbed my fingernails on the hairs of my chest where a coat lapel ought to be. "I'm not all that famous. I've not been on the tele much, I promise."

But she didn't laugh. She just said earnestly, "One of the crew pointed you out to me in the hotel."

"Ah, so you marked me down!"

She smiled a little then, but uncomfortably, as if I might have believed it. We talked a bit about Nassau, and the hotel and the food, and then we slid off the raft and swam back to the shore. As our feet slapped over the pink sand again, I said, "Can I invite you back to my hollow?"

"I'm awfully sorry . . . but I'm meeting a friend for lunch."

"Well, maybe I'll see you around."

"I hope so."

And that was that. I watched her nice brown hair and her nice blue swim suit and her long legs get smaller and smaller. With a sigh of regret I saw her figure finally merge with the shadows on the palm trees along the road. I actually began trying to unravel the roster to forecast when I might hope to be out on a trip with her.

But the heat was too good to be spoiled by mathematics,

and though I tried for a while I never did figure out when I might see her again.

But I could have spared myself even that small trouble. I saw her that evening as I boarded the aeroplane. She took my cap and raincoat and said, "Good evening, Captain," as she stowed them away in the vestibule. She looked as good in the Company's uniform as she did in a swim suit.

"So you're taking Miss Parkin's place?"

"That's right, sir. She's still not well."

All I could think to say was, "The way things happen to me!"

I didn't see her again all trip—a routine one. Clear weather all the way across to Norfolk, and then airways to the holding pattern, ending up with a smooth landing on Runway 04. But I found out from the First Officer that she was new.

At Kennedy when I was collecting my meal money ($10 a day) I had a natter with a type in Ops. And I ran into the eastbound crew who told me Corby was in New York, doing a take-over, they shouldn't wonder, of the Autoland factory. I didn't have a chance to talk to Alison.

But I rang her the next day about noon. I said, "I wonder if this time I could be the friend you're meeting for lunch?"

We went to a little place off Sixth Avenue, where they have red check tablecloths and goulash on the menu, so I suppose it's Hungarian. The head man stuck us in a little corner where it was so dim I couldn't see the colour of her eyes, which was a pity because overnight I'd decided I liked that nice safe shade. We must have looked romantic, because they didn't serve us for about half an hour. In that time, I found out quite a lot about her. A lot of facts anyway—though not much maybe about her.

You can kid yourself you're getting to know someone by asking and answering the sort of questions you find on any form from any Ministry.

I asked her where she came from. And she replied Saffron
Walden, did I know it?

"I've been there. I seem to remember a tidy little pub in the
square. I've had the odd session in the bar."

But though she knew the pub, she hadn't been inside. Her
father was an estate agent. His office was just off the square.
He was a partner, so his name was up on the board. Blackett,
Porter and Humphrey—I'd probably seen it without noticing
it. She'd been a doctor's receptionist for her sins before she
managed to persuade the stewardess selection board to have
her. Oh, she adored flying, it was absolute bliss, and she
didn't regret it, not for one moment. Of course her parents
worried, but then I knew what poor darlings parents were,
didn't I?

She was twenty-four. Only one year younger than Anne.

"What I can't understand, Alison, is why you're not married." On that excuse I picked up her hand, and pretended
to look for a nonexistent engagement ring.

She pulled it away, with a mild Saffron Walden Amateur
Dramatic Society gesture labelled *drama*. She looked down
at the tablecloth and fiddled with her fork. Her brows were
puckered. She hadn't the sort of skin that made definite lines.

"I was engaged once," she said. "But I'm afraid he was
rather a bad type. He went off the rails."

I didn't know what to say. I knew what I wanted to say.
That we're all bad types, and the rails aren't all that much
cop to stay on anyway. Instead I murmured pompously that
it was a Good Thing she'd found out in time. I began to find
it was rather too easy to drop into her idiom.

When at last the waiter came, we had goulash, followed
by apple pie and ice cream, followed by coffee, followed by
the bill. Three dollars-ninety. She thanked me for a lovely
lunch and said she was just going to pop along to the little
girls' room. I sat and did invisible noughts and crosses on the
check tablecloth, and I wondered if there was a flick she

might want to see, and if I might kiss her in the dark—and then I wondered if I wanted to.

By the cash desk, the waiter stood looking at the clock and cleaning his nails with a toothpick. He had a grease stain on his apron, and I remembered his breath smelled of beer. Everything seemed suddenly mundane and dull and I felt drowned in ordinariness.

I think it was that which made me say it. A desire to be really vulgar. I don't honestly think I had any intention, as it were, of exorcising Anne.

Whatever it was, when Alison came back, washed and combed and lipsticked, I said, "I know! Let's go to Coney Island!"

Once I'd suggested it, I wondered why I hadn't thought of it before. It was a real tangy New York day outside with the air crisp as celery. Coney Island in the early fall, with the lime leaves blowing over the roundabouts, and the first chill of winter to ice that hot lemonade. It didn't enter into it that in nine years of coming to New York, I'd only been there once before—with Anne.

"Coney Island?" she said doubtfully. "Why, yes. Yes, of course. I'd simply love to."

We had a slight argument after I'd paid the bill, because someone or other had told her aircrew expected the stewardess to go Dutch. She took out a clean dollar bill from her handbag and tried to present me with it.

"What on earth . . . ?" I stuffed it back in the pocket of her jacket as she made ineffectual little pushes with her hand. If I'd given Anne her lunch at the Waldorf, she'd have accepted it like a queen. It was odd that what was, after all, only this girl's generosity should irritate me. But it did. And as we boarded a taxi, I already had the haunting taste in my mind that the expedition would be a failure.

It wasn't that Alison wasn't pretty, or even sexy in a restrained sort of way. It wasn't that she didn't try either. She didn't yawn. She didn't get bored. She didn't ever lapse into sheer bloody-mindedness as Anne would have done. She kept her eyes attentively on me, blue and wide as the tinder-box cat's, till I found all my chitchat running out through them.

We went over the Queensborough Bridge. Her eyes encompassed it. She wriggled on her bottom and sighed and said she wouldn't fancy falling off *that*. I moved a bit closer. Her perfume was the lavender-blue, lavender-green sort. I took her hand. It was bigger than Anne's. More capable, not so boneless. I changed to the other hand, and slid my arm around her shoulders.

"This is Queensborough . . . if you look over there . . . you can see the United Nations Building."

I dropped my hand lower. I could just feel the curve of her breast. I could also feel her heartbeat through my finger tips. It was hurried and unhappy.

I took my hand away. I felt her relax. The taxi swung through Queens and Brooklyn, turned left to the coast, and already over the housetops we could see the giant wheel with its little cups of containers going round and round. Alison said, "Heavens, isn't it huge! I'd no idea! What fun!" And took out her compact and put another layer on her nose.

We stopped at the same gate Anne and I had stopped. We put our money in the same slot machines. Alison was a bit chary of the fortune-telling one. "I'm rather against them really." But when hers came out, and it said she was going to marry an important man and have three children, she slipped it in her pocket, along with the new dollar bill. She was quite right. I'm against those bloody machines too. Mine came up with the same one as before. I stared down at it disbelievingly . . . *your wife doesn't understand you.* I felt as if Anne or Corby had suddenly tapped me on the shoulder. I didn't read it aloud to Alison. I just tore it up and threw it away.

I suggested hamburgers. But Alison said, "What, after that enormous lunch?"

We bought some clams though. She didn't like them. But she didn't spit them out then and there on the sidewalk as Anne had done. She chewed them and swallowed them and pronounced them an acquired taste.

Nothing happened spontaneously. We didn't just wander around and have things happen to us. She was waiting eagerly, engine running, with ready anonymous ownerless enthusiasm for me to engage the gears. Her eyes asked, "And what shall we do now?" Like a child on whole holiday with an indulgent crackpot aunt.

So we did what I'd done with Anne—though I didn't really mean to. We went on the cakewalk, and though we held hands because everybody had to, her grip was weak. We went on the thing that blew the girls' skirts up. But they didn't get hers, because then her grip was strong and she anchored it down. I couldn't even imagine it was Anne in the darkness of the Ghost Train, because she didn't cling to me or scream or wriggle—she laughed. She didn't mind the wet sponges or the trailing cobwebs. The only thing she minded was my hand on her knee, and that she soon got rid of.

We went on the Dodgems, but she spent all the time adroitly avoiding everybody. She never hunched forward like a black-haired fiend. I never said, "You got me, pal!"

When we stepped out, she laughed and slipped her arm in mine and asked, "Wouldn't I make a fine navigator?"

Before we went on the Big Dipper, she bought a cheap head-scarf of white artificial silk to protect her hair. She wouldn't even let me tie it on for her and fasten it with a bow under her chin, in case I tried to kiss her.

We had come to the Pillar of Fate. They wanted a dollar each for you to go right up to the top, where they promised

you a panoramic view of New York before sending you corkscrewing down on a mat.

"No, Philip, don't. Honestly, it's not worth it!" She sounded
like a budget-conscious little wife already. "Besides, we've
had enough fun for today."

As if *fun* were like vitamins, a daily dose for the health of
your body and the good of your soul. It had been a mistake
to come to Coney Island. It was like trying to superimpose
black and white onto a coloured photograph. The merry-go-
rounds whirled around us. The music sounded like a sky-size
tambourine. The coloured lights glowed brighter and brighter
as the daylight faded. People jostled and shouted and laughed.
But the girl by my side was in shadow.

The last time I'd been here, I felt thirteen. Now I was
ninety-three.

The outing fizzled out like the fag-end of a Sunday School
treat. We walked along for a while, arm in arm. I watched
the stream of coloured lights running over Alison's face like
liquid dye trying to get in. I watched our feet as they
tramped through the churned-up ground and the sea of
paper bags and cartons and straws. I tried to hear the distant
sound of the Atlantic through the roar of the jolly noises. I
found coins in my pockets and I put them in machines and
I found myself owning a funny hat and a carton of foreign
cigarettes. Alison got a cheap glass ring out of a machine
that clawed up presents out of other cheap trash. She looked
as if she'd struck gold on the Yukon. We had a chicken-and-
french-fried supper in a neon and plastic booth. We had a
marshmallow sundae made of cotton wool.

Then it began to drizzle and Alison said, "Heavens, I must
keep my hair-do, or you'll snag me tomorrow!"

She smiled prettily to show it was really a compliment to
my authority, and then she gave a little sigh of pleasure
when we settled ourselves in the cab. "Oh, it has been fun!
Why didn't I do this before?"

"Because you've only just met me."

"Yes, perhaps." She let me hold her hand. "I think a lot of the fun must be in *who* you go with."

Now it was full darkness outside. The stippled film of rain on the taxi windows magnified the march of variegated lights into a fine cascade. I watched them for a moment. To me their melting colours seemed inexpressibly sad, like some valuable painting going to pieces.

I turned back to Alison. I could only see her blurred outline in the half-light. A glint of hair caught in a stray flash of light. The skin of her face gleamed almost phosphorescently. I pulled her to me suddenly. I felt her breath squirt on my cheek, as if I had knocked it out with the quickness of my movement. I felt the back of her neck stiffen under my hand. I couldn't at first find her mouth because she kept moving her head from side to side. When I did, I began to kiss it so hard that it was painful even to me. Then I became aware of *her*. I could taste her lipstick, smell her powder, feel her small cool lips under mine. A nice girl's lips, a bit bewildered, lost in the complex behaviour of a man's, doing their best under difficult circumstances.

Abruptly I stopped kissing her. "I'm sorry," I said. "I'm very sorry. I won't do that again." I pushed her away gently. "I don't know what came over me."

The strange thing was that she didn't mind much. Not once it was over. She got out her tools again and did up her face. She didn't speak for a long time. Then she said, "That's all right, really." Rather nervously, she patted my knee. "Honestly. I understand."

When we got out at the hotel I glanced sideways at her face. She had a curiously happy, contented look about her. As we crossed the foyer together, she looked suddenly matronly.

I wasn't yet sure how the evening was going to end. I wasn't sure how I wanted it to end.

"Heavens," she said, looking at the clock by the elevators. "How late it is!" She pressed the button. "It's been a marvellous day. I've enjoyed it all. Everything."

She was smiling, but watching me. She was wondering if I would try to come up to her room with her. I was wondering that, too.

"I've got my uniform to press and my packing to do. Then I shall have an early night." She smiled in half-mocking, half-meant severity. "I think we should *both* have an early night."

I was still wondering when the lift whisked her legs past eye level. Nice legs, nice ankles, nice feet. Where I'd come in, only the other way round.

I caught the next lift up to my own room. But by that time I had stopped wondering. Now I knew exactly what I was going to do.

I had a couple of drinks from the bottle in my suitcase to steady my nerves first. We always pick up a bottle of hundred-proof rum from Nassau, and it always goes straight to the spot. Then I went over to the telephone and lifted the receiver and said, "I want to make a call. . . . Where to?" I was almost surprised the girl didn't know. "To England. Hanfield, that's near London . . . Hanfield 2732."

"There'll be a delay. But I'll call you."

"How long a delay?"

"I'm sorry. I can't just say," said the singsong voice. "But I'll call you."

I took my glass over to the window. As usual, I found the central heating unbearably stuffy. I threw open the sash. A cold drizzle trailed my face like Ghost Train cobwebs. The buildings opposite shone like seals. The cloud was lowering. Across the way, the Chrysler Building had lost its head, somewhere round the sixtieth floor.

I stood there for a moment slowly drinking. There's something Edgar Allan Poe-ish about fog creeping lower and lower. It had reached the highest neon signs now, reflecting their colours on its underbelly before slowly putting them out.

I walked back and picked up the receiver. "Surely you've got my number now?"

"Sorry . . . but I'll call you."

It was over an hour later when she did. I heard the tinkle of bells and the clank of changing lines. And then above a buzzing of other voices, all at once very clear and high, Anne's voice, "Hello?"

Now that I'd got her I didn't know what to say. I cleared my throat, and shook my head to scatter the rum fumes away.

"This is Hanfield 2732."

"Your number is answering," the operator prompted, and clanked out.

"Is that you, Anne?"

"Yes. But who's that?"

"Don't you recognize my voice?"

Warily, a legacy perhaps of Maurice and his tricks, "No-o . . . not sure, anyway. Who is it?"

"Philip."

A long pause.

"But where on earth are you speaking from?" Her voice had a sleepy fretfulness.

"America. New York, to be precise."

"Is . . . is something wrong?"

"Not that I know of."

"Then why are you ringing? Philip! D'you know what God-awful time it is?"

I looked at my watch. "It's midnight here."

"It was midnight when I went to bed. Now it's past five." She paused. "Hang on while I light a cigarette. That's better. God, Philip . . . what's got into you?"

"You."

"I didn't hear what you said."

I bellowed into the phone. "I said *you* have."

I heard her high giggle come floating above weird under-
lying sea-sound effects.

"Anne?"

"Yes?"

"I went to Coney Island this afternoon."

"Alone?"

"No."

"Who with, then?"

"The stewardess."

"Did you phone me up to tell me that?"

"It was bloody awful. I was bored bloody stiff."

"Good . . . I'm glad."

"It wasn't like last time. Last time was fun, wasn't it? D'you
remember, Anne?"

"I seem to have some vague recollection."

"You've got more than that, haven't you?"

"I suppose so. I'm glad you enjoy my company better than
Miss What's-it. Did you wake me up to tell me that?"

"No . . . not exactly. But that day we had . . . couldn't we
do it again?"

She laughed. "Oh, yes. Nothing simpler. What d'you expect me to do? Hop on a plane? Get a cheap fare with Maurice's signature. That *would* be fun."

"Of course not. I'm leaving tomorrow. Boston and the U.K.
There must be places like that in England. Scarborough or
Blackpool or Brighton . . . yes, of course, Brighton, that's an
idea!"

"Brighton's frightfully wicked. Besides, what about Maurice?"

"He's this side . . . you know that. He'll be hugging his
Autoland over here for a long time yet."

"Well, that's certainly one place—" Her voice was drowned
in sea noises, but it sounded like *he can't come home early
from.*

"What was that? I think I missed that. Something about coming home early?"

"It's all right. It was nothing."

"When is he coming home then?"

"Not for a week."

"Anne, speak up! I can hardly hear you."

"Are you suggesting an improper weekend?"

"I don't really know what I'm suggesting. Just a day out, if you like. Or an afternoon. Or an evening. Anything."

"Well, I shall just have to consult my diary, won't I?"

"Anne . . . for God's sake." I paused. "Anne!"

"Yes?"

"You remember that look you gave me?"

"What look?"

"When we were sitting on the sofa . . . last time . . . just before we went into dinner."

"What about it?"

"I've been thinking about it. I can't get it out of my mind. It seemed to me . . . Anne, are you listening?"

"Yes."

"It was asking something . . . a sort of appeal . . ."

"Was it?"

"And I wanted you to know . . . whatever it asked . . . the answer is . . . yes."

There was a long pause. Then: "How do you know it *can* be?"

"Because I do."

"You're very sure."

"Quite sure."

She clicked her tongue and laughed. Then she said, "Why?"

"Don't you know?"

"I haven't a clue."

"You just want me to say it."

"I won't *know* what it is till you do, will I?"

I held my breath for a long time. Somehow I knew I

shouldn't say it. I waited so long that Anne's voice—tempting, prompting—came through again.

"Are you still there?"

"Yes."

"Well, then?"

"I've fallen for you. That's why."

"I don't believe it."

"It's true. And not just the usual sort of falling either."

"What sort of falling then?"

"Head over heels."

She didn't say anything then. But she gave a funny long-drawn-out sigh. I can't describe what it conveyed. I don't want to. Maybe it was just all that ocean between that distorted it.

"Aren't you going to say anything, Anne?"

Her voice had a satisfied drowsiness. "What is there *to* say, darling?"

"You'll see me when I get back?"

"I don't know. We'll have to see."

I began to shake with an anger that came over me like a sudden sweat. "Look, Anne, d'you know how much this call is costing me?"

"Oh, a fortune, I should think."

"Three dollars a minute!"

I had a vision of her lying back among the pillows, the phone idly held against her cheek, a pink frilly lamp casting a deeper pink light on pink sheets. She was so quiet, I wondered if she'd gone back to sleep.

"Three dollars a minute!" I shouted into the mouthpiece. "D'you hear that?"

And back her voice boomeranged, cold, disdainful, bored. "Well, if I'm too expensive, Captain Matherson . . . I suggest we terminate the call."

Then I heard her put down the receiver—and the line go dead.

I waited for a moment, with the earpiece still pressed against my ear. Vibrations, voices, sibilant sounds surged up like the sound of the sea in a shell. Then clickings and louder voices. My operator came up. "Your number has cleared the line. Have you finished?"

I said, "Yes, thank you," and put down the receiver.

Then I went back to the window. The fog had used the time I was talking to creep halfway down the Chrysler Building. It was coming lower all the time. I stood there with a drink in my hand until it reached my floor in the Coronet Hotel, and I had to shut the window to stop the stuff pouring into the room. As I walked over to the bed and started to get undressed, I thought that at long last, after looking for the stuff from Iceland to Timbuktu, the weather was going to be bloody awful for the New York-Boston-London ride.

FIVE

"THERE are those twelve pax waiting at Boston, Captain."

"I hadn't forgotten them."

"If you're going to overfly—"

"Who said anything about overflying?"

Even in good weather, this despatcher was as fidgety as a monkey on a stick. Now he stood by the window, blinking at the mist, while I went on drinking cardboard-flavoured coffee from the ten-cent automatic. Over his left shoulder, I could see 909 Victor X-ray twined about with refuelling hose: and just beyond, jutting out into the fog, the fantastic T.W.A. building looking like a vulture petrified on take-off.

"The met are doubtful about Boston weather."

"It's not exactly radiant sunshine here."

The despatcher began to get worried. He screwed up his little monkey eyes at the possibility of a nightstop, at the horror of trying to fit eighty passengers into New York hotels. "But, Captain," he said, coaxing me with a dud banana, "it's above Kennedy take-off limits."

I raised my brows doubtfully. I wasn't in my best of moods. I'm not used to being dangled on the end of a string—not by a girl, not by anyone. The night before still rankled. My sleep hadn't been long enough or deep enough, though my drinking had. Wide awake for hours, round and round in my mind went the fact that nobody—certainly no woman—had ever hung up on me. Standing there with the dead receiver to my ear, calling *hello* down a wire that never answered, I had felt such a damned fool. As for the Herbert who kept reaching out for the disappearing grapes . . . that was *me*. And now I felt unsure of myself, cut down to pint-size, unmanned, if you like—with the one clear thought inside me that I *must* take up that 909 this evening, no matter what.

I suppose when they feel like I was feeling, everyone gets a slight perverse pleasure watching someone else sweat it out. I watched the despatcher's pale face dispassionately. I did not mean to let him know too soon what was in my mind. He was oscillating between the met reports, the flight plan, the weather outside and me, making little sizzly noises like he was roasting on a spit.

I let the last dribbles of coffee drop onto my tongue, tossed the carton into the trash can, and put him out of his misery. "Tell the tanker crew . . . Boston fuel."

"Boston fuel! Boston fuel!" His voice rang out like wedding bells, and next moment he was off before I changed my mind.

Leaning on the window sill, I watched him emerge from the block, dash across the sopping ramp waving at the refuellers to stop, lest they make me overweight for a Boston landing. I watched them roll in their hoses, mount the tanker and disappear into the mist. Now the word would have gone out to Traffic, to Operations, even to those twelve assorted pax—business men probably, some tourists, a bright-eyed student maybe from Harvard—that Captain Matherson was coming.

One short sentence of mine, snowballing into action.

I remember Wilson saying when his wife was having a baby, you just did one small thing, and it started so much for so long. Well, that's what a pilot did when he said he was going. Most of us, of course, get one hell of a kick out of it. I've read somewhere that women spend their lives looking for love, and men for power. Driving a 909, not to mention all the decisions, gives you a spot of power all right. Up there, you're master. I've known captains who couldn't say boo to their wife's charwoman, who come on board like Jupiter straddling his thunderbolt. Maybe it's something on the same lines as teen-age kids, bewitched by a hotted-up motorbike into Ton-up boys. Or an impotent underwriter at Lloyds when he drops behind the wheel of his silver-grey sports car.

Your girl might hit you in the teeth, or your wife move in despair to the spare room . . . but, boy, you could make that machine respond! And, brother, does she give! Maybe there is something after all in George Preston's theory about why pilots resent criticism on their skill, about the connection between sex and flying.

I stared out at the 909, left alone now in the drizzle. I thought wryly . . . God knew, I was in much the same boat. I *needed* to make that machine respond. And suddenly, just because I wanted to, for the first time in all these years I wondered if I could. I actually rubbed the palms of my hands together, flexing my finger muscles. I felt as if all the ability had run out of them. Briefly, I eyed the 909 as warily and assessingly as if she were a woman.

Then like these nonsense ideas do, the feeling went. The next minute I could actually smile at it. It was nothing. All part of the hangover. Yet it left behind a small dent in the normally tough skin of my confidence.

"Captain Matherson!"

The tannoy was calling for me now. They were wanting the load sheet signed, the flight plan signed, the serviceability sheet signed, the customs declaration signed. If anything was going to happen to me and the aeroplane today, they wanted their acquittal before we even started.

"Empire Airways announce the departure of their Flight 507 to Boston and London."

The tannoy had a flat note to it as though it were muffled by the mist. I put my pen back in my pocket, picked up my brief case, and went out the side door to get on board before the passengers. Apart from its aeronautical hazards, fog always gives me the creeps. I hate its soft insidiousness, the way it subtly undermines your confidence in your own eyes and ears, distorting distance and muffling sound, the way its coldness creeps right into your bones.

It even combined with the oil on the tarmac now to make the surface slippery as an eel's back, so that I had to walk with a short uneasy stride. It took me twice as long to get to the steps, and I could hear the echo of my footfall bouncing back at me off the 909's huge blade of a wing like a tinny drumbeat. It had a curious ominous quality. It seemed to hammer at that dent in my confidence and get through it with a sizeable hole.

All the way up the steps, I tried to rationalize it. I'm neither Celtic fringe nor Cornish fey, so I don't suffer from premonitions, or bad dreams, or mermaids combing their hair on my wing tips. If I was feeling uneasy, I knew damned well it was because I'd had too little sleep, too much raw liquor, and an unexpected brush-off from Mrs. Anne Corby. All of which could be settled by two hot coffees and a more-fish-in-the-sea philosophy.

Just to put the latter into practise, when she took my cap and raincoat from me, I gave Alison Humphrey a warm and special smile. She gave me her own brand of special one back, discreet as her lavender perfume, proprietorial as a luggage label.

I said, "I'll have coffee as soon as we're airborne. Black, please. And make it strong."

She raised her brows reprovingly as she said, "Yes, sir." I

remember thinking there might be plenty other fish, but some had a much less exotic flavour than others.

All the same it was bright and cozy inside the aircraft. The lights held the weather at bay and the cabin smelled of new upholstery and rosy air freshener. The thick carpet obliterated my footfall. I waited like someone who's just taken a couple of aspirin for my uneasiness to lift.

But it didn't. Then I pushed open the flight-deck door and I knew why.

The crew were already in their places. The navigator was a shadowy figure behind a hand in a round pool of yellow light. Milligan was at the engineer's panel. First Officer Holmes was sitting in the right-hand seat, his arms folded, whistling softly through his gap teeth. All round, the fog pressed against the huge wide windscreens so that they looked like steamed-up bathroom windows. To all intents and purposes, I had dropped through a freak slit in time, and I was back in the simulator.

It was scarcely reassuring. I had difficulty getting into my seat. I fumbled with my straps before I managed to fix them. When I put on the earphones, I half expected G.P.'s voice to come crackling over from his place behind the green tin desk.

"Passengers all on board. Rear door closed. Preliminary Check Lists complete. Shall we light the engines, Captain?"

"Of course."

I knocked the Check List off the throttle box then. Holmes and I jostled round the cockpit floor to get it. As one by one the engines burst into life, I began tapping round the knobs and tits, reorientating myself almost like a blind man on Braille.

"Victor X-ray cleared to Runway Zero Four and hold."

With a noise like plaster being torn off skin, the brakes came off. We started to move uncertainly forward, bucking up and down on the oleo legs. I'd pulled the side window right back and pushed my head out to see better. I could smell the fog dank as mushrooms and feel the dew of drizzle on my face.

The mist was coming and going—so that at times I could see quite a long way, glimpse down to the salt marshes as the slight wind momentarily tore holes in the overhanging mist. Then back came the wet blanket, pricked by the innumerable blue holes of the taxi lights.

"Coming up to Zero Four now, sir!"

We came slowly round the corner and stopped. As Holmes and the Engineer got on with the Check Lists, I stared out at what looked like a Victorian backyard lit by flickering gas lamps.

Lights and mist have a curious effect. Let them fascinate your eyes long enough, and they drag you right away from reality like a will-o'-the-wisp over the marshes. I had the queer sensation of being half in a dream and half out of it. I was back in the simulator and therefore I was bound to make a balls-up again. Only this time it mattered because it wasn't a simulator at all—it was an aeroplane with eighty-eight souls on board. It all had that awful illogical certainty of a nightmare. And even when by gritting my teeth, I forced myself back into reality, it seemed to boil down to one single sudden certainty—that I couldn't fly the damned thing.

I remember turning to Holmes and croaking, "How about doing this leg? Good instrument practise for you!"

Holmes looked at me appreciatively and laughed. I have a reputation for a dry flight-deck wit when things get bad. The Navigator laughed. The Engineer laughed. The Controller in the Tower seemed to laugh as he gave us the clearance in one great blowout "Victor—X-ray—clear—take-off—cleared-to-Kennedy—Vortac—054 radial—to Sound Intersection. Cross-La Guardia—VOR 135 radial—at or below 4000. Cross—La Guardia—VOR 092 radial—at or above 5000 . . ."

I blinked my eyes several times to clear my vision and my

head as Holmes repeated it all back. I felt little prickles of
sweat break out under my arms and at the back of my neck.
I clenched my teeth so hard together I could feel the lumpy
muscles working at the end of my jaws.

Then I pushed the throttles up to 10,000 r.p.m. Victor
X-ray began to shake and shudder all over. I released the
brakes.

And then somehow the 909 took over. I got a punch in the
small of my back. I was seized by the small hairs. With a
roaring away of *no-more-nonsense*, Victor X-ray began
pounding into the fog. The normal process was reversed.
This time *her* power seemed to flow into *me*.

Back of us now would be streaming four black coils of
smoke from the water injection. As always, the take-off was
slow and majestic—the engine note booming out over the
countryside like a giant's foghorn, the wipers beating time
to and fro across the myopic windscreen.

One by one, up came the runway lights, muzzy as candy-
floss balls. I counted them go by, like pep pills I'd taken. By
the eighth I was beginning to feel more confidence. Not so
much in myself as in the aeroplane. Ninety per cent her, ten
per cent me—somehow we'd make it. I felt like the reluctant
virgin who'd been lucky enough to get the most experienced
operator in the brothel.

"V 1!"

We couldn't stop now, even if we wanted to. We were
committed, yet we were still six knots short of flying speed.
This was always the five seconds when I bit my lip.

"V 2!"

She came easily up onto her oleo legs, but still I could hear
the brushing of her tires along the tarmac. I let her ride along
like that, halfway between sky and ground for a couple of
seconds. Then I pulled back—and up she went.

"Gear up! After take-off check!"

With the mist streaming over us, at two thousand feet a

minute we began to climb. The needle on the airspeed indicator read 180 knots—that was all the indication we had that
we were moving. All vibration had stopped now. Everything
was steady. It was as if we were in some submarine cell trying to get from the bottom up through a dirty great sea. For
some reason, though the 909 was climbing fast, the time
seemed endless to me.

The needle was creeping round the altimeter dial. It's only
a forty-minute hop from New York to Boston and the flight
plan called for a height of only eleven thousand—and yet it
seemed we would never make it.

The First Officer was reporting going through nine thousand into the microphone when the greyness outside lightened. The windscreen dried up, turned pale grey, then white,
then yellow, then in a sudden explosion—bright gold. And
the next moment, we had broken surface, and the whole aircraft was illuminated in the sunshine of an early autumn
afternoon.

Holmes smiled. "This is more like it!"

I nodded. I couldn't have described to Holmes what I
really felt. Nor would I have wanted to. Down there we had
struggled, the aircraft and I, not only with bad weather, but
with a kind of mental gravity that momentarily had me
pinned to the earth's surface like a moth on a specimen paper.
Now we rode high in the clear. I could feel a nervous exhila-
ration running under my skin. I had the sensation of actually
feeling air and sun and speed of flight, as if we flew in a
cabinless craft. While through my finger tips, through the
seat of my trousers, the soles of my feet, came not exactly a
vibration but some sort of powerful emanation from those
forty thousand pounds of thrust under the aircraft's skin.

"Levelling off at cruising altitude. Shall I put George in?"

"Not on your life!"

Now it was my pleasure to keep her on a dead accurate
course. Now my finger tips had that touch which brought a

hairsbreadth accuracy. The aeroplane might have helped to bring me up. But now she responded obediently to my every touch. Now she knew who was master. I moved the control column slightly back and saw the answering tilt of her nose. I moved the stick to the left, and as rapidly and smoothly as if it had been an extension of my body, the port wing gracefully tipped down. I pressed the rudder bars as gently as a girl's foot under a café table, and felt that shimmying twitch of her huge tail. I was possessed with the glee of flight, with the accord of a perfect partnership.

"Steady on the southwest leg now, sir. Shall I report to Boston centre?"

"Do that!"

I heard voices crackling over the R/T. I wished the poor fogged-in bastards down there could see this. I'm no romantic, but even I have eyes. We were flying above a grey wig of stratus—quite alone—as the warm front below us now gave drizzle and fog and confusion, no doubt, to all earthbound inhabitants. Further in the west, there towered the huge black anvils of a cold front, their monstrous sides outlined in fiery gold as yet more sunlight tried to burst from behind them. And high in the blue sky above, were a bevy of plump round clouds that looked like the pink-tinted bottoms of Michelangelo's cherubs.

"Boston are giving 8/8 cloud at two hundred feet, visibility a thousand yards in mist."

"As I expected," I said. But the information seemed to come from another planet.

"The I.L.S. . . . localizer and glide path . . . fully serviceable."

"Excellent!"

A small lone cloud broke over the nose, momentarily filtering the sunlight. The 909 shook herself clear of droplets like a dog on a mat. As never before, I felt the clear high ecstasy of lonely flight. I felt ageless. I was the boy on a dolphin. I was a cosmonaut with galaxies, not clouds, slowly falling away under my feet. My vision was horizonless, my problems dispersed like clouds. I had conquered another element. The machine and I were perfectly mated.

But *I* was master.

The 909 seemed to be sniffing at the sunset. Just below the clear-vision panel, I could just see a sliver of her silver nose had been transformed into gold. I began moving my right hand over the well-known contours: the smooth square-ness of the throttle box, the rows of levers, the hard bony feel of the control column, the myriad switches above my head, each crowned with its little jewel, wondering how I ever thought I could not cope with them. More even than my flat, this was my home: the round faces of the instruments like good children in a class before me, and the red illumina-tion over the curved cockpit warm as a coal fire on a winter day.

"Boston are asking . . . do you want a Ground Controlled Approach?"

I looked at Holmes for a moment, bemused. It was like being deep in a clinch with a girl and asked if now some stranger stand-in should take over. Besides, after a bad start —as often happens—this was a day I was on form. This was a day when the fluence came out of me, the sort of day that middle-aged ladies have green fingers, the sort of day that a painter knows he can paint a masterpiece, or a show jumper's got that perfect feel of his horse. The 909 had brought me up. I was taking her down. I wasn't handing over to someone squinting into a radar box.

"No . . . thank you very much. Tell them . . . just the I.L.S.!"

At two thousand feet above Boston, Victor X-ray and I began to dance the Blindman's Twosome. We were back in the stuff again, not grey this time but a sort of eerie bronze.

That's because of all those beer signs, the cigarette slogans, the neons flashing on and off, the bonfire effect of a million lights from a million windows. Not that it matters really what the colour was—you still couldn't see a thing.

I'm pretty cagey about Boston. I go warily. Too many sky-scrapers sticking up out of the ground like tank traps for my liking. And I've never been the one to commit hara-kiri.

All the same taken carefully, an instrument landing is just like any other dance. There's a pattern behind it that you and your partner follow. And if a hundred and eighty miles an hour is rather fast, the floor's good and big and Control have seen to it that there aren't any other characters to bump into.

We'd cut the beam at 45 degrees. We were doing our procedure turn. I was keeping my eyes glued on the two-sided face of the I.L.S. indicator—the left half yellow, the right half blue, which could have been gum, the way at present the indicator needle seemed stuck in it.

"Bit of a crosswind, sir?"

"Could be."

I studied the map of the airfield on the throttle box, noting the obstructions—a 1349-foot TV tower west of the airport, a building 505 feet high one and two-fifths miles away, blocks two hundred feet and upwards in the dock area, not far away from where the instrument runway jutted out into Boston harbour.

"Coming into the beam now."

The needle had decided to come unstuck. It flickered twice, then began to sweep rapidly towards the centre. I steadied Victor X-ray out of her turn and edged into the beam onto 035 degrees. Two minutes later, out of the corner of my right eye, I saw the radio compass needle twist right over and point behind us.

"Over the Outer Marker," Holmes reported. "At eighteen hundred and twenty feet."

"Victor X-ray Number One to land. Visibility now five hundred yards."

Holmes looked at me to see whether I'd heard.

"Still on limits," I said.

From the top of the dial, the horizontal needle of the I.L.S. had started to move down. Now it formed a cross with the vertical needle, right in the centre of the instrument, and I had eased back the throttles.

Victor X-ray began descending, gear and half-flap down, all checks complete—dead in line with the runway, dead on the glide path, dead on a rate of descent of six hundred feet a minute.

I said to Holmes, "Keep your eyes out of the window. Let me know when we're contact."

"Will do."

I kept my head down, my eyes hypnotized by the instruments. My muscles acted on exactly what they told me. There was no visible join between me and the machine. Our course was 031 degrees—4 degrees starboard drift and steady as a rock. It was unlikely there would be much wind—that's one compensation about fog.

"Five hundred feet. No sign of approach lights yet."

The usual city grime was mixing with the drizzle on the windscreens. But the course never wavered, the two I.L.S. needles still crossed central. My eyes moved rapidly over the cockpit, checking the airspeed at a hundred and forty, the altimeter slowly unwinding. This blind approach was going to be a classic.

"Four hundred feet . . . nothing."

I shifted myself in my seat, making myself more comfortable. Half the battle in these letdowns was to be completely at ease. To be fidgety, tensed up or to try too hard was fatal. I saw the horizontal needle rising—but I didn't jump to pull the stick back. In my own good time, I corrected up onto the glide path.

"Three hundred and fifty feet . . . still nothing."

The localizer needle on the I.L.S. crept over to starboard, well into the blue sector. But those dots are only half a degree each. The deflection looks bigger than it really is. I was in no wild hurry to get back into the beam. Again I made small movements. A sliver of left rudder slowly brought me central.

"Three hundred feet."

"See anything?"

"Not yet."

The aircraft and I were completely in tune. The 909 was responding to my every movement. That vast wing span I could sense merging into the mist on either side of me, the long fuselage that tapered behind—they were all part of me. All I could hear were familiar noises: the hiss of outside air flowing over the nose, the quiet murmur of throttled-back engines, the slapping to and fro of the wipers, sluicing away the rain on the windscreen.

We were over the Middle Marker beacon—height two hundred and seventy feet.

"Surely you can see the approach lights now?"

"Still nothing, sir."

The beam was narrow here, not much wider than the runway itself. And at slow speeds, like all aeroplanes, the 909 tends to wallow a little. I saw the needle creep into the blue sector again. Down here there was more drift—maybe as much as 6 degrees.

"On limits . . . and still no lights, sir!"

Holmes was hinting we'd probably have to go round again. After that smooth approach, we might be foiled at the last moment. We were still edging into the blue sector, despite the new course of 029. And very slightly, we were below the glide path. As I eased the stick back, my mind was split up in two like the blue and yellow of the I.L.S. indicator itself.

Half was preparing to land, half was preparing to overshoot and climb back into the overcast.

"Two hundred feet!"

I tightened my grip on the throttles.

"Still nothing!"

I was on the point of pushing all four throttles forward, when suddenly Holmes called out, "Wait a moment!" Then: "Lights!"

I raised my head from the instruments and looked out. This was always a tricky time. The familiar sight of the lighted instruments gave way to a dripping cave. For those seconds, we were being guided neither by the instruments nor by the ground. I blinked my eyes at the gloom ahead, saw a buoy floating on the harbour water flash below us. Nothing else.

"Where?"

"Over to starboard."

"Ah, yes!"

I saw them then—two watery yellow eyes running into the greyness. We were over to port, and just a little high. Not so much starboard drift down here. I moved the control column, putting the right wing down.

"Full flap!"

I felt the 909 slow up. Reluctantly, a handful more lights were released from the darkness. I saw the green threshold like a brooch of emeralds, now dead ahead.

We were at fifty feet, slowed right down, committed to a landing. Coming down on the approach, time stands still. Nothing changes. Fractionally the instruments move, but the night outside still stays the same. Now everything happened at once. The threshold flashed past. I pulled the nose up and slammed the throttles shut.

We began floating softly just above the runway.

The mist was like a warm wet breath on the night. I could

see five lights to port, only three to starboard. I had a curious feeling of disorientation—no horizon, no sky, no earth. As though in a dream, not really believing it, I sensed a sideways movement.

It was then that I saw very slowly the lights begin sliding over to port.

Suddenly I realized we were going crabwise, drifting off the runway to the right. The buildings must have shielded us for that final part of the approach—now the night breeze was blowing full strength beam on.

Victor X-ray—nose up, wings level—was hovering on the stall.

I opened the throttles. I pushed the stick forward, putting on hard left rudder. But Victor X-ray still waffled, still drifted. I could feel her mushy under my fingers. She had practically lost flying speed. She was only half alive. There was no invisible join between her and me now. She had gone back to being eighty tons of ugly metal.

I *willed* her to respond. I tried everything I knew. Like she had with me on take-off, now I said . . . come on, for God's sake, don't give up now! I gave her all the power I could, so that she gave a great roar out into the night.

But there was no answering thrust. I felt the right wing sag. Frantically I tried to pull it up.

For a fraction of a second, she hesitated. Then with a tremendous crash, the wheels connected.

The whole aircraft tilted. The right wheel was off the runway, digging into soft mud. I could feel the drag as Victor X-ray slewed to starboard.

I pushed the nosewheel down, pulled back the speed brake handle. We'd be ground-looping in a moment. I jabbed at the left brake to slew her round. With a graunching bump, she began to come over to port. The moment we were back on the runway, I pulled up the reverse-thrust levers, and we began slowing down rapidly.

Too rapidly.

My mouth had gone dry. I had a sick feeling in my stomach. In ten years of flying, I'd never bent anything. I'd never even broken a plate in the galley or a bulb in the lights. Now I knew the record was over.

We weren't level. The left wing was very slightly down. Something had gone on the port wheel. Continually the aircraft was trying to hunt to the left. Two thirds the way down the runway we were at walking pace. Now Victor X-ray seemed to limp as we made our way to the ramp.

"Finished with the engines!"

In the silence that followed, I said nothing. Holmes and the Engineer got on with their Check List. I took my time, undoing my straps, pushing back the seat, getting out onto the Flight Deck floor. Then I walked down the passenger and crew steps, and saw the mechanics huddled round the port wheel, their torches flickering on a widening pool of oil.

The engineer officer looked up and saw me. "Burst tire and brakes gone . . . it'll be a wheel change I'm afraid, Captain."

I said, "How long?"

"We got no wheel here. It'll mean sending to New York."

The station manager came up then with his hands in his pockets, trying to take it in his stride. Though they were still taking off, Boston was now red to all landing aircraft. The wheel would have to come by road. The earliest it could arrive was tomorrow morning.

Side by side, the station manager and I walked towards the Reception Block together. Just before pushing open the glass swing doors into the warmth, I looked over my shoulder at Victor X-ray—standing there huge in the drizzle, glistening eel-silver under the high neon arc lights. The mechanics were already locking up for the night, taking away the passenger and crew steps.

There was no one in the corridors. My crew caught us up as we went into the Company Operations Room. The station manager started immediately on the telephone, organizing furiously. We just stood around, drinking the endless airline coffee, staring at the maps and signals and notices with which the place was festooned. The engineer began to make out an incident report for me to sign. First Officer Holmes started grinding out cheerful small talk about always wanting to have a nightstop to explore Boston. Alison Humphrey stood by the door, fiddling with her handbag, humming hard with embarrassment. Nice girls don't get into trouble—nor do they like being around when other people do.

Eventually the teleprinter broke in and relieved the strained atmosphere. I walked across the room to watch the words clack out onto the white flimsy.

TO EMPIRE AIRWAYS, LONDON AIRPORT, FROM BOSTON. IMME-DIATE PRIORITY. VICTOR X-RAY SUSTAINED BRAKE AND TIRE DAM-AGE IN LANDING OFF RUNWAY. REPLACEMENT WHEEL BEING SENT BY NEW YORK. EIGHTY EX KENNEDY AND TWELVE EX BOS-TON PAX TRANSFERRED TO PANAM LONDON SERVICE. REQUEST FUTURE DISPOSAL VICTOR X-RAY, CAPTAIN MATHERSON AND CREW: 02 49Z: ATTENTION CAPTAIN CORBY.

SIX

THE NEXT DAY, I flew Victor X-ray back home empty. And the day after that, Captain Corby had me in.

During the enforced stopover at Boston, I had prepared myself for the worst. Every time I closed my eyes in that damned luxury hotel, figures of Company losses were projected onto my mind: so much for repairs, so much for the loss of passengers onto other airlines, so much for idle time on the ground.

I had a feeling which almost amounted to certainty that Corby was gunning for me. I didn't stop to analyze why, though I had a sort of vague idea it might have something to do with being too loudly anti-Autoland. I knew damned well the real reason why he ought to hate my guts, so I suppose I took it as read that he did. Yet all the time I was perfectly certain that he didn't have an inkling about Anne and me. So much for the contradictory workings of guilt, I suppose. We had a chaplain at school, a mealy-mouthed bastard, whose favourite cheerful text was that we're not punished *for* our sins but *by* our sins.

So there I was putting words into Corby's mouth, meting out to myself imaginary punishments, and donning the little black cap. There was only one compensation. I flew Victor X-ray back to the U.K. without a qualm. I don't think I've ever flown better. A good instrument approach and landing through thick fog into London. The accident had been the slap in the face I needed. I'd somehow come back to my senses with a crump. And as far as Anne was concerned, I was cured.

The interview started slowly. Corby didn't greet me as a long-lost friend, nor did he give the impression he wanted to kick me down the stairs.

"This . . . this Boston affair." That's what he called it. "How did it happen?"

He asked me if I had any worries. They always do. Especially Corby, who was supposed to be, among all his other accomplishments, a dab hand at psychology. They start on a scale of descending sympathy.

Had I any family troubles? Was there anyone ill? *Very* sympathetic, that.

Not overtired, not finding the schedule too much? Able to sleep all right in spite of the time changes? *Quite* sympathetic.

No financial troubles? Had too big a flutter? Been buying a Bentley on the never-never? *Less* sympathetic, but a boys-will-be-boys smile.

Any civil problems? Police-court cases? The flower beginning to brown at the edges. Ending up frigidly with what they're sure is at the bottom of all airmen's troubles—wine and women.

No, I said, there was nothing. What else could I say?

I couldn't exactly tell him, "Well, yes, sir, there is. Between you and me, it's your wife, you understand. I've been having a bit of an affair with her. I slept with her while you were away. Oh, not on service, no, sir. While you were at your mother's, I think. You know how these things happen. She's a very attractive girl—I wasn't able to get her quite out of my system. But one very good thing about all this is that *now*, sir, I *have*. Something painful happens . . . a traumatic experience I think *you* would call it . . . and brother, you're cured! So now, sir, she's positively all yours. When all's said and done, what is ten thousand pounds for such a happy issue out of all our afflictions?"

No, I repeated, there was nothing. A sneaky little cross-wind that was blanketed on the last part of the approach, and then caught me with my trousers down just as I was holding off. An unpredictable wind. A bit of bad luck.

"But at Boston you have almost every aid under the sun. Runway centre line and side stripes, threshold and touch-down markings. Adequate lights. And Zero Four Right is not only a long runway, it's fifty-five feet wider than average."

I said none of those would have helped much, situation I was in.

"But what about the fact you refused a Ground Controlled Approach?" Corby went on smoothly. "That in my opinion was the root cause of this affair."

I said I didn't agree.

"If you'd monitored with G.C.A., you'd have been all right."

I said I couldn't see how G.C.A. would help on last-minute drift.

"It would have stabilized you on the centre line."

"I *was* stabilized on the centre line."

"You were obviously too slow to notice wind tendencies."

We argued it backwards and forwards. We went over the weather. We went over my report: what I'd thought and said and done, and what I hadn't thought and hadn't said and hadn't done.

"What we still can't find out is *why* you refused G.C.A. That continues to remain a mystery."

Behind his desk, Corby sat thumbing unhurriedly through the evidence. It had an immaculate uncluttered top, and my file shared pride of place only with a large silver-framed photograph of Anne. It wasn't a particularly good one. Her eyes, purged of wickedness, stared into an unfocused distance, drawing a pretty fair touchline between Corby and me.

I sat in front of the desk with the edge of the hard chair digging in my bottom. I hardly glanced at Anne. But I stared at Corby long enough and hard enough to count the wrinkles on his small grey eyelids. I thought up the protests I'd make when he gave me a reprimand, lost me some seniority or took me off jets altogether.

"But there is one thing at least this affair will have taught you . . ."

He had raised his eyes and was looking straight at me. They had an X-ray quality that seemed to penetrate deep inside me. And for one fantastic moment, I thought . . . *he knows.* He's worked it all out . . . he and his psychology books. But the next second, he'd finished his sentence, and the suspense was over.

". . . and that is to put your trust in machines. The Autoland would *never* have made a mistake like that."

I breathed again. I might have known. He began cleaning his pen carefully before he wrote his findings. He pursed his already skimpy lips. He did as bank clerks do—he made a swirling run over the paper before he began to write. I swore I would refuse to sign. I knew my rights. If an adverse report was too harsh, you could refuse. And that was precisely what Matherson was going to do. I clenched my fists. I would demand an interview with the Board. Go higher if necessary —right up to the Minister himself.

"And now," Corby blotted the paper, "if you would read this through very carefully and then sign it . . ."

He twisted the report round for me to see. Then he put the tips of his fingers together and waited.

Captain Matherson, I read, *is normally a conscientious and efficient pilot*—the sugar, I thought, before the bitter pill—

*and I have satisfied myself completely that the accident at
Boston was caused solely by his marked distrust of the instru-
ment aids which are available to him, a tendency which dur-
ing the next few months we hope to eradicate. Apart from a
Route Check with me for which he is in any case overdue,
I recommend that no action whatever be taken.*

I read that last line three times just to make sure. I wanted
to laugh out loud. No action *at all.* How people ever got the
idea that Corby was such a ruthless character, God only
knew! Talk about giving a dog a bad name! It was like that
night he had me out to dinner. He was just trying to get another plug in for his bloody robot. Far from being hostile, he
wanted to be friendly. He was saying . . . be converted, come
over on my side, help me sell the Autoland to the others.

Of course, he must be the original airman with a hundred
octane in his arteries. But the funny thing was, just as I'd
been wrong about him, he'd been wrong about me. I wasn't
all that against the Autoland, so long as I could measure up
to it—which now I knew I could. I wasn't as anti as some of
them. He should have heard Snaith and Williamson! Still,
if that was all he wanted from me—to make me the leader of
the pro-Autoland party, that was fine. I didn't care. It was a
peppercorn price to pay for getting off scot-free.

"I think that's quite fair, don't you?" He held out his pen
towards me. "I might even say lenient?"

I felt his eyes on me again as I signed. There was something old-womanish about Corby. His head made little waving swaying motions up and down as he watched the loops
of my signature. "We'll get the Route Check over as soon as
possible," he said. "Just routine. There shouldn't be anything
to that."

I nodded. I perked up enough to say, "I'll have to see there
isn't."

And then, by the way he began to close my file and stow it
in his drawer, I knew that the interview was over. I got up.

As I touched my cap to him at the door, I glanced back.

He looked very old and shrunk behind that desk, empty now except for the chocolate-box picture of Anne. That picture was turned away from me . . . and brother, that was how *she* was going to stay!

All the same I had a sudden pang of conscience as sharp as a bellyache. "I'm sorry," I said to Corby, though only God knew I didn't mean the accident. "And thank you, sir. Thank you very much."

I was wrong about Anne. I saw her that afternoon. I'd had lunch in the aircrew restaurant, and I was walking to the car park—head down—hands in my pockets, thinking about and planning the coming Route Check with Corby. I never notice much where I'm going when I'm not airborne. I only knew I'd reached the car park because the ground under my feet changed from concrete to that black ashy stuff. Then something made me look up, and I saw her. She was standing beside a white Austin-Healey Sprite. She was dressed in a pink suit made of some linen stuff that I'd seen her in somewhere before, with a little black fur hat and collar to match. The get-up suited her. When I came within calling distance she laughed and called out, "Hello, Philip. Can I give you a lift to Brighton?"

I wouldn't normally call myself a shifty character. I don't have to glance around before I kiss a girl, to see if anyone's watching. But today with the Check to be got over, and my nose to be kept clean, but *clean,* I had a bloody good look round all points of the compass before I as much as said *hello* back.

Anne saw what I did. "It's all right," she said. "No one's watching. Besides, you're allowed to say hello to the Flight Captain's wife. It's in Line Standing Orders. Ask Maurice."

It started me off on the wrong foot. I smiled frugally. I felt so big.

"I suppose you've come to collect him?"

"Maurice? No. As a matter of fact, Philip, I've come to collect *you*. I took a rain check on that day out, remember? I thought this is the perfect day for going . . . where was it again . . . Brighton?" And then as my face muscles sagged: "It's all right. Don't look so *painfully* worried. I was only teasing." She tossed the car keys up and down in her gloved hand. "I've been up to town. As simple as that. I dropped in to see Maurice on the way back. Does that make you feel better?"

I tried to be teasing back. "Not particularly."

My own car was parked three rows away, and I was just going to say something vague about being nice to run into her and maybe seeing them *both* sometime, when she said, "But alas, my poor husband has gone aloft!" She pulled a mock mournful face. Inconsequentially it struck me she might not have minded being a widow. "Then I saw your car in the park. That *is* your car, isn't it?"

"It is."

"I thought so. Maurice said you had a Wolseley." She smiled pertly. "So I hung around. You never know your luck, do you?"

I could see by the way her eyes moved over my face that she was disappointed in me, and she was trying to figure out why I was no longer so forthcoming.

"Where's Maurice off to?" I asked. "I saw him this morning. He didn't mention going anywhere."

"Oh, he's not off on Service. He's just flying around, testing his favourite thingummy."

"You mean the Autoland."

"Do I? I wouldn't know."

"I'd heard they'd installed it in the Astra."

"That sounds very heavenly of them."

"An Astra happens to be a light twin-engined aeroplane. He'll be testing the Autoland in it."

"If it's testing something, it'll be right up his street. He won't be down till midnight. But Maurice doesn't talk to me much. Not about the Company." Her voice had taken on a flatness as desolate as an Essex landscape. "Though he told me he was seeing you this morning."

"Did he now? And what did he say?"

"Just that you were in a spot of bother. And he hoped to help you out of it."

"Nice of him." I meant it, too. It was good of him not to tell her the whole grisly truth.

"Yes." She ran her tongue round her lips. "Did he say anything to you about me?"

"No, of course not. Why should he?"

"Oh, I don't know. Men do talk about their wives sometimes."

I took a step nearer her. In a low voice I asked, "Anne, you haven't told him anything about *us?*"

"Of course I haven't! Tell Maurice? You must be crazy!"

"Why did you think he might have said something then?"

"Because you've changed."

I smiled with relief. "Oh, I don't think so."

"To me you have."

"I still look pretty much the same to me."

She paused. Then slowly, "You're not the same man who phoned me from New York."

I patted her cheek playfully. "But you're the very same girl who hung up."

"Oh, that."

"Yes, *that.*"

"I was somewhat disappointed in you, that's all."

"I didn't give the right reply to the questioning look?"

"Something like that."

I said stiffly, "I'm sorry."

"Don't tell me you bear grudges, like Maurice."

"No, I don't. But I do know when I'm not wanted."

"God," she said softly. "Just how wrong can a man be?"

She turned slightly away from me to gaze out across the airfield. There's something about staring at flat distance which gives the human face a strange reflected ache. Without turning back towards me, she said softly, "Come for a drive with me, Philip."

"I can't. I'd like to. But honestly, Anne, I'm busy."

"Please."

I felt my good resolutions draining out of me like sawdust from a slit sack. She gave a shivery laugh. "After all, Maurice can't see you from up there. He's not the Russian eye in the sky."

It was such a pathetic attempt at her former jauntiness that I simply opened the passenger seat door and got in. "Mind you, I don't believe you. I think he *is*." I made binoculars of my fists and peered up over the side. "Or maybe he's the British answer to the Russian satellite."

Anne ran round the bonnet like a child and started the engine up.

"God," I said as she sent up a squirt of black ash. "I wish I'd taken that extra insurance out!"

She drove as I'd have expected her to drive—too fast, too hard on the gears, and yet with a certain careless flair.

"This is a nice little job," I patted the red upholstery. "New?"

"Brand new. This is her maiden voyage but one. Maurice bought it for my birthday."

"I didn't know you'd had one."

"Oh, I have them once a year. Same as most people."

I promised her that no one could tell.

"Isn't this fun?" she said after a while. "D'you want to see how fast she'll go?"

When I nodded, she put her foot hard down and we sped out along the Great West Road.

I've always known that speed is somehow therapeutic for

me. Besides, the wind itself seems to pluck at your face
muscles, saying *smile, damn you, smile*. About ten miles from
the airport, Anne turned left. I knew she meant to park on a
small rise that overlooks both the river and the airfield. I've
flown over it often enough, and been there for the odd drive.

It was a typical English early autumn afternoon, with the
sky bunched up with unimportant clouds, and the sun when
it came through weak as the beam of a twopenny ha'penny
torch. The river to the right was a curl of pewter, and in
front of us the airfield looked terribly detailed—a Bawdon
backcloth full of pale colours and sudden knife-edged
shadows.

Anne switched off, and put her hands behind her head.
"Ah!" she let out a long sigh of pure pleasure. "Bliss, isn't
it?"

For a moment, I watched our tiny tin aeroplanes taking
off . . . D.C.8s, 707s, 909s. The midget-sized Astra seemed to
be orbiting on a hidden wire, doing a disappearing act and
coming back to land. "All that seems unreal, doesn't it?"

I knew what she meant, but I didn't say anything because
I didn't want to acknowledge that I knew. She slid her eyes
round without turning her head. "Don't look at me as if I
were a bomb about to go off."

"I think you are. For me anyway. You're probably as dangerous."

She shook her head. "That's not true. I'll tell you something. I've been rendered harmless." She smiled slowly, moving her head nearer my shoulder. "Kiss me, Philip." And
when I did nothing. "*Please* kiss me. Just once. I won't ask
you again."

I cupped her face in my hands. "Listen, Anne," I said
steadily. "This has got to stop . . . understand?"

"I don't want to listen." She covered my hands with hers,
moving her head, so that my fingers seemed to travel slowly

over the softness of her skin. "I don't want to understand. Anyway, what are you being so solemn about? What has got to stop? There's hardly been anything *to* stop." Then she stared at me fixedly. Her eyes looked very large, the pupils distended. Her lips were wet and parted, so that I could see the tip of her tongue between her teeth. "Kiss me," she said again, hardly moving her mouth, never taking her eyes from me. "Kiss me, Philip."

I gave her a quick kiss, just brushing her lips.

"Kiss me properly."

Her voice had a low insistent quality. I had the feeling that she sensed I was determined to escape, and was therefore suddenly determined that I should not.

I felt I was sufficiently cured to be able to put my arms around her. The moment I did so, her body seemed to melt against mine. It became as soft and boneless as a cat's. I could smell her perfume that dragged me back more than any spoken reminder could ever do to that night in their house.

This time, I kissed her as she wanted. Properly. I felt her lips moving against mine—demanding, retreating, soft and gentle and then savage, while in and out darted her quick expert little tongue.

Like a high-pitched one-note song, excitement sang in my ears. Slowly my hands began to move down lower over her body.

Then as every good resolution in me began to topple, abruptly she snatched herself away.

She gave a sudden harsh laugh. "There's something," she said, "I must tell you."

Her breath came in little uneven gasps. Her eyes were still black and sensuous. It was as if she had snatched herself away from me to pursue some secret inward climax. Then very clearly, the words spaced and hard like separate falling stones, her face close as she could get to mine: "I thought you ought to know. I'm going to have a baby."

I never know what to say at times like these. I couldn't say what was uppermost in my mind, because the feeling I had was one of irritated relief.

In a way, nothing could be better. I couldn't imagine Anne and Maurice in the roles of mother and father. But the very idea rendered them immediately homely and manageable.

"Well?" She gave me a wry little smile. "Aren't you going to say anything?"

"Congratulations," I said. "I'm very glad."

"Are you? Are you *really?*"

"Of course I am. I'm delighted."

"Good."

"If *you're* pleased, that is."

"Oh, I'm pleased." She fiddled with the gloves on her lap. "I'm very pleased."

"And Maurice? He's pleased too, I should think?"

"Maurice? Oh, I haven't told him yet. You're the very first person to know. I only found out today. For certain, that is! That's why I called in."

For a moment I was sorry I'd been brusque with her—then I thought about her behavior afterwards and I wasn't.

"But you weren't to know that," she said. "You're not psychic."

"Well, he'll be pleased when he does know. Maurice, I mean."

"Oh, simply delighted. I shall tell him tonight. He always wanted to found a dynasty."

I laughed uncomfortably. I wondered how soon I could suggest driving back to pick up my car at the airport. I found the conversation suddenly difficult. Silence fell around us like a collapsed tent.

"When is it due? The baby?"

"Now let me see . . ." She counted on her fingers. "May."

"Oh, a long time yet."

"Eight months."

"Lots of time to get knitting . . . and all that."

She gave me a cold little smile. But I don't find a woman's confinement inspires me to any great conversational heights. I'm not like some men who find it attractive. I find it off-putting. The word pregnancy has about it a smell of boiled milk and urine and nappies.

"Of course," Anne said, not looking at me, "it's rather soon to be certain. Not being married, you wouldn't know. But I had one of those nasty little tests done."

I hoped she wouldn't go on. But she did.

"They inject a frog . . . no, a toad, and if the test's positive the poor beast lays eggs all over the cage floor."

"I hope," I said just for something to say, because I was embarrassed at being embarrassed, "for the toad's sake, they don't all hatch out into little Annes."

She shook her head. "Oh, they kill the toad. Or my stuff kills it. I forget which." Just fleetingly a curious pleasurable look crossed her face. Her lips were parted, her eyes dreamy. Suddenly she revolted me like the touch of the toad she was talking about. I shivered. I remembered thinking . . . Christ, but I'm glad to be out of it all!

But what we talked about after that I forget. I was itching to get away. And when at last we did move, on the way back she simply couldn't drive fast enough for me.

"Go on," I kept urging her. "Put your foot down! Get her all out!"

When we said good-bye at the airport, she said, "Good-bye for now, Philip. Don't let what I've told you stop you coming round."

"I won't."

"Promise?"

I promised. And I made up my mind to send her lots of

flowers when she went into the nursing home, and get a decent christening present for it when it arrived—just to make up for not keeping that promise.

When I got into my old Wolseley, I felt weak with relief. God, was I grateful I'd made the clean break! I had a shower in the flat, and then I did a flick and took myself out to supper. I enjoyed that evening. Just being on my own, without complications, without anyone to fasten their tentacles around me.

All the same that drive with Anne had left something in me. Information had been fed into that damned computer that works submerged under everybody's brain. It woke me in the night. I switched on the bedside lamp and looked at the clock. It was just after two. At first I thought it was only a bad dream, until my conscious mind started checking certain dates and facts with that subconscious calculator. Then I lay there in a cold sweat. "Christ!" I said it aloud just to exorcise it. "Oh, no . . . no, it couldn't be! It's *impossible!*"

SEVEN

There's nothing like the clear light of day for getting rid of nightmares. When the alarm roused me the next morning, I had that grey mental hangover you get when you've just discovered something unpleasant before you go to sleep. Then I pinpointed the trouble and wondered why in hell's name I'd been in such a state about it. I got up, bathed and shaved and then I sat with the morning paper and drank coffee. Between take-over bids and murders and articles on emergent nations, I rationalized my guilt right out of my system. It was a hundred to one against that baby being mine.

Oh, the time was roughly right, as far as I knew, but so what? Luckily, Maurice was home. I might have had cause for sweating if he'd been on a five-week trip to Honolulu and Japan. But thank God, he wasn't. He was there in person, no doubt doing his stuff. Conventional and safe in her cocoon of motherhood, Anne had probably forgotten it ever happened with me.

What in the world did *I* have to worry about?

Then with nice timing the morning post arrived, and there was a flimsy from Operations notifying me for Service BE 808 (the Midnight Tourist to New York) the day after to-

morrow, with a footnote at the bottom to say that Captain
Corby would be on board as Route Check Captain. The date
would be September 13th, but unlike most airmen (most airlines for that matter—there's no Seat 13 on Empire Airway's
aircraft) I'm not superstitious, and all this news did was to
fairly put me on my toes. If I'd had any lingering worry—
which I hadn't—about Anne and her condition, that would
have given it the boot. I was one hundred per cent determined to give Corby the ride of his Check Captain career.

I wasn't out of the Boston wood yet, I told myself. You
were never sure with Corby. He might still have something
up his sleeve.

So I spent those two days before the trip getting everything
on the top line. I took my best uniform to the eight-hour
cleaners, and I bought myself some new black shoes which
I really didn't need. I went up to the airfield the day before,
and I dropped in on G.P., who had a spare period so I did
a buckshee hour on the simulator. Unlike other big simulators, this one can be operated pretty well single-handed,
though this time I took along a gash First Officer who happened to be hanging around. I did a couple of instrument
approaches, and G.P. failed two engines on one side during
the last one.

"Good going," he said when I got out. "You're on form."

I told him about Corby and the Check flight, but being
G.P., he knew already. "That's all right," he said, "I can't
see you've got anything to worry about."

Nor did I. But to make quite sure, I spent a while in Met,
and all evening I studied my Route books, Line Standing
Orders and the 909 manual. I got all my emergencies taped
and on the top line—if there was an engine fire or our hydrau-
lics went, I wouldn't turn a hair. I even foreswore my usual
nip of scotch. With a midnight take-off, it's tricky to get your
sleep right, so it wasn't till the small hours that I mixed
myself some Horlick's and climbed into bed. I went out for

the count and slept like a baby till lunch time. Then I stayed where I was all afternoon, dozing and reading.

Round about six they rang up to say the incoming aircraft had been late arriving, so there'd be a three-hour delay. I didn't really mind. It meant three more hours in bed, and I actually went into a deep sleep again for all that time. Then I got up and had a hot bath. As I dressed into uniform, I had a good look at the weather: though I didn't want at this stage to be too optimistic, for take-off anyway I didn't think I was going to have any complaints. I went downstairs and had a meal in the restaurant. My bag, my brief case and I were all ready in the hall when the transport arrived.

I was the last to be picked up, because the rest of the crew lived miles further out and Corby was driving himself to the airfield. When I got into the empty seat left for me beside the driver, the crew all seemed in good form. Holmes was my First Officer again. But the stewardess was different.

I said hello and rubbed my hands and said the weather didn't look so dusty. Though it was pitch dark outside, the stars were shining as though someone had been polishing them with Brasso, and the visibility was brilliant. A busy little wind was sweeping the sky clean and keeping the tufts of cloud on the move. By the way it was bending the trees along the neon-lighted Great West Road, it was an easterly, which was all to the good. Nor did I have any complaints about the weather they had for us in Met. That wind would be behind us for a good halfway over, which should give us a fast crossing. New York was forecasting one-mile visibility in intermittent rain—which in my present mood was neither here nor there.

Coming out of Operations, I met Corby just getting out of his car. He was amiable to the point of affability.

"Hello, Philip," he said. "No more snags, eh?"

I shook my head. "None."

"Righto, then! See you on board." He had a book in his hand. "I'm looking forward to a nice restful trip!"

My opinion of Corby had undergone considerable changes in the last few days. He really *did* want to be friendly. I even shut Holmes up when he grumbled about having Corby on board, as we did our Checks.

"Oh, he's all right," I said between *jet pipe temperature limiter switch override* and *fuel transfer switches off and guarded.* "So long as you do your job, he leaves you alone."

In fact, he left us alone until an hour after take-off. I was a bit disappointed he had. Thundering down the runway, I held her down till the very last moment, and I don't think anyone knew exactly when she was airborne. Up she skimmed into the sky like a swan. I got a hell of a kick myself out of it—a sort of artist's delight, though Heaven knows that's the last thing I am. I remember glancing at Holmes and seeing his face in the red glow of the instrument lighting.

"Nice work," he said, breaking into a smile. "I hope Corby put that in his pipe and smoked it!"

If he did, he didn't say so. When he came up front at last, very high cirrostratus had put the stars out, and though there would be a moon up later, the windscreens were like giant masks cut out of black velvet. I heard his voice saying something to the navigator and I turned round. He was bending over the table, checking our position. I couldn't see his face for the peak of his cap. But he nodded his head several times as though in approval, and then came up and said hello to me.

"I was almost asleep back there," he said. "I thought I should come and do some work before I finally dozed off."

Holmes gave a sycophantic laugh, and got out of his seat. "Would you care to sit here, sir?"

"Thank you." Corby slid himself into the right-hand seat. "And now, Holmes, you go back and have some rest yourself. I'll do what Captain Matherson tells me for an hour or so."

He was so pleasant and informal that I could feel everyone

relax—me included. I had been hand-flying, but now I put the automatic pilot in, and there was nothing to do but for Corby and me to think up small talk to say to one another.

In fact, that was more difficult than flying.

After a few sporadic starts, perhaps to cut out the more animated conversation the Navigator and the Engineer were having, Corby drew the curtains behind us.

And there we were, cut off from the rest of the crew and the passengers. Just Corby and me in what was rather like a confessional box, with only the black night ahead of us and the dark Atlantic down below.

Corby began chatting about a show they'd seen. Anne knew the leading lady, a rather neurotic type called Essie Somerville. I might have heard of her.

I hadn't.

Nor had I missed much, Corby said. We talked about films, some television shows. Golf. The fairway at the club the aircrew used in Bermuda. Then the stewardess parted the curtains, and gave us our dinner trays. It was like being fed in a cage.

Shrimp cocktail, steak and mushrooms, tinned strawberries, coffee dispensed for a while with the need for conversation, but when the girl had cleared away, Corby started up again —this time on social questions, such as the laxity of our society, the crime wave and the need for severer penalties.

It's not a subject I'm up on. I'd eaten quickly, and I began to feel sleepy. I smoked one cigarette after another to help keep me awake. But all it did was to make my head thick. After another half hour of it, I began to feel uncomfortable. For all his affability, I wished Corby would get to hell down to the back. He kept talking in his soft rather expressionless voice and I found I couldn't concentrate on what he was saying.

Eventually, as it always does with Corby, conversation got onto flying in general and the Allen Autoland in particular.

"You see, you accept George." He was still trying to make me his disciple. "But the Autoland is only the logical extension of it. Evolution in the instrument world, if you like."

It was what G.P. had said—obviously he'd had the same lecture—and I didn't argue.

"I think pilots are by nature reactionary. They have to do things the way they've always done them, or they wouldn't be alive."

Vaguely, I agreed.

"But they have to have a modicum of science, technology, call it what you will. They have the little knowledge that isn't so much dangerous as besets the mind with fear." He lit a cigarette. "How many times for instance have you heard fears and fancies about high flying?"

"A good number." I shrugged. "But I think there may be something to it."

"There *you* go! Aircrew say it causes everything from corns to cancer. But there's more danger in this, Philip—" He thrust his cigarette under my nose. "Yet I don't hear pilots binding about *that*."

"But there are things high flying *does* cause," I said. "Or appear to cause. Undoubtedly the radioactivity produces, well . . ."

"I know *exactly* what you're going to say. Impotence and infertility. Oh, there's always been talk about that. For the last twenty years, I promise you. There are other causes of infertility besides high flying. Disease for instance." He paused, running his right hand along the ledge of the windscreen before saying softly, "Why, there is a very happy couple I know of. Well matched. Utterly devoted to one another. They have everything they could ever want. Except one thing. The husband caught some beastly bug when he was adolescent. Now he's not impotent . . . but unfortunately he is sterile."

"Bad luck," I said. "Damned bad luck."

I was wondering when he was going to stop. The weather in New York was deteriorating a little, and I didn't want to do a Checked Instrument Landing without rest or mental preparations. The monotone of his voice was such that I could hardly keep my eyes open.

More for something to say than anything, I went on, "Maybe they don't want a family though."

"Oh, but they do! In fact, the husband—they are comfortably off—has consulted specialists in London and Rome. And only recently he went to see a man in New York."

He waited for me to say something. I just grunted.

"The verdict was still the same."

"Pity."

"A *great* pity." He paused. "Of course, the wife doesn't know."

"Oh."

"D'you think she ought to?"

"I . . . er . . . well, I don't know."

"I thought by the way you said 'oh' you sounded condemnatory."

"I didn't mean to."

"Nevertheless you think he should tell her?"

"It's difficult to say . . . I mean, without knowing them."

"But you *do* know them!"

Suddenly he seemed oppressed by the darkness. "D'you mind if we have the lights on?" he said. "I like lights on. In a car, I like the head lamps full up. I like to see what's ahead of me." And without waiting for my answer, he went round the switches and the rheostats in the cockpit, turning them all on. The flight deck was suddenly drenched in light, dazzling me, hurting my eyes, making me blink, taking me back a month in time . . .

"You do know them," he repeated, and now I could see he had turned right round in his seat to face me. "You see, Philip . . . I'm not talking about strangers."

He glanced behind us at the thick closed curtains. He lowered his voice. In hardly more than a whisper, he said, "I am talking about myself. About Anne and me. I have not told this to anyone else. I am telling you now in the strictest confidence. I am . . ." He spoke as Anne had done the last time I saw her, the words very clear and spaced out in time. "I . . . am . . . unfortunately . . . unable to father a child."

"But—"

The protest was out before I could stop it. For the fraction of a second my only thought was that Anne, pursuing her secretive ways, had not after all told him the good news yet. And then like lightning, the full implication of what he had told me fell into place, and I stopped dead.

With a terrible silent menace, Corby's face moved closer to mine. I saw the expression of his eyes.

"But *what?* Finish what you were saying . . ."

I could say nothing. My mind seemed to have seized, so that I could think of no way to pass it off. The enormity of what had happened engulfed me. I knew as clearly as if I had confessed it aloud that everything on my face was there for Corby to read. Back my mind harked to everything that had happened. Those searchlight head lamps, now I knew they had been Corby's: the invitation to dinner had just been to bring me to the scene of the crime: the reason for his interest in the Wolseley with its telltale illuminated oval on the bonnet was now obvious, even his leniency over Boston was suspect. And following my thoughts as though he could see right through my skull came Corby's soft purring voice, his hating, judging, convicting eyes.

"But . . . ?"

Corby had said it again, throwing the word round my head like a noose. Then as if I were of no more interest than a lump of dead meat, he got out of his seat, and without saying another word left me alone in the curtained confessional.

BOOK THREE

Maurice Corby

ONE

"BUT—"

That single-syllable word seemed to fall through my body like a lump of lead. Every nerve screamed out against it. I felt unable to breathe. I wanted to put my hands over my ears. Had I been a man of less control, I would have struck Matherson there and then. For I seemed alive only in the desire to do him violence.

Instead, I kept perfectly still, perfectly master of myself.

I watched the swiftly changing expressions of this young man's face, and not only did their clumsy alterations confirm everything which I had hitherto feared, but they demonstrated him an unworthy contender for Anne's affections. Anne's unfaithfulness had sliced through my life. But her unfaithfulness with *him* not only injured but insulted my manhood.

I suppose that up until the climax of our conversation together, I had hoped to find Matherson Not Guilty. I suppose that even in my well-balanced, cynically pessimistic nature there must lurk the illogical eternal optimist. And that optimist—feeble though he be—offered that entrancing idyllic prospect that all the experts were wrong, or the one hope in a million had happened, and that our child by law would indeed be ours by love and by nature.

That feeble optimist died like so much of me on the block of that single word *but*.

In the course of my fifty years, I have built up among my few friends and my many associates a reputation for justice and coldness. The latter is not totally true. I think I am without many of the emotions which bedevil the lives of so many men. I am neither lustful nor greedy, nor can I remember when I felt physically afraid. All the emotion I have is concentrated in my love for Anne. My love for her is the perfect circle that is supposed to be divinity. My life begins and ends in her. She is the be-all and end-all of my life—and everybody else's for that matter. Now that I knew he had seduced her, the reverse of that emotion was projected upon Matherson.

I do not know if he felt it. I am not of the opinion that he is a person who is sensitive to the feeling or emotions of other people. However, one thing I do know was that he felt unhappy and guilty. He had not moved since that last word between us. When I got up to leave the flight deck, he glanced at my face quickly. But he still said nothing. I took back with me to the lighted cabin a memory of his very ordinary face puckered with apprehension. I think what I could forgive in him least of all was that he did not even love her, that this to him was a transitory affair of no importance, a trifling pleasure, yet for which he could with only a passing guilt entirely destroy my being.

As I walked to my seat in the passenger cabin, I kept my eyes lowered. When one has been done an abominable injury, reality seems to slip away from you. It is the mental and spiritual equivalent of losing consciousness after a corresponding physical hurt. I could not bear to meet the eyes of the passengers who watched me, worse still have inquiries made of me—which they invariably did of anyone in uniform

—as to the progress of our manifestly quick and smooth flight. I was in a cold grey limbo, and I preferred to remain in its quite merciful nervelessness.

Back in my seat, I stared out at the night sky. Moonlight shone through giant caverns in the cumulo-nimbus build-ups. Distant formations contained the horizonless darkness like stage pieces in an empty set. The night Atlantic sky has always seemed to me a near eternity of aching loneliness, colder than the Arctic wastes, moaning quietly into infinity. Now my heart was stretched to encompass it.

It was on a moonlight night like this—traditionally, for I am at heart a traditionalist—that I proposed to my wife, and she accepted me.

I put my hand in the inside jacket pocket of my uniform and felt the smooth leather covers of the diary I had kept up since I first met Anne two and a half years ago. I took it out and opened it up. There was no need for me to read it. I knew it all by heart.

It begins with her name . . . *Anne Beaumont was introduced to me at the Prentices.*

That was all. A small entry for the biggest event of my life. Five days go by and there are just blanks. Then . . . *rang up A.B. and asked her to lunch. To my surprise, she accepted.*

I can remember that day well. There is some song that Maurice Chevalier used to sing, where the man gets everything wrong and it is only the woman who remembers. With us, I sometimes fear the reverse applies. I wonder if Anne still remembers that day as I do.

I hope so.

It was early in April, and the crocuses were out in Green Park. As I walked along the sunlit pavements, I was not unaware of the particular magic of the time of year. Indeed, I had cause to be aware of it. As early in our acquaintance as that, I felt a new surge of youthfulness and joy in life. My worries, of which in the administration of my job I even then

had many, seemed suddenly of no consequence. My entire
problem was whether or not I was taking Anne to a place
she would enjoy.

Happily, because my great-grandfather made a considerable fortune, expense was no object. But partly because of
my ungregarious ways, I was not all that *au-fait* with the
London scene. Then besides the success of the lunch, I had
the small problem of flowers. I wondered if she would think
me old-fashioned, of another generation perhaps, if I bought
her some. I stopped outside Moyses Stevens. Everything
seemed somehow too big, too overpowering for Anne's fra-
gility. In the end, I settled for a single perfect red rose, which
they placed in a cellophane box and tied with a red ribbon.

I was to meet her at the bar of the Café Splendide. I had
not expected her to be on time, and I sat at a table in the
corner alone with my red rose in front of me. I consider it
impolite to start drinking before your guest arrives, but I
was somewhat nervous so I smoked one cigarette after another. Ten minutes went by . . . then twenty. The place was
getting crowded. People were always coming over and trying
to sit at our table, and I was kept busy sending them away.

I was beginning to think she had forgotten, when in she
came. She has a very special light way of moving. I had the
feeling that she had hurried along eagerly to our meeting.
Now she paused in the doorway. She was wearing a blue
silky sort of dress, very tight at the waist, and she held a
ridiculous little flower straw hat on her dark hair. From her
small shell-like ears there hung sapphire earrings that
matched her eyes. It was then—at that moment, framed in
the door with the sunlight behind her—that I fell eternally
in love with her.

At first, she seemed shy and embarrassed. Or perhaps she
had been hurrying too much, for her cheeks were flushed.
The rose appeared to both surprise and delight her. She
made a great fuss of opening it. She took it carefully and lov-

ingly out of its wrapping and pinned it on her lapel. She was
a delightful recipient of gifts.

Then—it being well past time for the table I had booked—
there was some trouble with the headwaiter which, however,
I very soon settled. We got a quiet place by the window,
and there was a long silence while she studied the enormous
menu.

For such a dainty shepherdess of a person, she had a
youthfully healthy appetite. She had smoked salmon, and
filet mignon, very rare. I made a mental note of the items she
hovered over, and how she liked those she eventually chose,
so that one day in the future I would surprise her with my
knowledge of her tastes. Out of politeness—though I was not
hungry—I ordered the same as she did. For wine I selected
a full-blooded red burgundy, 1959 Nuits St. Georges.

I will not pretend that conversation came easily. I was only
too aware that she was twenty-five years younger, so that all
the time I strove perhaps too hard to avoid boring her. The
food and the wine, which now absorbed her attention, provided conversational material for the odd remark. Then, as
she nibbled a dishful of *petits-fours,* I drew my attention
away from admiring her pretty little movements, and asked
her about herself.

"Oh, well—" She had laughed disclaimingly. "There isn't
really anything interesting to tell."

All the same, she had chattered on.

Her father had been in the Colonial Service, but had died
when she was five. Her mother? Oh, yes, she was still alive.
She hadn't seen her in years. She was in Cornwall, she believed. There had been some other man. Anne had been edu-
cated at a small boarding school in Worthing. An aunt had
brought her up. What was her occupation? Oh, well, she'd
done masses of things. She had a tiny income of her own. Her
father had left her what bit he had. But it came in useful.
She'd been a secretary for a while but that was frantic, then

a model, then she'd done a couple of trips as a courier on these European holidays. But that wasn't her cup of tea either.

It being my turn to talk, I tried to entertain her with word pictures of the places we flew to—New York, San Francisco, Honolulu. Since she had never been beyond Europe, I thought such a topic would be a happy choice. She listened politely, asking no questions, eventually saying, but with a nice smile, "You sound like the commentator in a travelogue. And now we must say good-bye"—it was the first time I realized how talented she was as a mimic—"to the golden shores of *wunnerful* Hawaii."

Then perhaps noticing my slightly discomfited face, she threw back her head and laughed, but not unkindly. "I want to hear about *you*. And what you feel on these trips. I'm more interested in people than places."

I was not unflattered that she should bring our conversation onto such a personal level so soon. I talked a little about the problem of being the Captain of an airliner, and about the even greater details attendant on Flight Captaincy. I was inclined to filter out the more distasteful side of the crew's perennial peccadilloes and discipline in general. But she would have none of that. She wanted to know what happened when a passenger got obstreperous. Did I have the power to clap him in irons? What about the crews? What was all this stuff she read about the girls on American airlines sitting on the pilots' knees? What on earth would I do if I came up front and I found the stewardess sitting on . . . what did I call my assistant, the First Officer's . . . knee? And she giggled happily into her coffee at my exaggeratedly outraged face.

She seemed to have read every scandal in the last few months pertaining to airline personnel. That business in Panama, when a pilot was beaten up by a prostitute's boy friend . . . what would I have done if I'd had to discipline him?

Did I keep a whip behind my office door like the manager of some obscure airline in Africa?

I said mysteriously that she must come to my office one day and find out for herself. And she promised to do just that, and she gazed at me with eyes that held at least some sort of admiration. It was then I noticed she had this fascination, odd in one of her generation, for discipline. It was later that I found she had, equally strongly, a desire to flout it.

In my diary I wrote . . . *took A to the Café Splendide. Was quite a hit, after all. Bill (including tip) £7. 10. 6.*

I didn't ring up again for a fortnight. I had to go on a trip to New York—we were in the initial stages of the Autoland contract—and this time I suggested a theatre. I prefer a straight play, but she wanted something lighter, so in the end we went to a revue. My diary notes that coming out of the theatre . . . *held A's hand.*

I saw her twice more, the last time a dinner dance at a large hotel, where Anne tried to teach me the cha-cha-cha. I am a competent dancer, and she appeared to enjoy herself. It was after that evening that I wrote in my diary . . . *have decided to ask A to marry me.*

It was a big step. I had given up thoughts of marrying some years ago. Although from time to time I have enjoyed the company of intelligent and sophisticated women, I had not found any need for their constant companionship. And my sexual appetites, though normal and perfectly healthy, I have always been able either to control or to satisfy on a commercial basis—a basis which I believe to be infinitely more moral than to involve another human being in a promiscuous affair with all its ramifications of deceit and misunderstanding. And in which sooner or later one partner or other will feel they have been inadequately recompensed for the emotional expenditure involved.

But apart from having no marked predilection for the company of women, I also suffered from this slight disability, which made me doubtful of the ethics of marrying at all. I had always been of the opinion that marriage without children is a barren existence for a woman. But on the other hand, Anne had by no means a highly developed maternal instinct. I had in fact watched her face on those rare occasions when walking through a London street we had come across quite presentable children. Her expression was utterly blank and unmoved. They meant nothing to her. All the same, I further tested her reactions. Several times, via her own childhood, I brought the conversation round to children in general, but she had no opinion on them, knew none, and I received the distinct impression that she had no wish to remedy the deficiency. But a far more cogent point, I felt, was that Anne is the sort of person who has something of a Peter Pan complex. A quality which I, for one, find very endearing. She is much more the perennial child, to be loved and spoiled, than the mother-figure yearning for fulfilment.

It was for these reasons, rather than the numerous young men whose names she occasionally let slip, and who all appeared to have the same intentions in mind as I, that made me decide to say nothing to Anne about the results of my illness.

It was June. I had taken her along to a small party at the Carruthers'. He's a colleague of mine of long standing, the Training Captain of the Company. Everybody had been very taken with her, and Carruthers—so Anne told me on the way back—had informed her that as far as British Empire Airways was concerned, I was God himself. She seemed quite delighted, and once again I was touched by her admiration of my authority.

I suppose it was long past eleven when we stopped outside her aunt's house at Marlow. It was moonlight. She, not I, pointed out the two horns of a waxing moon. She told me about some country superstition that the waxing of the moon was the time for planting the corn, and for starting new enterprises. I had kissed her twice before, but tonight was different. Instinctively I knew that this was my chance. That night, I noted in my diary (the writing is almost illegible, because I was so shaken with emotion) . . . *asked A to marry me and she has accepted.*

There followed a period of intense activity. I had radically to alter my whole way of life. There was a house to buy—Anne and I chose this one of which we have become very fond—mainly because it was some distance away from the little cells of Company families that cluster round London Airport.

The news of my forthcoming marriage was announced in Empire Airways. I received the usual felicitations. The aircrew bought us a small engraved salver in silver plate. I am not a man for close relationships, so I had no particular friends among the pilots. Carruthers was good enough to be our best man. At the wedding, which was small—my mother was indisposed just before the big day and felt unable to make the journey from Norwich, and Anne, like me, has few relatives and close friends—everything went very prettily. Carruthers jocularly referred to the fact that no one in British Empire Airways had suspected that under such an exterior as mine—for some reason I am regarded as being cold and remote—there beat such a romantic heart.

But anyone, I think, would have had a romantic heart if they had seen Anne then. She was all in white—white lace dress (which she and her friend Essie had flown to Paris especially to buy) with a short train and white flouncing veil, and she carried long-stemmed white lilies. She looked quite ineffably pure and lovely. Beside her, as the only bridesmaid, Essie Somerville looked a garish tinselly thing.

My diary notes the most important fact of my life . . . *2:50 p.m. A became my wife.*

It is unnecessary for me to add that this was the happiest

day any man could ever have had. My diary records no more, except a small cross. But my mind holds every detail.

Being a person of considerable fastidiousness, it is not easy for me to record, even in the privacy of my own diary, the times of sexual congress between Anne and me. I therefore devised the small symbol of marking the nights so blessed with a small cross of which only I know the meaning.

After the ceremony, we had motored down to Lydd, taking the car ferry across the Channel, and driven very fast to Granville, a French resort, where at a hotel at the water's edge, we had what is normally described as the first night.

Naturally as this was the culmination of my love, and I specifically say *my* love, I had looked forward to this moment with considerable ardour. During the long-drawn-out French evening meal, I had given Anne, by touch and gesture, every reason to suppose that I was eager to consummate our union. But Anne, due perhaps to shyness, or to the primeval reluctance of a young woman to approach her defloration, had lingered unduly over coffee. She had asked for (and naturally I had so ordered) extra liqueurs, and finally as we drank them, we were drawn into conversation with a very raffish couple in the bar.

When finally we had got to our room, I had the distinct impression she was alternately leading me on and repulsing me. She allowed me to kiss her ardently, but slipped away from me when I tried to touch her breasts. She let me take off her top garments without a murmur, but fought like a little wildcat for the remainder. Then when I tried to hold her naked body in my arms, she became child-like and afraid.

This behaviour I found at first exciting, then disquieting. And when finally I caught her, and coaxed her and our union was accomplished, in that very act it seemed as if she had slipped utterly away from me, over the edge of the world as I knew it, into some distant realms of her own imagination.

And in that final moment, she was lost, and I was alone

and bereft. I remember lying awake, listening to the pounding of the surf, my mind filled with two unhappy thoughts—that my wife did not love me, and that though she was so young and innocent, already there had been other men.

My diary then records the efforts I made to win her love solely for myself. My little symbol appears quite often, but so, too, do the encounters which I could not ignore with other men.

I was always a dutiful and attentive husband. I lavished presents on her. Far from only giving her the things she had seen and wanted, now I was continually devising and imagining the things she might like. And happily the whole world was my shopping market.

August 19th. Trip to New York and Chicago. Saw a silver and cultured pearl bangle in a Fifth Avenue store. Bought it for A. Cost 251 dollars 32 cents (including sales tax). X.

August 30th. At a party with Mr. Marks, A talking a long time with a tall young man with brown hair and loose mouth. As I had not been introduced, asked her about him in the car on the way home. All she could tell me was that he was a solicitor. She did not even know his name.

Similar entries appear again and again throughout that first year. The twelvemonth that followed was much the same. Out of a kind of ironic interest, I looked up to discover what had happened on the date of which today was the first anniversary, and this is what I read—

September 13th. Trip to Washington. Brooch of rubies in rather an exquisite setting caught my eyes in secondhand shop. Was more than my dollar allowance, so borrowed from Company office. 366 dollars 33 cents. X.

And then, not a week later—

September 19th. Walking up Piccadilly taking A to lunch at Claridge's, saw her watching one of those young business types—blue suit, bowler hat and umbrella—all the time he was approaching. Then she turned her head as if she was inter-

*ested in his back view. Am aware of this sort of thing in some
men, but am disquieted to see it in my own wife. The man
was quite unknown to both of us.*

*November 8th. A drove me to the airport for a Jamaica
Service. Captain S came over to the car for a talk. Anne was
very flirtatious. Gave him several oddly appraising glances,
which he seemed to enjoy but which I found distasteful.*

*November 24th. Brought back beautiful pearl necklace for
A from Hawaii. Great bargain, I think, at 58 dollars. X.*

*December 23rd. Returned from Service with a diamond
brooch for Anne. Rather extravagant, but it is almost Christmas. (I put no price.) X.*

There then happened a rather curious episode. I was feeling particularly happy and relaxed. I was lucky enough to be
home for Christmas, a privilege which perhaps Anne did not
fully appreciate, and I had decorated the house with holly
and mistletoe. We had a silver plastic tree from Harrods',
quite beautifully decorated with every conceivable bauble.
And locked securely in the cupboard of my study was a mink
stole for Anne of very nicely matched pelts.

We were both tired after our decorating, and we were relaxing in front of the television. The programme was of a
nature series about the Antarctic which I find quite excellent.
I was absorbed in the fine photography of a group of pen-
guins on an ice floe. A male penguin, his flippers stiff and ex-
tended from his sides, was going through their interesting
courtship procedure of diving for a large pebble and laying
it at the feet of his intended mate.

Suddenly in a harsh, uncontrolled voice, Anne leaned towards me, and cried, "There, Maurice! Take a *good* look!
Don't you recognize yourself?"

I thought about my reply very carefully. I was alarmed by
her expression. I had never known before that the coldness
of antagonism and the heat of rage could exist side by side
at the same time in the same face.

I said in a neutral voice, "I am aware that human behaviour and animal behaviour demonstrate similar patterns. But the particular likeness to myself escapes me."

I had hoped to disguise my deep hurt and at the same time to soothe her. But at my rejoinder she became completely hysterical. Far from the soft answer turning away wrath, it was as if my lack of anger disappointed and inflamed her. She laughed and cried and pounded the sofa until I had perforce to smack her quite hard with my open hand. At once she quieted and clung to me, and I carried her upstairs. My diary records the last cross of the year.

The New Year brought its own joys and problems. I was busy with the arrangements for the Autoland. I was busy taking Anne on little outings and shopping sprees. My diary records two flights with Anne to Paris and one to Rome, and another to Barcelona. Surprisingly for such a sweet person, Anne decided she would like to go to the bullfight. There was a particularly famous matador performing that day, and we had the best seats available, a choice which, though to Anne's, was not to *my* liking. Beneath these expensive seats they make a point of killing the bull.

I am not overfond of the sight of blood and I found the constant repetition of the slaughter tended to turn my stomach. Anne, however, was in her element. She talked about it all day. She was particularly impressed with the leisurely (and highly dangerous) way the matador despatched the bull. And that night she insisted on having the light out. She tried to fight me when I came to her, and in the final embrace, by her squeals and cries at my gentleness, I had the curious idea she imagined some man like El Torero was having his way with her.

It was about this time that I hit on a new way of dealing with Anne. Up until then, I had been only too ready to show a jealous interest in her predilection for other men. Now I either ignored it or encouraged it. So that like the spoiled adorable child she is, she lost interest in a toy that was too readily given. There followed several months of great bliss for me, when I feel sure Anne and I moved closer together.

Until that fateful entry in my diary of August 1st.

We gave a small cocktail party. In the mirror above the mantelpiece, saw A looking at Captain M.

I think that even as one writes a simple entry, one feels instinctively the beginning of a new chapter. But my feeling was not strong enough to serve as a warning—or else my presumptuous intellect foolishly rationalized it away. Had I known then what I know now, fair and honest though I pride myself on being, I think I would have found a way to get Captain Matherson out of the Company.

All the same, I watched carefully. Anne is much more transparent than she imagines. So with a coldness in my heart, I watched and waited. I watched them together. I watched the effect on her when I mentioned his name. I had an idea that Anne had been out with him that time in New York, for the aura of some childish pleasure clung to her like a cheap perfume. Deep down inside me, I suspected she wanted me when she could not have him, and although that suspicion never broke fully through the surface of my mind, yet because I am a man of very high principles, instinctively at those times I held her at bay.

August 17th. Returned earlier than expected from Mother's. A curious incident almost on my doorstep—in the headlights of my car, I think I saw Captain Matherson. He drives a Wolseley. There is a small lozenge badge on the bonnet of this car that is illuminated with the side lights. There are of course thousands of this popular type, so one cannot be completely sure.

Everything that night had been in order at home. The house was welcoming and warm. Anne was on her best and loveliest behaviour. But like a man who knows before he opens the front door that his house has been burgled, I knew something had happened. Anne pretended to be asleep when I came to bed. All about her suddenly, or so it seemed to me, was an aura of deep and tranquil satisfaction.

But I could not be quite sure my imagination was not playing jealous tricks.

August 18th. Purposely went along to watch Captain M in simulator. Made poor I.L.S. approach. When he saw me at the control table, seemed put out. My suspicions become deeper. Suggested he come to dinner, so that I might endeavour to find out the worst.

August 26th. Had not told A the name of our guest. In the mirror over the mantelpiece, watched her come in. Am satisfied there is something. But am not sure now how serious.

August 27th. Spoke to Mrs. Thorpe. It is not my usual wont, and she seemed surprised. Said to her that our guest of last night had thought he had left a scarf, the last time he had come to dinner here. The poor woman must have thought it some slight on herself, for she most vigorously denied it. So it was Matherson in the Wolseley. So he was in my house that night. So much I know.

September 8th. Captain M involved in incident with Victor X-ray at Boston. Cost to Company for passenger transfers, lost aircraft hours etc. cannot be far short of 50,000 dollars. Shall see Captain M on his return. Shall endeavour to find out possible connection between this accident and recent events in this diary.

It is a strange thing, but when you become involved in a problem which requires all your intelligence and observation to solve, you can become utterly detached and follow it through as if for the moment it is of no emotional concern to you.

Until, of course, the problem is solved.

And my problem came to its unhappy solution with this last entry in my diary . . . *September 10th. Anne told me she is pregnant.*

Then it is that the full floodgates of emotion burst open and prepare to drown you. Even Anne noticed that I was deeply and terribly moved. She drew me down beside her on the sofa. She held both my hands. She asked me if I was pleased, shaking my hands a little as if to force me into joy. I could not look at her. I kept my eyes down. After a while, I recovered sufficiently to say it was tremendous news and naturally I was overcome. I said I had always wanted children, but that I would be deeply worried about Anne's health and well-being. All of which was true.

Then I got up and poured myself a drink, and Anne said goodness, I looked as if I'd seen a ghost. I asked her if she herself was happy about the baby, and she said . . . ye-es, so-so, provided she got her figure back and we could get a good nanny. I asked her if she felt well and she assured me she did, and I was at a loss for anything more to say.

I remember standing on the hearthrug with alternating waves of love and hatred breaking over me. I still loved her just as much. But I hated him, and in some way I hated myself. My only thankfulness was that I would be out on Service with him on Sunday, that soon I would know. Until then, just for tonight I could hold Anne in my arms and pretend she was mine . . .

And now I knew for certain that she was not.

Dawn over the Atlantic touched my eyes with the physical pain of red-hot sparks. I slid the diary back into my pocket. I touched its covers lovingly. I wondered if I would ever write in it again.

Around me, the passengers who had slept were waking up. Like them, I stretched my limbs to try to get back the feel of life. I walked to the back and washed and shaved. My teeth chattered with the chill of shock, or the low ebb that seems to come with every dawn.

When I had made myself neat and clean, I went up front, and, waving Holmes aside, took the seat beside Matherson.

I said good morning to the rest of the crew. I said nothing to Matherson.

He appeared to be intent on his flying. He flew with that self-conscious care which under the circumstances I would have expected. He exaggerated his command of the aeroplane as if to show me, and maybe himself, who was master.

The dawn was a brief one. Cloud soon muffled it out, and the weather was deteriorating. We were half an hour in the stack before being cleared to Runway 04 at Kennedy.

There was no particular difficulty about the approach, but he performed it on instruments with overmeticulous accuracy. We broke cloud at seven hundred feet and the lights of the runway were straight in front of us.

I acted as his First Officer, carrying out his commands. It struck me as ironic—the two of us helping to bring the aircraft and all souls on board down to the ground in safety.

The landing he made was smooth. He taxied to the ramp. He stopped the engines. Then he looked at me inquiringly. There was now a sort of defiance about him, though there was nothing I could exactly put my finger on. His whole attitude seemed to be asking . . . what are you going to do now?

But I did not tell him what I was going to do. I just unstrapped myself and began in silence to get out of the right-hand seat. I saw no good reason to do anything else but keep him in suspense.

TWO

THE DAY after my return from that Route Check Flight, I walked into Captain Carruthers' office. As usual, he made a great show of being pleased to see me. He came out from behind his desk, and clapped me on the shoulder.

"Hello, Maurice! You're soon back. My, oh my, how time flies! Well, you're looking very fit, old chap. Found a bit of sun, by the looks of it. Did you have a good trip, and all that?"

I sat down on the spare chair by the window and accepted the cigarette he offered me. I said that I was in perfect health, never better, and that the trip had been relatively smooth and without incident. I did not think Carruthers noticed anything odd about me. In fact, I know he did not. Neither did anyone else—not in New York, not during the flight back to England, not even home last night with Anne.

Not anywhere.

The knowledge that I seemed exactly as before gave me a sense of personal triumph, akin to what I imagine actors feel after putting on a particularly good performance. And yet I would hesitate to call it a performance. I was not acting a part, so much as imitating a character. A very familiar character. In fact, myself.

For I was not the same person who had set out from London. Halfway across the Atlantic, that one word *but* had brought about a strange metamorphosis.

To act oneself is more difficult than anyone imagines. And yet when one carries it off, you have the added triumph of really being two people. The live one and the dead one. For just below the surface, below one layer of skin, one sliver of bone, one tremor of a nerve, lay a Captain Corby who was as dead as mutton.

And yet I was quite unconscious of any bereavement. Rather did my mood tend to an almost hysterical gaiety. Each small action that I performed, like dressing or washing or eating or shaving, or even, as I was now, talking to Captain Carruthers gave me a peculiar and especial delight. The only delight to which I can compare it is that of being in love for the first time, like I was with Anne. Then everything . . . sound and sight and smell has a heady potency. A fog layer of perception is stripped away. Colours acquire a new strength and clarity, sounds a piercing sweetness, every smell seems fragrant and nostalgic. You rejoice in breathing, because the ultimate privilege is to be alive and to be in love.

Now indeed I saw everything with that exalted perception. I rejoiced in life because I was dead. And I saw everything with new and child-like eyes because everything is bright and wonderful compared to death.

And like being in love, I found I had an added perceptiveness towards other people. For the first time, I realized that Carruthers had never really liked me. I realized it suddenly, the moment he said, "Well, and how did our old friend Matherson make out?"

He was just handing me a cup of coffee, which his office girl had brought in, and I caught that whiff of antagonism coming out of him as strong as the smell of the coffee.

I stirred my cup thoughtfully before answering. I had the curious urge, like a physical spasm, suddenly to laugh. I actually had to hold my breath, and purse my lips, so that no sound escaped me. You see, until that moment I don't really think I had completely decided. I had made certain plans. I had satisfied myself that I had the perfect method, should the need to put it into operation ever arise. The plan was my squirrel-nut store against a cold winter. The cold winter had come. The need had arisen. But still the two halves had not quite moved together. The right hand of action, the left hand of emotion had not yet clasped themselves together to make absolute purposefulness. Until that moment, when the cold dead Corby inexorably moved the lips and tongue of the living one. I took a sip of coffee. I sighed. I said, "Frankly, Bill, that's why I dropped in. I wanted to have a talk about just that. I'm more than a little worried about Matherson."

Simple words, seemingly indecisive. Yet as clearly as if I had said it aloud, they spelled out *I have decided to kill him.*

There was a trick question at school which our science master always asked the new boys. You know that light travels at 186,000 miles a second. What travels faster than light? The answer was thought.

In those intervening seconds while Carruthers frowned and I sipped my coffee, my mind travelled around the intricacies of my plan, not only with speed but with accuracy. I had very little time to lose, and from now on whatever I did must be with a purpose, whatever I said must not only assist that purpose but also be safe to record and to remember.

"I haven't," I said, "been able to get rid of his overconfident streak."

"What overconfident streak?" I could hear the deepening hostility in his voice. It was amazing that I hadn't noticed this antagonism before. Of course, Matherson was a favourite of his. A natural pilot, born not made—I'd heard him say that often enough. In a way, they were birds of a feather. Like liking like. Brash and bold and not overthoughtful. But Carruthers was more ambitious.

Which was all in my favour.

"Don't tell me you haven't noticed it?" I said sharply. Anne used to complain that I have cold eyes, grey and hypnotic. Perhaps she is right. Certainly Carruthers' red face grew redder under my stare. I meant to convey by my question that if he was as unperceptive as that, well . . . was he all that suitable as the Training Captain? I got my point over.

"I hadn't noticed it very much. Not more than most of his age group."

"Then you *have* noticed it?"

"Not much. Well . . . maybe a little."

"Have you noticed it? Yes or no?"

"Yes."

I gave him a small wry smile. "That's all I asked. I said *streak*, no more. Now perhaps you will allow me to continue." I drew a deep breath. "And this self-confident streak tends to make him distrust the Autoland."

"Does it?"

I raised my brows.

Carruthers made an amendment. "Well, yes . . . I suppose it might. Yes, possibly it does."

"You remember that meeting we had about the Autoland? What Matherson said?"

"I can't really . . ." Carruthers' voice faded uncertainly away.

"He said . . . I'd rather trust myself than any machine."

"Oh, yes . . . yes! *Now* I remember. Well, of course—"

I cut him short before he said *that's what the rest of us think, too.* "I'd had him on the same subject at dinner with us a few days earlier. I told him to hold his horses till the meeting. Otherwise we would never have shut the hangar doors and Anne would have been bored to tears."

Carruthers laughed and said, "I bet!" And just for a mo-

ment, I looked at him sharply lest he had heard something
about Anne. But Carruthers meant no harm. He said something about Joanna, his wife, saying that pilots can't talk
anything but shop. And then I got up and walked to the
door, because I wanted him to remember every word I had
said.

That day, on my way home, I bought a new diary. Since
the momentous news a week ago, I have put away the old
one. Altogether I had to visit three shops before I was successful. It is difficult to buy such an article in September.
Eventually I found some remaindered away in a small sta-
tioner's. I got it for less than half price, only eighteenpence.

I wrote just a few words for that momentous day . . .
*September 17th. Saw Carruthers about Matherson. We are
both worried about his overconfident streak. Carruthers recalled his remark at the meeting.*

And then although since I returned I have experienced no
desire for Anne, I put a cross. For my pursuit of Anne's love
and the furtherance of my plan are now identically embodied
in the selfsame symbol.

"What are you going to do with Matherson?" Carruthers
asked me the following Wednesday. I was having lunch in
the Senior Mess when he came and sat beside me. I stared at
him for a moment the way one does when the subject of
one's most profound attention is suddenly casually mentioned. For in Matherson and his fate, I had lately lived and
moved and had my being.

"Oh, Matherson . . . yes!" I frowned as if dismissing the
host of other pressing problems that had until then vexed my
mind. "Keep him off the roster for a while. And then I think
I'll put a bit of work on him in the Astra . . . hammering in
the value of modern mechanical aids. Though I tell you
this—" I broke off a piece of roll and popped it in my mouth.

"In his present state of mind it's going to be damned difficult!"

Carruthers said he supposed so, and went on to ask what the roast beef was like. I recommended it, though I told him to be sure to avoid the horseradish sauce which was made of office glue. We parted smiling, and that night I wrote in my diary . . . *September 23rd. Have taken Captain M off roster for Autoland training on the Astra though it will be a hard job to get him to accept it. Training Captain endorses my decision. X.*

I had already begun a programme of bad-weather landings using the Autoland for pilot training. I had completed Jackson, Hart, Lashley and Railton. Though they would doubtless not completely agree, I think I had made the first dent in the acceptance of this blind-landing aid. Autumn had got going with a vengeance, full of mist and fog and rain. We would fly down from London in bad weather and then it was my practice, approaching Riverly in near zero-zero conditions with cloud practically on the deck, to leave the cockpit together with my pupil, after setting up the Allen for a landing. We would sit, just the two of us, side by side in the empty cabin with the flight-deck door open. It was always a most memorable and confidence-giving sight. It had all the magic and eeriness of a theatre magician without any of the hocus-pocus. No one sat in those empty pilots' seats, while an invisible hand jiggled with the control spectacles, firmly closed the throttles at the roundout, thrust back the stick, and gently stalled onto the runway.

It was a little show that never failed to impress, and afterwards the pilot I was training was always completely happy to go off into the overcast with the Autoland alone. Oddly enough, it never failed to impress me either. Each time, I always got a sensation half exhilarating, half hypnotic. Each time, I watched entranced while my heartbeat ticked off the seconds towards the time when each separate task must be performed. Each time, I got in a mild sweat that the instrument would miss a cue or an entrance, as my mother did on the occasions when I used to take her to see Joan Sutherland at Covent Garden. Always as with her, the second is split with the timing of perfection. And therein perhaps lies the answer. Perfection, even in an instrument, gives me a profound, almost spiritual pleasure. I, for one, have no undue fears about man being taken over by the machine. When that eventually happens, mankind might well benefit. There is already a completely automatic underground train giving service while London sleeps. Calculations, accounts, vast memorizings and other functions are already done by machines. The Bible is being scrutinized by a machine to give the truthful answer on authorship. Imagine a machine that could dispense perfect truth on any subject—religion, medicine, history, philosophy. Best of all, perhaps, imagine the machine that dispenses perfect justice.

Instead of taking your fights and squabbles and claims and counter-claims to a fumbling human authority bedevilled with prejudice, ignorance and moral turpitude, your case would be fed, each side in turn, into the justice machine and out would come the perfect ruling, together with a just sentence printed on a card, as from those fairground fortune-telling machines of which Anne used to be so inordinately fond. Then the sentence would be carried out by another machine. There would be no need for any appeals and the only human beings in authority would be those who kept the machines in perfect order and prevented anyone from tampering with them.

I suppose that was what had first given me the idea.

Undoubtedly it must have been during one of those demonstrations of the landing machine, that I realized the possibility of how, should justice be needed, the Autoland could be adapted to my purpose.

I can't remember the actual moment the inspiration came.

It seemed now that this idea of mine had been part of me for so long that, rather like being married to Anne, I could not clearly remember a time before it.

The day after that lunch with Carruthers, I saw Matherson. It was close to noon. I had been sitting at my desk, checking over and over again with my Autoland manuals that this theory of mine would work, when suddenly he came into view through the left-hand plate glass of my office window. He was making his way through the vehicles in the executive car park. He was alone. He was wearing a suede sports jacket, and those rather repulsive cavalry twill trousers affected by office boys on weekends. A wind from the southwest was blowing through his hair. There was about him a purpose-lessness, as though he had nowhere to go and nothing to do. I saw him stop, feel in his pockets, produce a packet of cig-arettes.

There is something pleasurable in watching a person who is totally unaware of being observed. But in the case of Math-erson and me this feeling of privilege and power was greatly enhanced by the special relationship in which we now stood. I have read that a detective frequently develops a close feel-ing towards the criminal he hunts, a judge towards the pris-oner, the hangman towards the condemned man.

I have also read, though I am by no means a student of criminology, nor do I have a morbid delight in such things, that the hangman peers through the keyhole of the con-demned cell, assessing the weight, build, and general char-acteristics of his victim, so as to prepare the proper drop and the most humane execution. That then he carries out a re-hearsal on the gallows next door, using a sack of sand of the approximate build and weight, doing his work with great quietness and tact lest the condemned man hear him.

I suppose that with my mind so occupied, it was only nat-ural I should look down again at those calculations I had noted on my pad. They applied to the electronic averager which controls the last two hundred feet of the descent, supervising the closing of the throttles, and the pulling back of the stick. This averager was not exclusive to the Autoland, but was used on other automation machines where averaging techniques of from one to ninety-nine per cent were required. It was easily supervised and serviced, being in the forward part of the main control box. On this averager my theory was centred; but it still remained only a theory, with no practical proof it would work successfully.

And for my own rehearsal, I would have to wait till the following day—when neither Matherson nor anyone else would be around to hear.

Even in a supposedly round-the-clock service such as flying, old mores and customs die hard. Weekends especially the tempo relaxes, and that Friday evening I found the Training Block as empty of people as if gone over by a giant vacuum cleaner. Even along the rubber-floored corridor, my footsteps echoed because no other sound waves interrupted or overshadowed mine.

I had been up early and breakfasted well. I had taken Anne a cup of tea in bed, and had sat for a moment beside her, touching the bare part of her forearm that emerged from all the froth and fancy of her peignoir. I said she was looking more beautiful than ever and that her condition became her. But I scarcely saw her. For the nonce, I could see only my plan and the beauty of its perfection. Now that I was committed to it, I felt alive and alert, full of energy and sublety. In the wholehearted manner in which I embrace all things upon which I have set my heart, I was as devoted in the furtherance of my plan as I had been in the courtship of my wife.

I let myself into the Simulator Room with my own key. Then I closed the door behind me and locked it again. I stood for a moment with my back to the door, looking around, drawing in that warm air, which smells to me (of all things) like the inside of my tuck box at school which was always unhygienically warm from being too near the hot pipes. I like the look of the room itself. It is empty and impersonal, without decoration, full of plain colours, plain yeas and nays. Unlike most of its cumbrous cousins, this simulator can be set in motion, flown and operated by one man. Its subtle simplicity has always reminded me of Henry the Fifth's courtship speech to his French bride . . . I speak to thee plain soldier, for I have not the wit to woo in other places . . . how did it go? I had meant to say it to Anne when I proposed. But in the end, emotion had choked it out of me.

For some reason, it choked me a little now. Perhaps it was the quietness of this room, the simulator waiting up there like a scaffold, the weight of this duty which I had to perform. Whatever it was, as I made the necessary adjustments on the desk control, tears welled up into my eyes. I felt very alone. I stood there, clasping my hands, and though I pride myself on being a self-sufficient person, I actually prayed for the strength and the courage to complete my task.

I walked up the steps with my head a little bowed. For a few seconds, I felt that I, not Matherson, was going to the appointed place of execution.

But once inside, a metamorphosis took place. Not deliberately but as if the memory had come into my head unawares, I recalled that day six weeks ago, when Matherson had sat in this selfsame seat, the time when he put up such an extraordinarily poor performance. The night after, if my calculations were correct, he had seduced my wife.

There is a very powerful hypnosis in doing exactly the same things in exactly the same places as someone else. Briefly if you are poised on the crest of a tidal wave of emotion, as I was then, you can topple backwards into the past or forward into the future. For a moment, sitting there, my back leaning where his back had leaned, my buttocks pressing where his had pressed, my eyes seeing the same things, my ears listening for the same sounds, I could feel I *was* Matherson, and that my whole being was filled with the same lusts and guilts that his must have been that day.

In fact all through that session in the simulator, reality shimmered. I was in the past. I was in the future. I was myself. I was him.

But it was I who bent down to the main control box of the Autoland—the "brain" of the thing where are all the circuits and slave motors—and undid the clips of its metal cover. When the inside was exposed, it looked with all its different coloured wiring not unlike a more complicated human nervous system.

Very slowly I inserted my hand, and carefully as a man turning the combination of a valuable safe or a surgeon operating, began manipulating the speed-control mechanism of the electronic averager. This is the clever machine that having observed the rate of descent from two thousand feet to two hundred down the I.L.S. glide path, then takes over control for the next one hundred and eighty feet as an exact replica of what it has observed for a tenth of the time. Its duration of command is normally about half a minute before it initiates the roundout. But by moving the speed control fully forward, theoretically it could be made to produce not a tenth of the time monitored but a hundredth, starting a landing almost instantaneously, only a few feet below the height it took over.

That is what I did. There was no need to put the cover back on again. For at the end of the experiment, I would have to readjust the speed control back to its normal position.

Now I switched on the main controls. Immediately the warm air inside hummed with the sound of imitation engines. I went through the Check Lists. I strapped myself in.

And then the rehearsal began.

Very slowly, I opened up the throttles, took off and made

a circuit, picking up the I.L.S. beam. I positioned the simulator at two thousand feet in the landing configuration. I
checked all the safety devices. One by one, I engaged the
three autopilot levers. Then I pushed back the seat and
watched.

Everything proceeded normally. Controlled by the robot,
rudders and elevators did their jerky little dance. The two
needles of the I.L.S. made their cross dead in the centre of
the instrument. Not one foot below the glide path did the
simulator go, nor did it wander into the blue nor the yellow
sector. The altimeter ticked backwards—1000, 800, 600 . . .

Nothing could be more reassuring. Airspeed 140 knots,
rate of descent 400 feet per minute.

500, 400, 300, 200 . . .

I was watching the instruments performing now, as he
would watch them in the Astra. My heartbeat was quicken-
ing. I could feel the blood beating thickly in my veins, in my
ears, in my head. The saliva in my mouth seemed to solidify,
caging my tongue. I kept licking my lips to try to get a little
moisture but the effort was strenuous, like moving under a
weight of water.

I knew the critical time was approaching. Now the electronic averager was about to take over.

I heard the click as the autopilot pitch coupler disengaged
itself from the I.L.S. glide-path signals. It sounded so loud,
I jerked my head. The moment was almost on me.

180, 175, 170 . . .

There was a whirring sound. Then back came the throttles
and up went the nose. Even though I was expecting it, hoping for it, praying for it, the sudden start to the roundout
took me by surprise.

Though I was Corby safe in the simulator, I did exactly
what Matherson trapped in the Astra would do. I lunged
forward with my right hand. Out of the corner of my eyes, I
saw the airspeed falling. All the nightmares of childhood

falling down and down and down into blackness advanced
out of the past and overwhelmed me.

I got hold of the first autopilot lever and pushed it out.
Then the second, then the third.

I had just got back manual control. Sweat was dripping
down into my eyes. I was pushing the throttles forward,
when the whole simulator shook with a violent juddering.

The next moment, like a trap door being sprung, the nose
had dropped and we were in a tight spin.

Going down and down and down. For one brief second, I
had all the pangs and terrors of certain death, boxed in with
a machine gone mad. I covered my face with my hands. My
whole body stiffened. My teeth bit through my lip and I
tasted my own blood. Then almost imperceptibly, the sensation merged into a pleasure like physical ecstasy. I was Corby
locked with Matherson in a death dive—only I would miraculously live. Through a pink haze, I saw the warning needles
of the instruments, indicating we were going round and
round. I felt dizzy but elated. The simulator was making a
terrible high moan like the wind screaming over a rough sea.
My head ached. I was putting up my hand to my eyes when
suddenly there was a noise like thunder, and we had hit "the
ground."

The simulator still went on whirling. I blinked my eyes,
squinting dazedly at the instruments. The altimeter was reg-
istering minus five hundred feet as though it were boring
deep into the earth. With a great effort, I managed to get out
of my seat, and turn off the main switch.

Abruptly everything was very quiet. Silence seemed to
come into the cockpit and lap into every corner of it like a
tide. I stood with my eyes closed. I was dizzy and disorien-
tated. Not only the physical experience but the emotional
one had left me spent. I was sweating and yet I felt curiously
cold. I could hardly stand upright. My north, my south, my
left, my right were all tumbled with being spun like a top.

Somewhere beyond the horizon of my immediate thought lay a sense of triumph like a sunrise, but it had not yet then burst upon my full consciousness. All I knew was that those few seconds had seemed a lifetime—which in a sense they were.

When I had rested a little and all was calm within me again, I went back to the simulator control box. Once again I took my time, manipulating the delicate mechanism back to its normal position. Then I replaced the metal cover.

I had a sudden attack of nausea as I left the simulator and came down the steps, but it soon passed. I still felt very cold. The bright lights hurt my eyes. All the same, I went over to the Instructor's desk. I looked down at the airfield map and the record of the flight I had just done. I saw the straight red line turn into a whirl of circles like a crimson spider's web, three hundred yards from the threshold of the runway. If I had wanted further evidence, here it was.

I took up a cloth and carefully wiped all traces of the ink pattern off the glass, making away with every indication that I had been here at all.

Then I took up my cap and brief case. I had just opened the door, when down the corridor came a voice, "Who's that? Who's in there?"

The shape of a man became clearer in the light leaking from the Simulator Room. I saw the brief reflection from a pair of spectacles. It was Preston, the simulator Instructor.

"Oh, it's you, Captain Corby!" He sounded breathless and at the same time relieved.

"Me," I said calmly and rather humorously. "Working on a Friday evening, Preston? I didn't know the Company paid overtime."

"It doesn't, Captain. But I was in the main building. I heard the noise, so naturally—"

"The noise, Preston?"

"You know, sir. The simulator. You can hear it from King-dom Come."

I began switching off the neons. I took out my key. I said, "Do you want to stay here?"

"Oh, no, sir. I just came along to see what on earth was happening."

I locked the door and dropped the key in my pocket. "I was just doing a little simulator practise. It's not often I get the time."

"No, of course not, Captain."

He asked no more questions. He was being tactful. Ob-viously he thought I had made some bad mistake in instru-ment flying which I would not want him to know about. We talked about the weather—how damp and misty it had be-come—as we walked out of the building together. We said good-bye. Then we climbed each into his own car and drove off home.

That evening, Anne ate little supper. I heated her some milk which she screwed up her nose at, but sat sipping by the fire.

I sat behind her at a small table, and while rather listlessly she thumbed through a woman's magazine, I wrote in my diary . . . *September 25th. Simulator confirms what has been most worrying me. An overconfident pilot might well distrust Autoland and thus come to grief. Must get Captain M's train-ing fixed up as soon as possible. X.*

THREE

THE weather map on the morning of Thursday, October 1st, showed a deep depression moving slowly northeast across the Atlantic, giving low cloud and fog for hundreds of miles ahead. The Riverly forecast—these days always on my desk—was a light southerly wind, 8/8 cloud at two hundred feet, visibility three hundred yards in continuous rain.

I put Matherson down for Autoland training next day, to fly down to Riverly with me in the Astra at 9 A.M. But by evening a fresh wind had sprung up, and the Low shifted rapidly east across the North Sea and Scandinavia, leaving a clear frosty sky behind it. The training programme was therefore cancelled due to urgent pressure of business.

October 8th was the next date. The thick blue and red line of an occlusion was almost stationary across the whole country. Riverly forecast was 8/8 at one hundred feet, visibility four hundred yards in fog. Once again, they were wrong. Cold air flooded in from the north, and the day was crystal clear. One hour before Matherson and I were due to take off from London in the Astra, I sent word that the flight would not now take place.

Six days later, Matherson phoned up. He had seen his

name again on the Training Detail, this time for tomorrow. His voice sounded edgy. He said, "What's going on?"

For the first time, I began to think how Matherson might be feeling. A plan absorbs you utterly. I was now wholly obsessed. But it was the details I was concerned with, not the final thing nor the aim. As I held the receiver to my ear, I could hear him actually breathing at the other end of the wire. People, they say, rationalize things. They put blinkers down over what they don't want to see. Matherson would be struggling to do that: trying to believe that what had happened with Anne had not happened, that I did not know, that the Boston accident had not occurred, that the Check Flight had been entirely satisfactory, that this Autoland training was not hanging over him. I listened to him hard. I had the sudden single certainty that he was afraid.

"What d'you mean?" I asked.

"This Autoland training of mine . . . it always seems to be postponed."

"I'm sorry . . . but I have been unexpectedly busy."

His voice hesitated. "So that's why."

"Of course. Why d'you ask?"

"No reason." His voice hesitated again. "Except that when we are due to fly, Riverly is forecasting practically zero-zero . . ."

"All the better for—"

". . . and our training is postponed when the weather clears." For the third time, he hesitated, this time for very much longer. Then: "I see the weather forecast for Riverly tomorrow is fog."

"A fairly normal weather forecast for mid-October unfortunately."

The fourth hesitation, this time the longest of the lot. Then: "I hope we can get it over and done with tomorrow."

"Third time lucky," I said.

I had not intended that utterance to be prophetic, but in

fact it turned out so. By working late in the office the night before, I had cleared my In tray, and there was nothing undone that needed to be done as next morning in thick fog I edged the Astra from blue taxi light to blue taxi light, with Matherson sitting silently beside me.

Just as I was doing the Before Take-off Check, he suddenly said, "Well . . . this time it *didn't* clear."

I turned and looked inquiringly at him.

"You got your pea-souper today."

"Fortunately . . . yes," I said. "You'll get the best possible idea how useful the Autoland is today."

He grunted, said nothing more, looked out of his side window as I opened up the throttles. Immediately we were airborne, the fog enveloped us in a cold clammy grasp.

It is a thirty-minute flight down to the south coast and Riverly. We flew on instruments via Dunsfold and airway Red One. All the time, Matherson was nervous. He was restless. He kept moving his hands over the controls as though he wanted to fly himself. Every now and then, he kept glancing across at me, as though he was trying to assess what was in my mind.

Over the Riverly range station, still maintaining altitude, I said, "The first thing I want to emphasize is *safety*. You've done all the checks and the safety precautions in the simulator . . . but now in the aircraft we'll do them all over again. Until I'm satisfied . . . and you're satisfied . . . that they're all buttoned up."

He was very attentive. Almost suspiciously, he listened to every word I told him. He asked questions—none of the other pilots had done—and it became apparent to me that he, too, had been studying the mechanics of the Autoland.

As I went over the radio altimeter tests, the autocontrol safety lights, I said, "Glad to see you've been doing your homework."

I had said it jocularly, a joke to lighten the tension that

was obvious in the cockpit. But he didn't smile. He gave a grim sort of little nod, and then we went on to the release mechanisms.

I said, "One thing I must emphasize . . . below a hundred and fifty feet do *not* take over from the Autoland. As you know, the human eye is subject to distortions. So below the height, *don't* move these three chaps forward"—and I tapped the autopilot levers—"and resume pilot control."

"I won't," he said.

"Unless there's some emergency . . . and you *have* to."

"I won't," he repeated.

It was over this part of the instruction that he was even more attentive than usual. I engaged the Autoland. He practised pushing the levers forward and regaining manual operation.

He said, "There's that lag . . . before you get complete control."

"No more than a second or so."

"Always have thought it's bad that the pilot can't overpower this autopilot when it's engaged."

"If he could," I pointed out, "the autopilot wouldn't be strong enough or positive enough to do the automatic landing." I paused. "Satisfied?"

"I think we'll run through those safety precautions again," he said slowly. "That is . . . if you don't mind."

I shrugged my shoulders. "I don't mind."

And we went through everything again. When at last he seemed satisfied, I got clearance from the Tower to descend.

Through all levels, the fog was still the same oatmeal consistency. At two thousand feet, I lined up on the I.L.S. localizer. I put the wheels and flaps down. Then I engaged the three levers of the Autoland.

"Come on, Matherson," I said. "We'll go and have a smoke in the cabin."

I had reached the "confidence-trick" part of the training—

when I sit with my pupil in the small passenger cabin, chatting and having a cigarette, while through the open door we can see the Autoland doing the work.

We lit up and puffed away. I made one or two observations which Matherson received in silence. He spent his time alternately looking at the pilotless controls, and then at the streaming porthole by his side.

As we got lower, he began to be more nervous, peering out as though he was expecting to see the ground come up on us at any moment. I told him to relax, everything was going to plan. But he still looked as though he was measuring the distance to get to the cockpit.

I could just see on the left-hand side of the throttle levers the needle of the radio altimeter creep anti-clockwise round its dial.

400 . . . 300 . . . 200 . . .

We were coming down through thick cloud.

150 . . . and we were still in the stuff.

Then suddenly—and this was always the most dramatic moment of all—the cloud lightened, the edges became wispy and broken up. I saw a hedge, a muddy field, a leafless tree that seemed almost on top of us. It was always the same—released from a foggy prison the ground always looked closer than it was.

The next moment we were approaching the threshold. Momentarily I felt the roundout. Then almost before you realized what was happening, the throttles were slammed closed, the engines' noise died, the control column moved right back. For a fraction of a second, we glided nose up.

Then there was a very slight judder, and we had stalled onto the runway.

As the wheels hissed over the wet tarmac, I suggested, "Good landing, eh?"

"Not bad."

I then led the way up front, and we sat down again, side

by side. I disengaged the autopilot and taxied back along the runway. There was nothing else moving—not even the birds were flying.

We took off again. This time, he put in the Autoland. He watched it carefully, almost as though it was a mine that might go off at any moment. Once again, everything was perfect.

This was usually the time for our elevenses, after which the pupil would go off on his own, just to finish the job of building up his confidence in the machine. But Matherson wanted another demonstration. He seemed anxious for me to stay with him in the aeroplane. Only when the third landing was just as good as the others did he seem reassured and relaxed, and he said he was satisfied.

"Good," I said. And then, "Thirsty?"

"I could do with a drink."

"Then we'll have a break."

As I made my way slowly to the ramp near the airport restaurant, the mist worsened. Light rain was now dribbling down the windscreen. There were delayed airliners all over the place. I had quite a time, finding a place to park.

I shut down the Astra's engines, switched everything off, and put my left hand down to pick up my brief case. Matherson had got out of his seat, and had started to lead the way to the door at the back.

Then he stopped and turned round. He saw me still sitting there. "Aren't you coming?"

"In a moment." I had opened my brief case and now I held up three printed forms. "Just got this to do . . . a report on our three blind landings."

"Then I'll wait."

I put the forms on the throttle box. I said carefully, "There's always a queue in the café with these weather delays."

"I suppose there would be."

I began to take my pen out of my pocket. "Do you think you could lead the way . . . and bag us a place by the counter?"

He hesitated. Then: "All right."

"Thanks."

"What'll you have?"

"Coffee."

He began moving to the back again. "Black or white?"

"Black. Oh, and Philip . . . we better have your moniker on the serviceability sheet. It's on the table in the cabin. Just initial it, eh?"

"Will do."

For a few moments I sat there, listening to him moving around at the back. Then I heard the door opening, the thump of his feet on the tarmac, the slam as the door shut again.

I put my pen back in my pocket. Now the moment had come, what I was going to do seemed to be as normal as an item on a Check List. The plan had its own impetus. As I took off the cover of the Autoland control box, and put in my hand and began to do exactly as I had done in the simulator, it was as though I had done this many times before.

It was all over in a matter of seconds—as simple as that. And in a very short time after Matherson had left the cockpit, I was treading in his footsteps, as it were, to the back of the aircraft, and out on to the tarmac.

There I put down my head and hurried through the streaming mist towards the muzzy lights of the restaurant.

The place was not as crowded as I had expected. Matherson had managed to get two seats at the counter. My coffee was already in front of the vacant one.

"Thanks," I said.

I put sugar in my drink and stirred it slowly. Matherson looked out at the rain beating against the windows.

"Looks worse."

"Won't make any difference to the Autoland." I started drinking. "That's the beauty of it."

I got the impression that he was not so sure. He rummaged round in his pocket, produced a packet of cigarettes, took one and passed them over.

We both lit up. I had my elbows on the table, nursing my cup. Matherson said, "How many circuits do you want me to do?"

I looked at my watch. "Just the one. I don't want to make it too late, getting back home."

The mention of going back home seemed to reassure him. But all he did was to shrug his shoulders and say, "As you like."

"You see," I was still studying my watch, "if we get away from here at twelve . . . take us thirty minutes . . . say three quarters of an hour. Should make it easily for one o'clock lunch."

"Yes." He finished his cigarette. There was a silence between us as he ground it out in the porcelain ashtray. Then he said, "By the way, about the Route Check—"

I could not have been more surprised. With an affair of such enormity on his mind, here he was still worrying about his flying! It was hard to imagine the utter boneness of the man. An added spurt of anger was injected into me at such an attitude.

"What about the Check?"

"Was it all right?"

"What makes you think it wasn't?"

"You said nothing."

"Why should I?"

"The others do." He paused. "And I seem to be off the roster."

"That," I said slowly, for I had perceived that even this

character streak could serve its purpose, "was only temporary. Till your Autoland training was complete."

"You mean, I'll be out on Service?"

"As soon as you've done this flight . . ."

Immediately he seemed to brighten. As I had intended, he became reassured. He thawed somewhat. He almost smiled.

"Well . . . in that case . . . the sooner it's over, the better." He paused. "I could do with a spot of Honolulu heat."

He got off his stool, and took his cap and brief case off the counter. He had started to move away when I said, "You're sure you've got it buttoned up?"

"I think so."

"*Think* isn't enough. You're *sure?*"

"Sure, then."

The waitress had come up to collect the empty coffee cups. I saw her look at me, as I called out to him, "And remember now . . . *trust* the Autoland!"

He was at the door, turning up the collar of his raincoat. He said nothing, just gave me a queer sort of smile.

And then he had gone, and I was left with the sound of the rain outside mixing with some dance tune, hummed by the waitress as she prepared to wash up.

"I'll have another coffee," I said.

"Can you remember which one?"

"I had black."

She peered inside both cups. "Then it's this one." She looked at me enquiringly. "Another black?"

"Please."

She was pouring it out when the first engine spluttered into life. I passed over a shilling . . . and the next engine was alive.

She had put two sugars in the saucer. I unwrapped one slowly, placed it in a teaspoon and dipped it into the liquid. I watched the brown coffee swarm up into it as though drawn magnetically. I could hear him taxiing, the sound getting fainter and fainter, muffled by the fog.

He would be moving over to the far end of the airfield now, to take off position on Runway 25.

I said to the girl, "What are those cakes?"

"Those?" She pointed inside the glass showcase. "They're coconut."

"I'll have one. It'll go with my coffee."

I heard the engines roar up to take off power as she passed me one on a plate.

An army of small liqueurs, china ornaments, chocolate bars and glasses jostled for position on the wall shelf beside the upturned spirit bottles. Behind them was a mirror. In it, I could see fragments of myself as I drank. One eye below the Gordon's gin, my lips and the rim of the coffee cup between a pile of potato crisps packets and some blocks of Bourne-ville chocolate, my left cheek sliced away by Johnny Walker whisky, my hair, looking almost white in this illumination, just visible above a bottle of Double Diamond beer.

I stared at that mosaic of myself. I sipped my coffee and screwed up my eyes.

"Is anything the matter?" asked the waitress. "Coffee a bit strong?"

"It's a trifle hot."

"Have a drop of milk in then." She pushed over a jug in-vitingly. A few drops spilled on the counter. I shook my head.

I could hear the engines going further away. He would be downwind now.

I tried my coffee again. I didn't want to meet my one anxious eye in the mirror. I swallowed a couple of mouthfuls.

"Unpleasant weather," I said.

"Gets worse and worse." The waitress mopped the counter. She had big pinky-purple hands, swollen and drowned-look-ing. "Rains winter and summer. We never seem to get them nice hot days. It always seems to be winter."

He would be crosswind and on base leg. The engine noise was getting louder. He would be coming in at two thousand feet to intercept the I.L.S. localizer beam.

". . . and d'you know what? It always rains on my day off! You just notice! Sundays is nearly always wet . . ."

He would be putting down his wheels. He would be pulling back the three autopilot levers. He would be locking on.

". . . not that there's much to do. Not for young people these days . . . My mum was saying . . ."

He would be coming up to the glide path now. The Autoland would be beginning the descent.

". . . 'cept of course, Bournemouth . . . but then it's the buses, isn't it . . . ?"

The altimeter needle would be turning anti-clockwise. Every fifteen seconds another hundred feet lower. Coffee gets very sweet towards the bottom of the cup.

". . . no youth club, no nothing. Just that one cinema and they say they're going to close that . . ."

He would be at five hundred feet now, alternately looking out at the fog and checking the Autoland operation. I had finished the second cup of coffee. I said, "I seem to have run out of cigarettes. Would you give me a packet of Players?"

"Twenty?"

"Please."

She pushed over the packet. I put down two half crowns. She went off to the till. There was a ting as she put the money in. She was just moving back to me with the change, when there was the most tremendous crash.

Her round face distorted with fear. The features dragged and flattened as if they'd been splattered against the wall.

Immediately in front of me, the bottles and ornaments rattled. The mosaic of my face shivered in the mirror. My eye grew large and terrible, and then winked out. My skin crumpled into a thousand wrinkles, like the picture of Dorian Gray. My lips turned back on themselves like an animal's.

Briefly I seemed to look into something evil. For that split second, I was almost crushed by what I had done.

And then the mirror steadied. The gin and whisky bottles stopped rattling. It was my own face now, my ordinary face —worried, alarmed, as puzzled as the girl's. And as the fire bells started clanging, and the klaxon sounded out on the ambulance, like all the others I rushed to the open door of the restaurant calling, "What's happened?"

And then I started running into the fog towards the direction of all the noise.

That night, inevitably I was late home. There was one thing to do after another—seeing to the painting out of the name of the Company (always one of the first jobs to do after a crash), statements to the police, guarding the aircraft, keeping the Press as far as possible at bay, organizing all possible assistance and facilities for the investigating officers from the Ministry of Civil Aviation. I had rung through to Empire Airways to send a car down for me, but it was nine o'clock before we managed to leave Riverly and well past twelve before the driver left me outside my own front door. There was no light on in the house. Anne would be fast asleep in bed—and that was a blessing. I took the key out of my left-hand trouser pocket, and let myself into the dark hall.

Immediately I was aware that once again, this home was mine.

A scent of chrysanthemums greeted me. Of all flowers, they are, I think, my favourite. When I switched on the light, I saw that Anne had been busy, filling the white jade bowl we have in the hall with lovely extravagant blooms. It was the same in the lounge too. As I poured myself a whisky, I sniffed their fragrance appreciatively, soothed by the peculiar appropriateness of their poignant smell.

Not that I was conscious of feeling particularly sad. But I think that this day's doing would have been enough to unnerve most men. I think they would have been sufficient to unnerve me, had I not been sustained by the knowledge that I did this for Anne. I have in my time been present at a number of accidents. I was the first on the scene when a Constellation crashed on landing and forty people were killed. I was a witness when two aircraft collided. There were a good many more physically terrible things to see on those occasions, but today's comparatively minor tragedy—after all, only one man killed—took naturally a much greater toll of me.

It was not so much that I felt guilty. I don't think that apart from that awful moment in the café, when my whole being was split asunder and I seemed to look through into something dark and frightful inside me, I had felt more guilty than any other just judge would have done. It was just that faced with the actual scene of Matherson's death, that split didn't quite mend, and out of it came a terrible fluid which semed to imprint unwanted pictures upon my mind.

But gradually on that long drive home, even these disappeared. I became first of all convinced that I had done no more than any other husband would have done under the circumstances, except that I had accomplished it more cleverly and logically. It was the logic that now peculiarly delighted me and held my mind. From that, it seemed only a step to realize that I had not so much killed Matherson as hastened his inevitable end. I had speeded up time for him, telescoped it, as I had speeded up the averager on the Autoland. I had, in fact, only accelerated what sooner or later his own faults would have done for him.

Besides, what I had done was simple. Murder did not lie in the tightening of a spring. Murder was guns, bullets, knives, ropes—and hideous violence.

As I sat behind the driver, silent out of consideration for our tragedy, all the scenes that troubled me fell away like the dark road behind us. Not again did I feel I was running through a grey death-smelling limbo of my own making. The scenes of a few hours ago melted. That smell of petrol mingled with the graveyard smell of wet fresh-slashed earth, newly crushed grass, the sight of the fuselage made into witch-shapes of twisted bones and evil features, the dark faceless figures bending over what was left of Matherson, the hushed voices, the harsh shouts, the sounds of the rains sucking away and tinkling and gurgling through the clay—all went. Funnelled away like black smooth-flowing water, never to come back and trouble me.

Behind me now, with a little tinkly whir, the French ormolu clock on our mantelpiece struck half-past twelve. I turned my head and looked into that oval gilt mirror above it, almost as though I could see Matherson again reflected there.

The mirror showed nobody, of course. Only the straight-backed empty chairs with their beautiful Regency striped silk covering, the sofa where he and Anne had sat when he came to dinner, the little mahogany table where he had put his drink. It was difficult now to imagine he had ever been here.

I walked away from the mirror. I moved to the sofa. I put my drink on the table where his had been. As surely as smoke through an open window, he had gone for good. Elation suddenly began to edge my mood, as if a gold rim had been sprayed on a funeral card. I poured myself another drink. My mind was very clear. I was satisfied that I could not honestly call it murder, because it was justice and because it was perfect. Not perfect because it was seen to be done, but perfect because it was *not* seen to be done.

' The little joke delighted me out of all proportion. I began to giggle uncontrollably into my drink.

I was as bad as Anne. I mopped my lips and fingers where the drink had spilled.

Anne. At her name, the humour left me. I became more sober. One thing she must never know was that I had accel-

erated Matherson's end. I thought of her sleeping up there.
Miraculously, although it was as I knew it would be, desire
for her began to stir deep down in me. It was as though now
the plan had been carried out, the courtship was over. The
eyes of my spirit would become focused, and the two X's in
my diary would merge stereoscopically into one.

I would break the news to her myself. I would be very
gentle. I would never let her know what I knew. She was all
mine and I could afford to be generous. As gently as if the
flowers had been Anne herself, I fingered the soft silky petals
of the chrysanthemums. I actually touched them with my
lips.

Then for the first time I noticed their colour. For once,
Anne had made a mistake. Usually she was so good. But
white, *all* white was wrong for this room. I glanced around.
Every vase was full of huge white chrysanthemums. One,
two, three, *four* vases . . . the brass bowl, the silver rose dish,
all full of white chrysanthemums.

I walked through to the dining room. More white chrysanthemums, chrysanthemums on the stairs, on the landing window. Chrysanthemums everywhere.

Suddenly the place was like a funeral parlour. The smell
overpowered me.

And now I knew.

Anne had heard—the television, the evening paper?—that
Matherson was dead. And this was her way of showing that
she mourned him.

During the weeks that lay between the time of Matherson's crash and the inevitable Inquiry, I diligently searched
Anne's face, and sifted every word and action for signs of
grief.

It was with profound thankfulness that I had so far found
none.

That is not to say that she had no reaction to Matherson's

death. But what she had was too complicated for me to fully comprehend. She is much too feminine a person not to make me jealous. When I appeared not to notice (wisely, I felt at the time) her display of all those white chrysanthemums, she had pointed them out to me. She insisted on sending a great sheath of them to Matherson's funeral, and when I agreed that some such floral tribute would indeed be a kind gesture from us both, she insisted no, I could send *mine* officially from the Company if I chose. But she—*she* would send her very own. She had sat in the lounge at the little table under the lamp where I normally wrote my diary, and pondered what she should put on the card. She had asked for my suggestions, but I had not been able to offer any. In the end, she had written in her big flowing handwriting simply *from Anne.*

All the same, mixed in with this rather naughty way of trying to make me jealous with a dead man, was a healthier reaction. For somehow I think she *despised* Matherson for getting himself killed.

The night before the Inquiry opened at the Holborn Town Hall, we had watched another of my favourite educational programmes on television—this time about some obscure king in a forbidden territory near the Sudan, a king who never grows old. Once again, it was excellent. It was about a primitive tribe whose king rules by physical strength. Any chieftain can challenge him to combat, and if he bests him, the king is killed and the successful challenger assumes the uneasy crown. The king possesses over a hundred wives, whose little mud huts he visits secretly. At the first sign of physical failure, it is their duty to meet together and to suffocate him. This time Anne made no side remarks when the programme ended. She simply laughed and trailed her fingers over the top of my head, the way I love her to, and said, "Well, there's a lot to be said for the good old days!"

I tried to draw her down to me. I would like then to have

given her a foretaste of my own ardour and virility. For since I had dealt with Matherson, it was as though scales had fallen from my eyes, and Anne was not only as desirable as before, but if it were possible, twice as desirable to me. But though fully aware, I think, of my desire, she kept me at my distance—tantalized me a little, too, I must confess. She simply twisted her body out of the reach of my eager hands and went and sat on the sofa. "You've got a busy day tomorrow," she said, which is her way of saying *no*. "Besides, I want to come to the Inquiry, too."

I know I pursed my lips in a way she doesn't like, because I intercepted the scornful look that momentarily came into her eyes. I thought carefully before speaking. It was wholly for her sake that I did not desire her presence. The idea that there might be any difficulty for me at this Inquiry hardly crossed my mind. I had done what I had to do, and I had done it well. And now it was my duty to see that Anne would never, must never know.

"I think that would be foolish, my dear. An Inquiry of this nature is distressing enough to us who *have* to go."

"I still want to come."

She got up and moved to the door, as if the argument was closed. I was vexed in my mind as to whether I should forbid her or humour her.

"Why, my dear? Give me one good reason."

She came back towards me then, swinging her hips exaggeratedly from side to side. Then she bent down and brought her face close to mine. Like a naughty little girl, she pouted and said, "Because I *want* to. Because I'd"—a curious sensuous look diffused her face—"enjoy it."

For a moment, I had been almost shocked. Then I had realized she was teasing me again. I wondered if she had perhaps provoked my reproof, the way she sometimes likes to at first. I drew her down onto my knee, kissing her neck because her face was turned away from me, letting my hand gently stroke her thigh. But again, her mood changed. She became girlish and naïve. She *knew* the Commissioner, Mr. Justice Pelham, hadn't she told me? Oh, no, not personally, but she'd seen him before. When? At a *real* trial, a murder trial, a capital murder trial . . . oh, no, she didn't usually go to that sort of thing, but Essie had persuaded her, years ago before we were married. She'd queued up outside Lewes Assizes. She'd seen him put the black cap on his full-bottomed wig. And she wanted to see him again.

In the end, I gave in—as I always do with Anne. And she was seeing him again now.

I wondered what she thought of him. I confess I almost had a pang of jealousy at her admiration. But today he sat up there on the high desk—a very ordinary figure in a blue suit, his judicial manner scalped away with his wig. To his left was John Bakewell, an expert on instruments and automation machinery, in chalk-stripe flannel. And to his right was Rudwick, a senior captain of Atlantic Airways—whom I had suggested, as a matter of fact, to the Ministry as a possible assessor because of his interest in Autoland—wearing a double-breasted brown tweed. On the floor of the Court, the Attorney-General wore neither wig nor gown. And the only formality apparent at all was Mr. Butterworth's white bow tie, worn presumably to give the Pilots' Union—whose brief he held—a sense of value for money.

It was always the same at a Court of Inquiry. Someone in authority had decreed that if you were going to find the real truth on an aircraft accident, the only way to get it was in an atmosphere of informality.

Here were no police, no detectives, no suspicion. Here it was more like a Round Table Conference, or a Rotary Club Meeting. The anticipation of such an atmosphere, of course, had been part of my plan. And I knew that once the Commissioner and his two assessors had reached the decision I intended, it could never be reversed. An aircraft-accident Inquiry is never reopened. There have been accidents all over the world where in the opinion of many pilots later evidence should have been reviewed, and the findings of the Court changed. But after the insurance money has been paid, there are too many financial and political considerations involved, and sleeping dogs are always let lie.

So that once the experts reached their irrevocable decision on the cause of this accident, no Court of Law would ever be able to contradict them or hold session against anyone.

I had been the first to be called when the Court opened at ten this morning. My evidence on that last training trip had for the most part been listened to in respectful silence. Now the afternoon session had started, with an eyewitness account by some local charwoman. Here at the back of the Court we were far away from the radiators—the Holborn Town Hall is a mausoleum of a place in any case, quite unsuited to my wife in her delicate condition—and I whispered to Anne, "Are you cold?"

But she shook her head without turning, impatient of my interruption. All the same, she was trembling. I watched her out of the corner of my eye. She was sitting on the edge of her chair, leaning forward as if afraid of missing a word. Her lips were parted, the pupils of her eyes slightly distended. From time to time, she gave a little sigh, as I have heard her do sometimes at a play or film which had wholeheartedly captured her imagination.

I let my eyes slide back to Mrs. Kettlewell. I was satisfied that the trembling of Anne's body was caused by some inexplicable feminine excitement—and not by grief, as I had at first supposed.

FOUR

"AND NOW, Mrs. Kettlewell, you were coming up . . ." The Attorney-General screwed up his eyes and put his long fingers to his forehead in an attitude of concentrated memorizing. "Inkle-ferry-beacon-barrow-road."

"*Lane*, sir. Inkleferrybeaconbarrow *lane*."

Somebody laughed. Somebody else joined in. Finally a murmur of merriment rippled right the way round the Court Room. Unabashed, the Attorney-General stood smiling and bowing at the small middle-aged witness who had just contradicted him. Of course, Sir Alexander Lockwood Q.C. was an actor—they all are—and this was his stage. But even so, he certainly possessed the common touch. He was easy, relaxed, informed. He was gunning for nothing and no one. It was obvious that the Ministry of Civil Aviation had instructed him that here there was nothing underhand, no breach of the regulations. That everything was quite honest and aboveboard. That in fact the accident to Astra Golf Alfa Victor Mike on the fifteenth of October was nothing more than one of those unfortunate incidents which periodically bedevil the progress of aviation.

"Mrs. Kettlewell . . . I stand corrected. This . . . this *lane*—

I shall not venture again on its appellation—borders the edge of Riverly Airfield?"

"It does, sir."

On the long oak table in front of the dais were the control components of the Autoland system. I had been looking at them for some time, considering how battered, twisted and torn by the crash they were, almost beyond recognition. Everything was perfectly satisfactory. It was all rather like Church, with the Commissioner the preacher, and in the pews marked *Ministry of Civil Aviation, British Empire Airways Company, the Allen Autoland, the Astra Aircraft, Pilots' Union* sat the congregation beneath him.

There was for me only one fly in the ointment. It was a large fly, and had those big eyes flies have, enhanced by the thick round lenses of spectacles. It sat in the front row of the benches reserved for British Empire Airways, slightly to the left of us. There was no reason that I could see why George Preston should want to be present at the Court. I knew he had been friendly with Matherson, but then he was friendly with everybody. I had noticed him for the first time while I was giving evidence. He seemed to be intent on every word I said. Now he was listening, just as avidly as Anne, to what Mrs. Kettlewell had to say.

"You were accompanying your husband in order to go to the Inkleferry Stores?"

"That's right, sir. For a bottle of Worcester Sauce."

"And you and your husband had stopped at the pear tree in the hawthorn hedge . . . puffed because of the hill . . . just after eleven-thirty?"

"Couldn't 'ave been more'n a minute after, sir . . . 'cos me 'usband leaves our 'ouse prompt on the quarter past."

"And while you were standing there, you heard the sound of engines?"

"Yes, aeroplane engines."

"How did you know they were aeroplane engines?"

"Well, they couldn't very well have been car engines . . . not up in the sky, sir."

"And what did these . . . *aeroplane* engines do?"

"They came on all of a sudden very loud."

"Loud enough to startle you?"

"Not *startle*, sir. Takes more'n aeroplane engines to startle *me*. I was . . . well, surprised like. I looked up."

"And could you see anything?"

"Well, sir . . . it was still very foggy."

"You've told us that."

"The rain got in my eyes."

"So you saw nothing?"

"Oh, yes, sir, I did!"

"And what did you see?"

"An aeroplane just coming out of the clouds."

"And what did you do?"

"I shouted to Bert, 'There's an aeroplane going round and round and it's going to crash!' "

"Is your husband a marine, Mrs. Kettlewell?"

"A *marine*, sir?"

"I asked that because we have a rule in England that whatever is said to the marines is not evidence."

"He never has been a marine, sir! He's a groom, sir! A groom, sir, to Lord Thornaby, sir, up at the Big House! That's why, as I have already told you, sir, he has to leave at a quarter past the hour sharp to get the horses ready for Lady Thornaby and the Honourable Master Thornaby and the Honourable Misses Thornaby to ride in the afternoon!"

"Quite, Mrs. Kettlewell, quite!" Sir Alexander raised a large pacifying palm. "Far be it from me to discredit your admirably accurate evidence. And what did your husband do?"

"He shouted, 'Down, Effie,' and pulled me into the ditch."

"So he didn't see the aeroplane . . . as you so vividly described it . . . going round and round and round?"

"He was in too much of a hurry for that, sir."

"So neither of you actually saw the aeroplane crash?"

"No, sir. But we heard it. And we *felt* it, sir. Felt it through the soles of our shoes."

"And the time was . . . we have it pretty well exactly, thanks to your husband's commendably regular habits . . . eleven thirty-one?"

"That's right, sir. Regular as clockwork, my husband, sir."

"And what time did you climb out of your ditch?"

"Couldn't have been later than eleven thirty-four, sir."

"Then what happened?"

"We looked around for the crash, sir."

"And you found it?"

"Yes, sir."

"Where did you find it?"

"In the thirty-acre field next to the aerodrome."

"However by that time fire tenders and men were already there?"

"Oh, yes, sir. Lots of men shouting and hoses playing. The ambulance was there, too. We watched it leave."

"Thank you, Mrs. Kettlewell." Sir Alexander returned to the table in front of the Commissioner's raised dais and poured himself refreshment from a carafe of water. But Mrs. Kettlewell did not move. I think she had been enjoying herself, and now she looked like a prima donna awaiting her bouquet. Sir Alexander looked up, and had to smile at her and say again, "Thank you, Mrs. Kettlewell. That will be all," before with dignity she vacated the chair and, holding her big chin high above her rabbit fur, stalked off to the back of the Court.

Quite at ease, the Attorney-General stood silently studying his notes before looking up to the dais and saying to the Commissioner, "With respect, sir . . . having concluded our only eyewitness account . . . should we perhaps move onto the Ministry Investigating expert, and what he found at the scene of the crash?"

"That would appear logical."

"If Mr. Butterworth agrees." The Attorney-General turned to counsel engaged by the Pilots' Union. "I am perfectly willing to change the order of the witnesses if My Learned Friend thinks otherwise."

"Sir . . . I have no objection whatever to the Attorney-General's order."

"Right then. It's Mr. Stevens, isn't it? We'll have Mr. Stevens."

Stevens went up to take the oath. He had an intelligent-looking face, light grey eyes. We'd had a talk together down at Riverly. He had in fact occupied the very same stool at the self-service counter on which Matherson had sat.

"Now Mr. Stevens," said the Attorney-General, "you are a Ministry aviation expert, are you not?"

"I am."

"So before you tell us what you found at the scene of the crash . . . perhaps you would oblige the Court by answering some questions arising out of Mrs. Kettlewell's evidence?"

"Certainly."

"First of all . . . the noise she heard. The sudden loud noise of engines. What would that mean?"

"The pilot had obviously just become visual, and must have thought he had missed his approach."

"He would then disengage the three Autoland levers, resume manual control, and push the throttles forward?"

"Yes."

"Thank you, Mr. Stevens. Now Mrs. Kettlewell said that the aircraft was going round and round and round. That would be a layman's description, would you say, of an aircraft spinning?"

"Yes."

"The pilot then . . . we can safely say . . . for some reason lost flying speed, tried to regain it by putting on power, failed, stalled and spun in?"

"Yes."

"Now Mrs. Kettlewell saw the Astra emerge from cloud. We know the cloud base to have been a hundred and fifty feet. So that it spun in from about that height?"

"Yes."

"Thank you, Mr. Stevens. Now how would you describe the weather from an aviation point of view?"

"Not good. In fact, Riverly was closed at the time to all normal traffic."

"All *normal* traffic . . . yes, that's what I was getting at. But for the purpose of Autoland approaches it was all right?"

"It doesn't matter to the Autoland *what* the weather is."

"Quite. And the practise landings in such weather were to get the pilots used to the idea?"

"Yes."

"In fact in much the same way . . . you will forgive me if it seems fanciful . . . as troops are sometimes given live ammunition in manoeuvres?"

"Yes."

"Such conditions have to be second nature to pilots before carrying out Autolandings on large passenger-carrying aircraft?"

"Yes."

"And so . . . what I am getting at . . . it was perfectly legal for Captain Corby to authorize this training under such bad weather conditions?"

"Perfectly legal."

"In fact, he did it with the Ministry's blessing?"

"He did."

I listened to the evidence with satisfaction. The way it was proceeding, it seemed unlikely I would again be called to the stand. Now the Attorney-General moved quite naturally to the crash itself, questioning Stevens on what he found there.

"Where was the wreckage?"

"Eight hundred feet short of the threshold of the runway, dead on the centre line."

"Was there a crater?"

"Only a small one. The wreckage for the most part was flat on the surface, scattered in a circle of diameter sixty yards."

"That conforms with the aircraft having struck the earth with considerable force?"

"Yes."

"Was it in the landing configuration?"

"Yes . . . wheels and flaps down."

"There was no fire when it struck?"

"No."

"But there was extensive damage?"

The investigator nodded. "Both engines had been torn from their mountings. The pilot's cockpit was a crumpled shell. The fuselage had split in the centre, and the tail cone completely severed. The controls were fractured. Many of the instruments were so badly damaged it was almost impossible to take readings. But we were able to establish quite categorically that there had been no engine failure, no control failure . . . in fact, no aircraft failure whatever in the air."

You could almost hear the relief from the benches of the Astra aircraft manufacturers. They had been cleared. This was their release. In an accident Inquiry, it is as though all the suspects are corralled into one room, and one by one the finger of guilt is pointed at them. Should they evade it, they are forever cleared, and become spotless as driven snow— while the tension tightens amongst those that remain. The weather had been exonerated. Now so had the aircraft. The field had narrowed down to two: the man or the robot. And a shadowy third, of whom no one else in this Court Room had an inkling.

"What other damage was there?"

"The nose section was crushed inward, fracturing cables,

electrical and hydraulic systems." Stevens went into a long monologue of damaged parts, like a dirge ". . . both wings were severely buckled along the leading edge . . . the position of the pilot's body indicated he was in his seat, gripping the control wheel . . . the throttle levers were severed right off . . . the Autoland servomotors and mechanical linkage were damaged . . . the electronic averager was found in the fully fast position—"

Those last ten words came jarring out at me like an alarm bell. I had rather hoped from my inevitably cursory examination from my seat of the bits and pieces on the table that the crash would have eradicated all possible recognition of this anomaly. Momentarily I held my breath. I looked round the Court, scanning each face. But nobody appeared to have noticed anything unusual. George Preston sat impassive and unmoved.

". . . the radio and radar altimeters had been serviceable before impact . . . the clock had stopped at eleven thirty-one and twenty seconds." Stevens himself had obviously seen no special significance. He was still proceeding steadily through his litany of broken mechanisms. ". . . all Autoland warning lights were broken, the auto-throttle connections were severed, the flight compass was smashed . . ."

For the next five minutes, the monotone continued. Nothing stood out in that flat panorama of wreckage. Finally the meticulous Stevens came to a full stop.

"All this extensive damage was consistent with the aircraft striking the ground in the way described?"

"Yes."

"And you cannot, I presume, say that the Autoland was working correctly before the crash?"

"No . . . but nor can we say that it was *not* working correctly."

"The point's taken. Well . . . thank you, Mr. Stevens. I am obliged."

Carruthers followed Stevens on the stand. He brushed back his pale fair hair with his right hand, and began producing the right answers to the usual stuff. Matherson was properly certificated. He held a valid Airline Transport License: he had been medically examined on July 17th and pronounced fit: he certainly could not have been suffering from fatigue. He had been properly and completely instructed in Autoland operation.

"And what was your opinion of Captain Matherson's flying?"

"Well above average." He hesitated then. Perhaps he had suddenly remembered our discussion on the subject, because he went on, "He had his faults, as we all have . . . but all the same, he was a natural pilot."

"And being a natural pilot, he was perhaps somewhat against a robot pilot?"

"Most of the pilots are."

"And you, Captain Carruthers? Are you?"

"I can't say I'm enthusiastic."

"There would be no need of an officer in charge of training for the robots?"

"I see what you're getting at . . . but it isn't just that. A man is more adaptable in emergency."

"And more liable to make mistakes?"

"I wouldn't agree."

"Why not?"

"The trouble with a machine . . . it can't *recognize* mistakes. If it gets itself into trouble, it just gives up."

"But to all intents and purposes, this machine doesn't make mistakes."

"Again, I wouldn't agree."

"But, Captain, the statistical proof is overwhelming!"

"And it was Einstein who said two and two do not necessarily make four."

Another small laugh went round the Court at that, over

which the Attorney-General was not quite so pleased. "What about Boston? Didn't Captain Matherson land off the runway there . . . damaging his aircraft only a matter of weeks ago?"

"It was one of those things."

"What does that mean exactly?"

"A minor incident."

"And this . . . this crash we are investigating now?"

"There is no evidence it was Captain Matherson's fault."

"But you'll agree all three levers of the Autoland were *out* when the Astra hit the ground?"

"He had regained manual control . . . yes."

"Perhaps you will also agree that the wreckage was found dead in line with the runway, and Mrs. Kettlewell's evidence shows the Astra to have been on the glide path?"

"Yes."

"So there doesn't appear much wrong with *that* Autoland approach, does there?"

"We don't know for certain."

"As far as I can gather, however, you are implying that something *did* go wrong?"

"I think it did. And I think Captain Matherson managed to get the Autoland out, but could not avert the stall."

"There is a warning, I believe, against regaining manual control below a hundred and fifty feet?"

"Yes."

"This warning Captain Matherson would be aware of?"

"Of course. Apart from his instruction, it's also in the Operation Manual. But in an emergency, he would have no option."

"But what *was* the emergency, Captain?"

There Carruthers hesitated. He began fingering his slight moustache. "Well . . . of course . . . I don't know."

"You don't know?"

"That's what I said."

"Everybody talks about this emergency . . . but nobody knows what it was."

"To find that out is surely the purpose of this Inquiry."

"The purpose of this Inquiry is to find out the cause of the accident," the Attorney-General said sharply. "Which need not necessarily *be* an emergency." More coolly, he went on. "Now what were Captain Matherson's flying hours?"

"Eight thousand nine hundred and twelve."

"And how long had he been in command?"

"Three months."

"Three months . . . mm." Sir Alexander stroked his chin doubtfully. "He was a very *new* Captain?"

"He was still a very good one."

"And how many of those hours were on Astra aircraft?"

"Six."

"Six!" The Attorney-General sucked the word as though it was a sweet. "Only *six!*"

"The Astra is only used for occasional training. None of the Line pilots have much time on it."

"And no doubt those six hours are spread over a period?"

"Yes."

"Well, then in the Astra cockpit," Sir Alexander moved away from the witness box, and stood in deep thought holding the edges of the table, "Captain Matherson cannot have been exactly at home . . . would you say?"

"He'd have been all right."

Carruthers' tone sounded somewhat blustering. Sir Alexander gave another suck—longer and louder this time—before raising his head and saying, "Mm . . . well, thank you." And then looking up at the Commissioner. "Sir . . . I have finished with Captain Carruthers. And now no doubt My Learned Friend," he gestured towards the Pilots' Union corner, "would like to ask the witness some questions."

Sir Alexander retired to a seat on the front bench, and Mr. Butterworth emerged onto the floor, a small smile on his face.

"Now Captain Carruthers . . . would you be so good as to give an account of Captain Matherson's many flying accomplishments?"

He went over them all—training courses, instructor's endorsement, Company examinations, 180-day Checks—the lot. Butterworth was a man of mannerisms, always moving up and down, either holding out his lapels or bunching up his coattails at the back, so that he somewhat resembled a plump strutting cock. It was not until he had extracted every ounce of Matherson's merits that he allowed Carruthers to go, and in his place called for John P. Groger.

Now on the witness stand there was a very different character. Here was a lean craggy-faced American whose speech was as clipped as his close-cropped hair. I knew the Managing Director of Autoland very well, of course, and a more able man you would never find. He must have known the Autoland was on trial—perhaps for its life—but never a flicker of a hooded eyelid moved. While Butterworth behaved as though he had St. Vitus' dance, Groger kept icily still as he steadfastly maintained the Autoland's innocence.

"But, Mr. Groger . . . have you ever landed an aircraft?"

"Negative."

"Have you ever operated the Autoland in the air?"

"Negative."

"Then how can you consider yourself competent to voice such an opinion?"

"Been beside the pilot enough times."

"Landing in zero-zero conditions?"

"Hardly see m'hand in front of m'face."

"All the same, that's not the same as actually *doing* the operation. You're not a *pilot*."

"Are you a pilot, Mr. Butterworth?"

"I am not, sir. But I am not voicing an opinion."

"Don't see it makes a jot of difference here."

"Let's face it, Mr. Groger . . . you're not really sympathetic with the pilots' point of view."

"Mr. Butterworth . . . I'm the manufacturer of a robot pilot which I know is safer than the human one."

"The pilots don't agree."

"I wouldn't expect them to."

"There are other blind-landing systems that are a good deal safer than yours."

"In what way?"

"The pilot can overpower the autopilot."

"The stronger the autopilot . . . the safer the landing."

"Other systems have a press-button automatic release."

"We don't like that."

"Why not?"

"Besides other dangers . . . there's a chance of inadvertent disengagement."

"What about overshoot?"

"We don't envisage the need. We rely on controllers to keep the runways clear, just as we rely on 'em to avoid collision in the air."

"So that with the Allen Autoland . . . a pilot is virtually committed to a landing at a hundred and fifty feet?"

"Yes."

"What if something goes wrong?"

"Nothing would."

"Surely something *might* go wrong?"

"Only if there was interference from the human operator. Low down, we believe in trusting the machine, not the man."

"Mr. Groger, most blind-landing systems believe in keeping the pilot in the loop."

"That's only to get initial pilot acceptance."

"So you foresee the time in the very near future when all aircraft will be landed completely automatically?"

"I do. And automatically taken off."

"Are you trying to tell me that just as science has made

the radio officer and the specialist navigator unnecessary in an aircrew . . . now it is the pilot's turn to be redundant?"

"You're saying these things . . . not I."

"Your attitude, however, is quite evident. It is the attitude of a businessman."

"Sir . . . it is the attitude of a mathematician."

"An expert calculator?"

"Yes, sir." Groger held his head very stiffly. "Which gives me . . . more'n a pilot . . . the right to say this accident could not have been caused by the Autoland."

"That's a rash statement."

"Still happens to be true."

"If the autopilot failed—"

"The second would take over."

"And if that failed—"

"The *third* would take over."

"There could still *be* a failure."

"Statistically speaking . . . impossible."

"How can you say that?"

"We have done years of tests. The Autoland failure rate is one in a hundred million landings . . . compared to the pilot error accident rate of one in a hundred thousand bad-weather landings."

"You're saying then that it's a thousand to one it was the pilot?"

"Thank you for the arithmetic, but what I'm saying is it's a hundred million to one it wasn't the Autoland."

"All the same, a lot was found wrong."

"Delicate instrument. Got a bad belting."

At this, Mr. Butterworth's small smile seemed to enlarge a little. He started moving again, away from the witness, and now instead of his usual aimless jog trot there seemed a definite purpose in what he was doing. Before he stopped at the oak table with the remains of the Autoland on it, I knew he would. I knew he would put out one of those pink fat hands

—the left, as it happened—and pick up a metal mass of broken wheels and wire springs. I knew he would, as though in triumph, hold it under John Groger's nose.

"You will recognize this?"

"Of course."

"And what is it?"

"The electronic averager."

"The electronic averager," Butterworth repeated, "somewhat battered . . . but here we have it." He paused and looked down at the remaining pieces. "It is a pity this robot cannot talk, is it not? It appears to be able to do everything else." He raised his eyes, and perhaps it was my imagination, but he appeared to look straight at me. "Earlier this afternoon in Court, amongst so many other details of damage, this valuable piece of evidence went unnoticed."

I can remember a curious sort of feeling come over me. Not fear exactly, but an alertness, an awareness of danger. I leaned forward in my seat. I saw the faces all round the Court quicken with interest.

"Now this ingenious machine—"

Butterworth went on to explain what it did, how it took over for the last part of the approach on account of the weakness of the I.L.S. glide-path signals.

"Now this . . . well, clock, I suppose you can call it . . . was in the fully *fast* position—"

"We were told that earlier," interrupted Groger dryly.

"—and I am advised that this means that the aircraft"—he paused dramatically to draw himself up to his diminutive full height—"would start to carry out a landing nearly *two hundred feet above the ground!*"

"Now let's get this correct," Groger said, still unmoved. "The landing is monitored by the radio altimeter."

"But the electronic averager initiates the roundout?"

"Agreed."

"It pulls back both the throttles and the stick?"

"Agreed."

"Slowing down the aircraft?"

"Agreed."

"Practically to stalling point?"

"Look," Groger said, "it does all this just above the ground and—"

"*Normally*, Mr. Groger . . . but in the fully fast position it was found, it will do it around two hundred feet . . . won't it?"

"Well, now—"

"And if Captain Matherson tried in those circumstances to resume manual control . . . the aircraft *would* stall."

"It might."

Butterworth's small smile expanded enormously. "Well, then—"

Now a silence had fallen on the Court. I drew a deep breath. Listening to people groping towards a solution—now hot, now cold—of which only you know the answer is like being balanced on a wire that someone is shaking. I do not know if my expression had changed. Certainly Mr. Groger's had not.

The same deep unemotional voice: "Mr. Butterworth."

"Yes?"

"You will agree that this instrument had just completed its part successfully in no less than *three* landings?"

"Yes."

"Then will you kindly tell me how it was that after being serviceable and in the normal position for those three landings, it should suddenly advance itself to the fully fast position for the fourth landing?"

Butterworth began to wave his hands. "Vibration . . . some flying manoeuvre . . ."

"Mr. Butterworth."

"Yes?"

"The tail cone was severed from the rest of the aircraft . . . could that have been vibration?"

"Obviously not."

"The cockpit was shattered . . . perhaps by some flying manoeuvre?"

Butterworth did not answer. His face had gone bright red.

"Why would you say then there had been all this damage?"

"By impact with the ground."

"Exactly! Yet for that piece of the Autoland, you demand some other explanation. The aircraft would need a sledge-hammer blow to alter that setting on the electronic averager. That sledgehammer blow it received . . ." Now it was Groger's turn to pause dramatically. "When the Astra spun in and crashed."

Mr. Butterworth's smile seemed to wither at the edges. "But surely there might be another reason?"

"Other than the logical one? Tell me, Mr. Butterworth . . . tell me!"

But instead, Mr. Butterworth put down his trophy among the other broken pieces of the Autoland, said as though dismissing him, "Mr. Groger, I am obliged," and returned without his smile to his place on the Pilots' Union bench.

I breathed easily again. I looked round confidently, the danger past. It was then that I saw George Preston's head had turned right round. I could not see his eyes because those thick spectacles were opaque with the reflected light from the chandeliers. But they were fixedly—I do not think I was mistaken—looking at me. And I seemed to see above his head, like those balloons over characters in cartoons, the thoughts and ideas that were going on in his mind.

Once again, I felt the shaking of the wire.

And then—as though in slow motion—I saw Preston get off his seat and walk over to where the Attorney-General was conferring with the Commissioner. Sir Alexander looked surprised at the interruption, but turned his ear to listen. Then he was nodding, bringing in Mr. Justice Pelham into the conversation. Finally agreement was reached, and what I had most feared happened.

George Preston took the stand.

Preston was a pleasant enough, ordinary person. That night he had interrupted me in the simulator, he had seemed so incurious. But now, after hearing the previous evidence, had he put two and two together? How much had he guessed? And yet—Matherson was certainly not the sort for confidences—how *could* he have guessed?

"Raise your right hand . . . you do solemnly swear to tell the truth, the whole truth and nothing but the truth?"

"So help me God."

"You are George William Preston?"

"I am."

"And you are a simulator Instructor employed by the British Empire Airways?"

"Yes."

"You have listened to all the previous evidence at this Inquiry?"

"I have."

"And now you think . . . so you told me . . . you have some evidence of your own that might be relevant?"

"Yes."

"It was some incident, you say?"

"Yes . . . an incident involving the simulator on September 25th."

The Attorney-General moved over to the oak table and one by one began examining the pieces of Autoland. "Mr. Preston . . . perhaps you would tell us this incident in your own words."

"It was a Friday, and after office hours. Everybody had gone home. I happened to be in the Company Information Room reading a trade magazine, when suddenly there was a loud noise. I knew what it was. It was coming from the simulator, which I'd locked up only an hour ago. Somebody had got it out of control, because that high scream could only mean the machine was spinning. I closed up the Information Room, went down the stairs and out of the block across to the Training Section. I was just coming down the corridor when the door of the Simulator Room opened, and out came Captain Corby. Thinking he'd made some flying mistake, I asked no questions."

"And presumably were told no lies." The Attorney-General slowly returned to the witness box. "And then?"

"Well, then . . . Captain Corby locked up."

"Go on."

"We walked over to our cars . . . we . . . well, we said good night."

"Proceed."

Preston had given his account of the incident in a firm voice. Every now and again he kept looking in my direction. But now under the Attorney-General's questions, he seemed to lose the thread of what he was saying. Standing there in the witness box, he brought his story to an abrupt end. "Well . . . that's all."

"That's *all*?"

"It's . . . it's the similarity. The simulator spinning . . . then the Astra spinning."

"Mr. Preston . . . it's a simulator for a 909 aircraft," Sir Alexander looked up at the great stained-glass dome that spanned the roof of the hall, "is it not?"

"Yes . . . but in many ways an Astra would react the same."

"Mr. Preston—"

"Sir?"

"Captain Corby was quite within his rights to be there?"

"Oh, yes. He has a key. But it's not the practise for one person to be operating the simulator. Usually there's an instructor, crewmen—"

"It was Friday evening, you said?"

"Yes."

"And they had all gone home?"

"Yes, but—"

"Captain Corby must obviously be occupied in office hours. There's no reason why he shouldn't operate the simulator at other times on his own, I suppose?"

"Not really. All the same—"

"Mr. Preston . . . I suppose there have been other occasions when the simulator has spun in?"

"Oh, yes."

"Why was this occasion any different from the others?"

"It was . . . well, it just happened before the crash."

"In each case, presumably the pilot allowed the speed to get too slow?"

"Yes."

"And that's probably what happened to Captain Corby?"

"Well . . . of course we don't know."

"But unless the speed gets too slow . . . the simulator won't stall and won't spin?"

"That's true."

"So that *is* what happened to Captain Corby?"

Preston lowered his eyes. "Yes."

"Captain Corby said he was doing some practice?"

"Yes."

"He might have just been in there on his own . . . fooling around?"

"Not Captain Corby."

"Or experimenting perhaps?"

"Perhaps."

"In fact, there might be dozens of reasons." The Attorney-General moved back to the oak table. "You'll forgive me, Mr. Preston . . . but I'm still not quite sure of the intention of this evidence you insisted on giving."

"The simulator," Preston was making a big effort to make himself clear, "reproduces what goes on in an aircraft."

"Yes, yes . . . we know that is its whole purpose. But what else?"

"What made the simulator spin . . . might have made the Astra spin."

I had my eyes so carefully concentrated on Preston that I was only dimly aware of being watched myself by Anne. It was as if distantly the outermost guards of my consciousness registered her occasional assessing glances. But that these did not themselves penetrate into the council chamber that was the real thinking me.

But what *did* penetrate now was the curious sound she made as Preston spoke those words. It was half an indrawn breath, half a moan. It was almost as if she were trying to reproduce in miniature that very sound of the spinning simulator.

Jerked out of myself, quickly I glanced round at her.

I had thought that I had reached my bitterest moment, drained the cup, when I knew Matherson had seduced my wife. But now an even bitterer one came to confound me. For whatever the Learned Friends of this Court might or might not discover, Anne knew. Not the technicalities of course—but she had guessed what I had done. I saw it in her face. Faces can ask more loudly than any tongue. Eyes can prise open the secrets of any heart. I saw hers grow round and black and very terrible. I actually felt them digging like metal bores into my brain. Her cheeks were drained of colour. Her mouth remained open, as if still forming the sound that seemed to linger like frosted breath over her lips. In some odd way, her face had stretched and flattened and grown strange with an emotion too powerful for its muscles, like the face of the girl in the café the day of the accident. Those two faces—Anne's now and the girl's then—I knew I would remember all my life.

"Yes, yes, Mr. Preston . . . but we seem to be going round

in circles. The simulator spun because it got too slow. Everything seems to spin if it gets too slow, even this Court."

"My idea was . . . well, anything might set off . . ."—Preston was now hesitating badly—"an idea in someone else. We are all sort of . . . in the dark . . . groping for the true solution."

"That's so, Mr. Preston. I'm obliged for your efforts." As Preston vacated the stand, the Attorney-General was addressing the Commissioner, "And now, Sir, I don't know whether you want to call Captain Corby again?"

Mr. Justice Pelham conferred with his assessors before saying, "It is neither here nor there with us. But under the circumstances, perhaps Captain Corby might prefer to come forward."

I saw his eyes searching the Court for me. I stood up. "Sir . . . I would so prefer."

I have had in my life many moments of crisis. Two engines failed on take-off, one hot night in Khartoum. A fierce fire suddenly flared up in the passenger cabin on a winter westbound halfway across the Atlantic. I once circled Lima for four hours, using up fuel before doing a belly landing. I lost half a wing when an unauthorized military aircraft collided with me over the Channel. I had, you see, been well inoculated against occasions like this.

And yet, I had not. As step by step, I walked across the well of the Court and over to the witness box, I knew that nothing mattered.

I had lost Anne. I had lost everything.

"Captain Corby." The Attorney-General was coming towards me now, fingering his lapels. "You have heard Mr. Preston's evidence about the simulator?"

"Yes."

"Is it correct?"

"As far as it goes . . . yes."

"But I expect you would like to give your version?"

"I would."

"And what were you doing in the simulator?"

"I was experimenting."

"Ah, yes." The Attorney-General rubbed his hands together. "As I suggested. And what was the experiment?"

I hesitated almost as much as Preston had done. "Well . . .
it was quite simple . . . nothing mystifying . . ."

A cross-examination is a swordplay, a duel—no less. There
is feint, thrust, parry, lunge. You must think quickly, well
ahead of your opponent.

Just as I had intended, Sir Alexander sensed my reluctance.
Now almost tartly he said, "In that case, there won't be any
trouble explaining it to us."

"No . . . not really." I still spoke slowly. "There is an order
that a pilot shall not disengage the Autoland below a hundred and fifty feet."

"Yes, yes . . . we know."

"It is a sore point with pilots . . . this prohibition . . .
though it is for their own good, for the machine to all intents
and purposes does not make a mistake."

"Quite."

"The Autoland Company . . . whom I have the greatest
respect for . . . have always been somewhat vague on the
reason for this prohibition."

"I see. But to get back to that day . . ."

"That day I was finding out . . . what happens if the pilot
does disengage."

"So you were doing an Autoland approach in the simulator?"

"I was."

"Until a hundred and fifty feet?"

"Exactly."

"And then you disengaged the three autopilots and resumed manual control?"

I paused. "Yes."

"And what did you find out?"

"I found out . . . that unless he's quick, the speed is too low, the aircraft attitude is insufficiently nose down."

"And what happens then?"

"He stalls and spins."

A hush came over the room. It was evening time now, though you could tell only by the darkness that had settled over those dusty windows. The chandeliers still glittered like spotlights above us.

The Commissioner cleared his throat. "Captain Corby . . . you will tell me if I am wrong . . . but what Mr. Preston said may well, after all, have a bearing on the case."

"Sir . . . I think that may be so."

"Did you suspect that Captain Matherson might have . . . in spite of warnings to the contrary . . . taken over at a hundred and fifty feet?"

"Sir . . . I did suspect it."

My hesitations only seemed to inspire them. The more reluctant my answers, the more eager they became to gouge them out of me. The scent of a cause for an aircraft accident always sends a Court of Inquiry off like a pack of hounds in pursuit. It is as though they fail if they do not find one. And now it was as though Mr. Justice Pelham and his assessors had smelled the truth inside me. The Commissioner leaned right over the high desk to say to me, "You made no mention of this in your evidence."

I lowered my eyes. "Sir . . . I was the first to be called. There were other things one suspects."

"Such as?"

"Well, the aircraft . . . the Autoland."

"You are satisfied now it was not the aircraft?"

"Sir . . . I am."

"And you accept the Allen Autoland Company's evidence?"

"I cannot see how the accident can be blamed on the Autoland."

"So there remains . . . does there not . . . the pilot?"

I said nothing.

"Captain . . . did you hear what I said?"

I raised my head.

"Captain . . . you have had a strong suspicion it might have been pilot error all along?"

"Sir . . . one does not lightly blame a dead colleague."

"Were you friendly with Captain Matherson?"

"I am friendly with all my pilots."

"You knew him well then?"

"I did. And had a high opinion of him."

"All the same, he was a new Captain, was he not?"

"He was."

"And his experience on the Astra was limited."

"Yes."

"Captain Corby . . . I am aware that these questions are painful . . . but was there anything about Captain Matherson that had made you . . . uneasy?"

Again I kept quiet.

"Captain . . . you must answer my question."

"There was of course the Boston incident." I paused. "And—"

"Yes, Captain. Go on."

"Sir . . . it is not easy."

"Was there then some other incident?"

"Sir," I said in a voice so low that only the Commissioner and his assessors heard, "there was a whole pattern of incidents."

A rustle almost of excitement could be heard between the three men on the high desk. They had got what they wanted. Now they sat back, as I knew they would, well pleased— intent on the final dash to the kill. The Commissioner lightly tapped the tips of his fingers together. "And now, Captain, perhaps you would start at the beginning. Can you tell us the date of the first incident?"

"August 18th. I can remember it well."

"And where did it occur?"

"In the Simulator Room. I watched two I.L.S. approaches. One by the Autoland . . . which was good. One by a pilot which was . . . Mr. Preston will bear me out . . . poor."

"And the pilot?"

"Captain Matherson. He saw me standing there. He saw that I had seen. He seemed . . . upset."

"And what was your reaction?"

"Pilots go off form, you know . . . like golfers. I thought it was just one of those occasions."

"But Captain Matherson felt he had been shown up by the robot?"

"I was afraid so."

"And what did you do?"

"I asked him to dinner. We talked. I suggested he represent the younger captains at a meeting on the Autoland."

"And what was the purpose of this meeting?"

"Quite frankly, to 'sell' the Autoland to them. We were having . . . we still are having . . . intense opposition to it from the pilots. They feel that robots are taking over their jobs."

"And was the meeting successful?"

"We made some progress. I allayed some of their fears."

"And Captain Matherson?"

"He made only one remark."

"And what was this remark?"

"He said . . . 'In doubt, trust yourself, not a machine.'"

"And how did you feel about that?"

"Somewhat concerned. But I shrugged it off by saying to myself that Matherson was young."

"You were making allowances for him?"

Instead of answering, I poured myself a glass of water from the carafe on the ledge of the witness box, and drank slowly.

"And then, of course," the Attorney-General said, "there was the incident at Boston."

"Yes."

"Where in the worst weather, Captain Matherson *refused* a Ground Controlled Approach?"

"That is true."

"And what date was that?"

"September 8th."

"That incident was surely part of this pattern?" They were prompting me now. "Wouldn't you say?"

"I have to admit that had he monitored his I.L.S. approach by G.C.A., the accident might never have happened."

"This showed a certain overconfidence?"

"Something along those lines perhaps."

"What did you do?"

"I had Captain Matherson in. I talked to him. I had him sign a report. It is there, sir," I said to the Commissioner, "among the relevant papers on your desk . . . to the effect that he tended to disregard mechanical aids. Even so, I tried to keep it in proportion. Captain Matherson had hitherto an excellent record with the Company."

"And then?"

"I went on a Route Check with him."

"What happened?"

"Not a great deal. On the surface, it was all quite satisfactory. But below—"

"The same . . . attitude was apparent to you?"

"Unfortunately . . . yes."

"What did you do?"

"I expressed my concern to the Training Captain."

"And what date was that?"

I paused. I looked up at the dark ceiling. "Excuse me . . . I'm not quite sure." I put my hand into the inside pocket of my jacket and took out my second diary. I opened it up, turning over the pages. "Ah, yes, here it is. September 17th."

The Attorney-General was standing beside me, looking over my shoulder. I passed the diary over to him. "It's all there," I said.

Sir Alexander had taken it into his hand. "There's nothing personal in this?"

"No."

"I see Captain Carruthers was also worried about Captain Matherson's overconfident streak."

"Yes."

He began riffling through the pages. "You don't mind me looking through it?"

"Not at all."

He stopped at another entry. "I see you had another talk with Captain Carruthers on the 23rd. You suggested you take Captain Matherson off the roster to start his Autoland training on the Astra . . . adding that it would be a hard job getting him to accept it. Captain Carruthers agreed."

"Yes."

"And then I see you have an entry after your simulator experiment two days later."

"Yes."

"You note that a self-confident pilot who didn't trust the Autoland might well stall and spin. It is obviously on your mind."

"Yes."

"Captain . . . the moment a pilot becomes visual on a bad-weather approach . . . that's a danger period, isn't it?"

I kept silent.

"Captain, if you would be good enough to answer my questions . . ."

"Yes, it is."

"Why is that?"

"The human brain takes time to reorientate itself from instruments to the foggy outlines of the ground. The eye is subject to hallucinations in depth and vision. In addition, rain on the windscreen causes distortion, a refraction of up to five degrees. So at a hundred and fifty feet, a ground object half a mile ahead might even appear *above* the aircraft."

"On the Autoland approaches you were on with him, did he seem nervous?"

"Not really nervous. Perhaps a little apprehensive when the ground made its sudden appearance."

"Did you do anything about this?"

"I reminded him that this apparent close proximity to the ground was a normal phenomenon. And instead of the usual two landings I did with the others, I gave him three."

"You wanted him to trust the Autoland . . . not his own impressions?"

"Yes."

The Attorney-General drummed my diary several times on the side of the witness box before handing it back to me. "But in spite of that . . . he didn't."

"One cannot be definite."

"But that's what you think took place . . . isn't it?"

"It is still only conjecture."

"You think Captain Matherson, completely distrusting the Autoland anyway, thought he was going to hit the ground, and began to take over the flying himself?"

"Sir, it cannot be proved."

"And though he succeeded in regaining manual control, the airspeed had by then fallen below the stall, and he spun in?"

"There are only indications to that effect."

"In fact, what you had most feared . . . happened?"

"Sir . . . since you insist on my opinion, I think Captain Matherson trusted his human brain and not the machine's. He trusted something that thinks erratically at 370 miles an hour, instead of an infallibility that thinks at many thousands of miles a second."

"So the cause of the accident in your opinion was human error?"

"Sir . . . the cause of all accidents is human error." I paused. "But let me say again, this is only a theory."

The Commissioner leaned over his desk to say, "It is, however, Captain Corby, a theory . . . the *only* theory . . . that appears to fit the facts."

"If this *is* what happened . . . sir, I hold myself to blame." As I stood there in the witness box, I bent my head. "There was a pattern . . . it is now quite apparent to the whole Court. Why was it not earlier apparent to me? One after the other, the incidents build up to the inevitable climax. This tragedy I should have foreseen and forestalled. I have a great deal of experience. I know how pilots react. I had ample time to take precautions. But I did not. Mr. Commissioner . . . I blame myself. Right up to the end, I admit I was concerned about Captain Matherson. My last words to him were *remember now . . . trust the Autoland!*"

A silence fell over the whole Court Room. As I walked away from the stand, and Mr. Commissioner began conferring with his assessors, I knew what an actor must feel when, as they say, the audience is with him. Everyone in the hall that day, I think, was with me.

Except one. Except the most important one.

I kept my eyes down. I glanced at no one. Yet as if my eyelids were transparent, I was aware of their glances. I actually heard someone, Captain Rudwick, I think, murmur . . . if anything too conscientious. I had no need to exaggerate the gravity of my mien, nor the sense of my loss. That I forebore to glance at Anne as I resumed my seat was assumed, I think, to be a right and proper bearing in the face of the conclusions I had helped the Court to find.

Nor did I glance at her as Mr. Justice Pelham summed up. The report would not be published for several months, but here he was giving us the way the Court was thinking, the moment before it rose.

". . . it is natural after a tragedy for people to examine their consciences, and to say to themselves if only I had done this or that it would never have happened. Just as it is the duty of a Coroner to reassure people who are thus distressed, so it is now my duty to remind us all that no man can be his brother's keeper. It is quite clear that Captain Corby did everything that he could. His training was obviously careful and painstaking. He cannot and must not blame himself. It is easy . . . and often agonizing . . . to be wise after the event. In this accident, the aircraft was proved to be quite blameless. As must be expected with so delicate an instrument, many parts of the Autoland had been mutilated, but as Mr. Groger says, after three successful approaches, why should it suddenly go wrong? In the absence of acceptable evidence that it did, the odds of a hundred million to one, scientifically proved, *against* it going wrong, are obviously overwhelming. We live now in an age of speed. All over our civilization, not just in aviation, machines have been evolved to take over. They do the jobs quicker and more efficiently than men. It is not only a sobering and solemn thought . . . it is a fact that must be accepted. One cannot help being left with the impression that this accident was caused because Captain Matherson was a human being who *refused* to accept it. He knew better than the machine . . ."

Mr. Justice Pelham gathered his notes, and put them into his brief case. Then he stood up, together with his assessors. Everyone in Court rose to watch the three of them file out.

For a little while after they were gone, now it was all over, there still remained a hush over the hall, before people started collecting their things and moving to the door.

I helped Anne on with her coat. We walked out of the Court, side by side but in silence. In the hall, I thought it only right to have a few words with my colleagues, with officials of the Ministry and the Allen Autoland. They were all affable and kind. Once again, my manner was taken to be distress at the case, and a loyal distaste for the Court's conclusions.

The doorman was kind enough to get us a taxi. We were among the first to leave. Darkness had already descended. The night air was full of damp smoky smells. A few people were waiting curiously on the pavement. Their faces looked as strange to me as Halloween lanterns.

I did not dare to take Anne's arm as we stepped into the taxi. I sat as far away as I could from her, but the sweetness of her perfume almost suffocated me. We hardly spoke a word the whole way. I shivered as the taxi stopped outside our home.

All was dark inside, and the whole façade looked grim and alien. Anne stood back for me while I unlocked the door, and she did not glance at me as she stepped over the threshold. She gave me her coat in silence, and in silence I hung it in the cloakroom.

The house was very warm, but I still felt chilled to the bone. I closed the lounge door softly after me. Anne was already sitting on the sofa, staring in front of her at the mirror over the mantelpiece. I walked to the tray of drinks and poured myself a stiff scotch. Without speaking, Anne held out her hand for me to pour one for her, and I did so. As I stood in front of her, holding the glass out to her, I forced my eyes to meet hers. Or maybe she forced them, I don't know.

To my surprise, she was smiling.

Momentarily, I was so overcome by the unexpected softness of her face that I almost went on my knees in front of her and begged her forgiveness. But something in her expression kept me standing stiffly in front of her. In those few seconds as I stood there, I sought like a blind man groping through a minefield to analyze her mood. I could feel my heart beating very fast. My breath came noisily. I had the curious certainty that for the first time I was standing in the dock, and I felt weak with apprehension.

Then gradually I noticed the way her eyes travelled very slowly and deliberately over me. I had seen her look like this at Matherson, at men she liked the look of in the street, at Captain S., at that young solicitor. I had seen those half-closed eyes, that small secret smile, always turned away to someone else, and I would have given my soul to have them turned towards me. Suddenly like a bomb bursting inside me, I knew that for the first time in our lives my wife wanted me, desired me. With a profound sense of shock I realized that what I had done, far from repelling her, had given me stature—that the killing of Matherson had made me her man.

I stared at her disbelievingly for a moment. I put out my hand to touch her, to kiss her, then to take her. But I dropped it to my side again.

The day's doings had left me worn and spent. I felt very old. I had no desire left in me. I looked at Anne, and I wondered if I would in my whole life ever have desire again.

I turned away. I walked over and switched on the television. Anne looked at me in disbelief. And then after one bitter scornful glance, she picked up a magazine and began to thumb idly through its pages.

Now as I sat on that sofa, I could see only myself—myself and the flickering grey-green shadows of the television—in the gilt mirror above the mantelpiece.